'The perfect s...
Chris '

'Grabs hold and...
Phoebe Morgan

Praise for Ross Armstrong

...ish and ... ... it'
Mick Herron

'Ross Armstrong delivers a twisty mystery through the
perspective of a fractured brain. Original and gripping.
Tom Mondrian, and his unique outlook, will stay with me'
Peter Swanson

'Absolutely loved *Head Case*. Couldn't put it
down. Tragic, funny and frightening. Ross
Armstrong has written another cracker'
Chris Whitaker

'An eerily atmospheric reworking of
Hitchcock's *Rear Window*'
Guardian

'Addictive and eerie, you'll finish the
book wanting to chat about it'
Closer

'Ross Armstrong will feed your appetite for suspense'
Evening Standard

'A dark, unsettling page-turner'
Claire Douglas

Ross Armstrong is an actor and writer based in North London. He studied English Literature at Warwick University and acting at RADA. As a stage and screen actor he has performed in the West End, Broadway and in shows for HBO and Netflix. Ross' debut title *The Watcher* was a top twenty bestseller and has been longlisted for the CWA John Creasey New Blood Dagger.

@Rarmstrongbooks

Also by
Ross Armstrong

The Watcher
The Girls Beneath
Beach Bodies

THE GETAWAY

ROSS ARMSTRONG

ONE PLACE. MANY STORIES

HQ
An imprint of HarperCollins*Publishers* Ltd
1 London Bridge Street
London SE1 9GF

www.harpercollins.co.uk

HarperCollins*Publishers*
1st Floor, Watermarque Building, Ringsend Road
Dublin 4, Ireland

This edition 2022

1
First published in Great Britain by
HQ, an imprint of HarperCollins*Publishers* Ltd 2022

Copyright © Ross Armstrong 2022

Ross Armstrong asserts the moral right to be
identified as the author of this work.
A catalogue record for this book is
available from the British Library.

ISBN: 9780008232511
US: 9780008538354

For my father, John Armstrong. Quite unlike
any father depicted here, fortunately.

'What difference does it make how much you have?
What you do not have amounts to much more'

SENECA

Cast of Characters

The Rathwells

Robert: *The Millionaire Magnate*
Sofia: *The Trophy Wife*
JR: *The Gifted Son*
Bobby: *Cousin Bobby*
Jeanette: *Beloved Aunt*

The Staff

Isabelle: *The Lifestyle Assistant*
Amelia: *The Super Tutor*
Ben: *The Father Figure*
Kostas: *The Security*

Journal

11 August, 2.05 p.m.

I'd always thought that if I saw someone drowning the instinct to save a life would kick in automatically. And that's true, it does. But you can suppress it.

As I write I'm sitting on a yacht, having just watched someone flail helplessly above the waves. They were close enough for me to reach out a hand to help. But I had to pretend to be complicit, to save myself. I bit down on my tongue as I watched the body disappear beneath the turquoise water, leaving only spots of blood behind.

Was in a kind of trance after that. Someone yelled and then the engine started to roar. We turned in a wide arc. Felt a creeping under my skin, from all that guilt and fear.

Other girls at boarding school used to awkwardly ask if I could get sunburn. I told them I could, and did, and joked that I must've got that from my father's side.

I stared at my sunburnt arms. Thought about what heredity gives us: little messages written in the genes for future use. Or maybe they're just bad habits. Or debts to be paid.

Mr Rathwell was once quoted in the paper, saying: in this life you're either the shark or you're the chum in the water.

His private island came back into view, a dot on the horizon.

I thought about how this all began with a new addition to the family, a holiday to get away from it all, and a dinner for eight.

And how it was on the day I found out I'd been so naïve that I decided to start documenting what was happening here, so I had timelines, details, so my testimony would line up with the order of events.

We cut through the water. I felt a wetness on my top lip and realised a single stripe of blood had fallen from my nose. Reached for a white handkerchief to stem the flow. Sat there looking at the red on white linen.

I went to sit on my own on the starboard side. I closed one eye against the sun as my meditation app played in my ears. My fingers quivered, pushing my ringlets under my sunhat. I wiped my prescription sunglasses clean and began to write this. The Rathwell family often see me making notes, earbuds in, every inch the diligent English tutor. People will think I'm planning ahead – some kind of self-soothing – and in a way I am.

I try to breathe, try to stop my hand shaking, try to stay calm.

I feel eyes on me, that sixth sense we have, that shiver on the back of the neck.

Need to keep writing.

But now I know someone's watching me for sure.

They're standing over me.

They're trying to—

PART I:

Just an ordinary dinner for 8

At a grand house

I

The LA

Isabelle

Rule one of taking a flight on a private plane is don't arrive after the owner, but that is exactly the mistake our new addition, Ben, made.

As an LA (lifestyle assistant) I had done everything I could. The lights were set at the correct level, the drinks cabinet was full, Herb Alpert and the Tijuana Brass was playing, which meant we were ready to wheel on Robert Rathwell (wealth estimated to be in the high nine figures, business interests include: the ownership of fifty London mansion blocks, a red-top newspaper and an aluminium mine). Tropical swing music spilt out onto the runway in the morning sunlight, as he sat blowing out his lips, wearing the Louis Vuitton sunglasses that were a gift from the lady of the house. No matter how much cream I applied, he would get sunburn. It defied science at this stage, but with a job like mine you soon begin to ignore what *should be*, and focus on what *is*, then start putting out the fucking fires.

Amelia smiled at me from the back seat, such a lovely girl

and a wonderful tutor, but I had a feeling I'd need to keep an eye on her. Kostas, our security man, was peering over his aviators, a newspaper he wasn't reading in his hand. Robert's wife Sofia, forty-five years his junior, was staring out of the window at the hot concrete, arms folded and perfectly still. *TW2.0*, so *Tatler* had dubbed her, was a new brand of trophy wife armed with a law degree, a sustainability foundation and outspoken feminist leanings. Hardly the kind of spouse expected of controversial magnate Robert Rathwell, she's a brilliant woman and is even distantly related to Queen Margrethe II of Denmark.

Their nine-year-old boy, little JR, was spread out over three tan leather seats, drowning in electronics – tablets, laptops and computer consoles; his eyes, brown with a hint of green, switched between screens. Though he had the look of a mysterious child genius analysing the stock exchange, and was indeed prodigiously smart beyond his years, his internet consumption mostly consisted of skateboarding accidents and people lip-synching on TikTok. I noticed a little sadness in those eyes, as ever. He had claimed he was depressed as soon as he knew what the word meant, and it broke all our hearts. This was why he visited the child psychologist. It was one of the reasons, anyway.

Robert sighed, his tongue sought out his top lip, something about the way he blinked. Unrest. This was a dangerous state, and I knew I had to put a stop to it at once. But my options were limited as Ben was late and uncontactable. Ben had been employed as JR's new father figure, not that we used that term around his biological father, Robert. Ben was to be the body that his father couldn't be. An actor by trade, which seemed appropriate. A strong, young presence. Unfortunately, his lack of presence on the plane was a problem.

My phone pinged and I only had to glimpse the title of the email from Ben to understand its meaning. *Sorry* … it read. Not a call, not even a text, an *email*. He was pulling out.

I immediately shouted to the man on the runway in the high-vis, in the politest way I could muster: 'Lose the stairs, we're leaving.'

'Air traffic control won't like ya, love,' the man chirped back. 'If you hear a bang, that'll be you colliding with a Boeing 737 bound for Crete.'

I laughed with a tight smile and strode away from the man mansplaining air travel to me. I banged on the pilot's door and called for them to get going, then made a beeline for Robert.

Such are the pressures of the job I do find it hard to control my anxieties sometimes. This could be explained by my parents; my mother was Irish and the soul of diplomacy, my father a Frenchman who was given to plain-speaking at loud volumes. I often feel them fighting within me to get out. I mostly let her win, but he does get his way sometimes.

Strapping in next to Robert, I took one of my pills and soon the corners of my world softened. I felt a crack between my shoulder blades and pushed back into my seat, all stress receding.

To say my work extended beyond what I was told it would be ten years ago is an understatement. I certainly had no idea that 'carer' might be added to my duties, but I suppose that's why he used the title lifestyle assistant, because no one knows what one is. But Robert is a deeply charismatic and kind man, no matter what the papers say. Even if there are days when I feel like *pisser dans un violin*. That's a phrase my father used that translates as things being so futile it's like you are pissing in a violin.

There was a small black box next to me. Robert smiled and tapped at it, beckoning me to open it up. Inside was a thin silver necklace bearing a huge amethyst, my birthstone. I held the teardrop of purple quartz up to sparkle in the light and blushed. He enjoyed that.

'It's beautiful,' I said, feeling quite moved. 'I'll try it on later.'

He just nodded, almost shy, as I placed the gift in the inside pocket of my black blazer, making sure no one saw this preferential treatment.

What touched me was that, whereas other men of his stature would delegate such gestures, his presents showed just how well he knew each of us. Michelin-starred food from my favourite restaurant was casually placed on my desk. Unguents, cosmetics and masseurs arrived at my home unannounced. That's what people on the outside didn't see, the give and take. I'd been getting more attention at the time, because of the extent of my work, but he was always thinking about us all, deeply.

As the plane levelled out, I opened Robert's pill box and recounted the contents meticulously: three white pills, an orange, a yellow, two blues. His eyes, as brown and green as JR's, looked on with a sense of remorse.

'Three swallows,' I whispered, 'then done. All's going beautifully to plan. Now, would you like something nice to wash these down?'

'Yes please, darling heart,' he said. I found the rasp in his voice quite debonair; it suited his long, studied vowels.

'And what would you like, darling?' I said. 'What would please you most?'

He tapped at his scuffed and scratched iPad ...

B-L-O-O-D

Firstly, I wondered why he had chosen to type. He hadn't used it much since rallying after his last stroke. I decided his voice was tired. As my eyebrows rose at what he'd written a figure appeared above me holding a red drink.

'Bloody Mary?' Sofia said, holding a crystal glass of dusty red liquid, a black straw and a stick of celery.

She had a habit of sneaking up on you.

'I've held the spice but not the alcohol,' she said in her curved Danish.

I took the cool glass from her and adjusted his special table, so it was around the level of his chest as he held her eye. He's no invalid but does appreciate ease in all things.

'Perfect, darling girl,' he rasped. We were all darling girls or darling hearts. I think it made him feel like he was a wartime fighter pilot, and we were the nurses who looked after the brave hero when he came home. 'Now go on,' he said to her. 'Fuck off.'

I averted my eyes, not for the first time when in the presence of the two of them.

'I love you too,' she said with a slow blink and a gentle pout. It was his little joke. He had begun to use the two-word expletive as a term of endearment in recent years.

I had to tuck back into my seat as she leant across me to kiss him softly on the mouth, her right breast gently touching my left shoulder. Out of the corner of my eye, I saw her press her forehead to his, her thumb gliding firmly across the creases of his skin.

Then she drew away, sliding back into the seat adjacent, and the ambient light from her phone lit her face.

When all was still, Robert showed me another message he had been composing on his little screen. He only did this when he really didn't want to be heard.

Is JR happy? it read.

'Thoroughly,' I whispered. My words were protected from other ears by the white noise of air travel. 'Well, he's getting there. And Sofia is ecstatic with the new man. Ben is … arriving later.'

Good.

'Ben said JR has a real sparkle behind his eyes.'

Robert's vacant eyes flickered, his fingers stirring again.

Ben. I wish to meet him.

He eyed me. He didn't often make such requests. What Robert didn't know was we seemed to have employed the one person more elusive than himself. But I was determined not to bring it up until all was lost and I absolutely had to.

'Are you looking forward to your birthday?' I whispered, moving swiftly on. 'They say eighty-six is the new sixty-eight.'

Don't mention my birthday in the house. And I will be 83.

'Oh, I know. It's just that you've been eighty-three for a while.'

'I may look like a bag of bones,' he quipped, 'but that doesn't mean I'm not vain.'

I laughed. He still had the power to make me feel like a schoolgirl. 'Very good,' I said. 'You've got your giggle out of me. Now save your strength.'

But he kept typing. *I have concerns.*

And now I sensed this was why he had chosen to take to his keyboard.

'About?' I muttered.

The mood of the party. Let's keep our wits about us. Yes?

I paused as I took in the implication. 'Yes, of course,' I said, as casually as I could. 'Noted. Anything else?'

'No, no, darling girl,' he whispered.

With a gentle touch on his shoulder, I left him to sleep and took a seat at the back where I could see everything. It was then I read Ben's email.

Occasionally, I glanced up at Kostas as I read, who was undoing his panama suit jacket and tying back his hair, then rising to the drinks cabinet for a Tom Collins. Every so often I'd forget he was with us, but then that was part of his remit.

By the time I finished analysing Ben's message, I was furious. He'd fucked us like we were an eHarmony date. I could only imagine how this would affect Robert. Everything I did was to keep his mood as consistent as possible. Hot white pains and dull aches returned as I read the message once more.

I got a part I couldn't turn down. I thought it best to be honest.

I didn't believe it for a second. Ben had had second thoughts about the oddity of the position, OK, I understood, father figure is not a role many people are familiar with, but he had been informed what he was in for, and we had paid far over the odds for what the job entailed. He had a hell of a sense of timing. I couldn't spirit up a replacement at such late notice. Sofia was clear about how important this summer was for JR; they wanted to see him come out of himself in his last holiday before leaving home for boarding school. And Robert was already unsettled by something.

I'm aware how this makes me look, but I have my future to think about.

As the phone connected to the wi-fi, then started to ring, I considered how firm to be with him. Twelve rings later, 'Hi. I'm so sorry,' Ben said. But he wasn't really going for it. This was a poor show from someone whose job it was to pretend.

I checked around to see if anyone was watching, then had a glass of water and my second pill, wondering how to delicately explain the position he had put me in.

'I really am so, *so*, sorry,' he repeated, after my tactical silence.

'Oh darling. What happened?' I cooed into the handset so he could hear the kindness in my voice, as I thought of chokeholds and the best places to bury young men.

2

The Super Tutor

Amelia

As we boarded the yacht bound for Korpios, Mr Rathwell's private island, the sun broke through a cloud and the sea glittered like foil. It felt like a sign of good things to come.

Kostas helmed the yacht single-handed. Mr Rathwell liked to keep his entourage in single figures and his private life as private as possible. And privacy was particularly important here as this getaway was planned to coincide with a story breaking about Robert back in England. He wanted to be out of reach of every zoom lens when it hit.

Korpios was a haven from the digital world. JR got to have his last splurge on the plane, but this would be his detox. They thought it might help with his moods, but I always felt they worried too much about those anyway. It's a difficult age for any kid, particularly a gifted one born into unusual wealth. People seized on a few morose words and that time he told another boy he would 'have him shot'. But I'd heard worse.

The Grand House only had a landline. It would be like living in a period drama set in the nineties. No mobile signal, no wi-fi, no chance of him being dragged into what was being dug up on his father. Which was being strictly kept from me too, in fact I overheard even Sofia had chosen to protect herself from it because of her nerves.

It would be my last trip with the family and I knew I'd miss JR so much; he didn't act or talk like other boys and I didn't see that as anything to be afraid of. People often mistook me for his big half-sister and that helped him treat me similarly. I'd shielded him from the tensions in the house – 'the Atmos', I called it to friends – sheltering him in books, conversations and trips. We held hands under the soft light of aquariums and museums.

I saw this holiday as one in which we would both finally escape the Rathwells.

In a final push towards manhood, it was decided he needed more special attention in his last months before boarding school, so two of us were meant to take turns looking after him. The problem was that this Ben, who I'd never met around the London house, was nowhere to be seen on the yacht either. The Rathwells never explained anything to me, but I could barely imagine their world of interpersonal relationships anyway, where it must have seemed like everyone had something to gain from you. Must have been difficult to know who to let in. This was why I tried to be respectful about things they didn't want me to know, gleaning everything I might need to from the gaps between words and doors.

It had taken some time to fill Ben's position, far longer than Sofia had expected. She had known that finding the right young man would be difficult, having chosen to avoid the specialist agency for super-tutors I came from (we're all Oxbridge grads with decent knowledge of a wide tract of subjects) because she wanted someone *a bit more real*. I had come to accept that it was her accent that made everything that came out of the mouth of Sofia Rathwell, née Durkblum, sound blunt and philosophical. Even simple questions like *how are you?* could take on complex meanings. But most of her intentions, I came to realise, were very innocent. You couldn't blame 'the Atmos' on any one of the Rathwells in particular, it was the potion of putting them all together that caused it. Individually, they were wonderful. Or maybe wonderful is being too kind. My friends tell me that's a habit of mine.

The result of Sofia narrowing her search was that only one man had made it past the telephone interview stage and been invited to meet face to face on the morning of Easter Monday. Just one, it fascinated me. His agreement to the date suggested a lack of a strong traditional family, I overheard Sofia telling her husband, Mr Rathwell. And I heard him agree that that seemed like a very good thing.

Ben arrived with the inevitable awe that comes with a visit to the mansion on Billionaires' Row, just a cricket ball struck in anger from Hampstead Heath. The new man took it all in as he flashed past the doorway of the study, trailing Sofia to the library, where she liked to take visitors.

I heard their soft voices carry across the wooden floor-boards ...

'This isn't a job that experience could prepare you for,' I heard her say. 'But I'm sure your training as an actor will help. You mentioned you have a part coming up at the Royal Shakespeare Company, but it doesn't start for a while, until September, is that right?'

I couldn't see him or make out his words, despite the fact that I'm a deep listener, a quality all musicians need, to hear what's really going on.

'JR is the most wonderful young boy, you'll see, he's quite remarkable,' she said. 'But then there's the lack of discipline. Problems with concentration. *Rage*.'

The word hung in the air. It was true, I'd seen it myself. Had cleaned up the broken glass after his birthday party.

'You see ...'

She paused, musically to my ear, as orchestras sometimes do before launching into the main theme.

'... JR's father, Robert, is a good deal older than myself. He lives a fine life but not a very physical one. At least, not in the traditional sense. So, you see, we need ... a role model to ... provide a positive influence, to support him on his journey from youth to young manhood, and for the outdoor parts of life that are so important for boys. A father figure if you will.'

He drew breath to speak, coughed, took a sip of water.

'Korpios is a very real, very rustic island, just west of the bustle of Lesvos,' Sofia said. 'The population when we aren't on it is zero. Two maids come over to service the Grand House daily whether there is anyone on the island or not, though the word maid is insufficient for what they do: they cook, clean, serve. They are a marvel. No one is allowed near the island without our say-so. You would spend the whole month of August there with us.'

'Well ...' he said. He wasn't sure what to say at first, but then suddenly the words seemed to come easily.

'Well ... I know it could seem unusual to employ an artist for this, but I happen to tell stories for a living, and I think

18

everyone needs stories, everyone needs a little escape, especially young boys. I'd be coming into his life at a time of real change and that can be magical, and it can be fragile. Luckily, I remember being his age myself, and there's nothing more extraordinary than a young man realising who he really is. And that's a story I'd like to be a part of.'

His voice was calm. I thought the answer was perfect for a client like Sofia who requires a bit of stardust, it didn't seem by rote, I could tell he was thinking through it all as he said it. He was charming, that was certain, but the other mysteries of Ben remained hidden to me. And that was by design, because I was always in another room or out of the house when Ben visited. The Rathwells kept the staff apart for control's sake, the kind exerted by an experienced businessman for practical reasons. All of us could know a little about how things worked, but if we formed a union, we might put the pieces together and end up knowing too much. Consequently, having been employed by the family for two and a half years, and Kostas having been with them for ten, we'd never even had a single conversation. It was a remarkable feat. So typically Rathwell.

On the boat, the sea was millpond still as we made the crossing, only disturbed by us. The air was static. As this was a gulet yacht, meaning it had both sails and motors, Kostas nodded to Mr Rathwell and soon the engines cracked into life. I'd noticed Kostas was so keen on Rathwell he often walked in step a couple of paces behind him. I've even seen him occasionally taking on Rathwell's gestures, like any good shadow would.

Isabelle and Sofia were deep in conversation on the yacht's cream leather seating, some metres away, as white ribbons of water shot up either side of the boat. I leant forward, trying to make out if they were talking about this Ben, but the white noise of the ocean made it impossible. Isabelle turned, catching me staring, and I looked away immediately. The Rathwells' lives were full of secrets and anyone trying to delve into them seemed to regret it. A quality of relaxed awareness was required, Sofia told me on my first day. By which she meant you have to appear relaxed, while being very wary.

I started massaging my ankle just above my prosthetic foot, as the altitude of planes can make it sore afterwards.

'You don't mind, do you, J?' I said, pulling at the sleeve.

He wet his bottom lip, his eyes so fixed he didn't even blink. He'd seen my smooth prosthesis before but never seen me remove it.

'Can I ask something, Am?' JR said. 'If it's not too rude?'

He'd been gearing up to the question for the entire time I'd known him and had clearly decided that we now knew each other well enough for him to ask it.

I laughed softly as I kneaded my thumb into the skin where my leg ended: 'Is it about my ...'

'Yes,' he said, hardly taking his eyes off it. 'How did it get like that?'

'An accident in a car,' I said, keeping it as breezy as I could. 'Don't worry, it won't happen to you. Cars are safer than when I was your age.'

'Oh, I'm not worried,' JR nodded, not taking his eyes off my foot for a second. It was a little strange, but I found his quirks endearing. 'I wish that hadn't happened to you. I wish I could take the pain away.'

It was things like this, so unusual and empathetic, that

moved me. 'Thanks, J. It's done now. Don't dwell on it. Think of it as a mistake from olden times.'

He nodded, the light in his eyes fading a little. Serious things tended to drag him into a reflective mode.

'I hear that's what Ben's like,' I said, to snap him out of it, having barely ever brought up the subject of Ben with him: 'Old-fashioned somehow. Like an old-time movie star, someone said. Is that right?'

'Yeah,' J said, that spark coming back. 'Tall, nice. Like Edward G. Robinson.'

I laughed at that name coming out of his mouth. I almost forgot watching old films was something he did to bond with his father.

'So, you met him on his interview, and he's come by the house three times since, to get to know you a little? What do you think of him? Is he … interesting, cool?'

'Cool? Wouldn't say that,' J said, he really found that funny. 'No. Nice, but not cool. Like you.'

And soon we were both laughing at his cheek. I was happy to see him smile again and quietly delighted he didn't find Ben more impressive than me. Recently, I'd started to fear that I was like his blankie with the clowns on it; no longer good to be seen with.

Maybe it was sad to want the love of a little boy, but I cared about him a lot, and knew he was in a transitional stage. I remember the fit he threw when he was first told Ben was coming to meet him, the cricket ball that broke the glass of the Modigliani painting. He gets 'social anxiety', I explained. However, despite JR's worries, the day Ben arrived I remember hearing him and JR laughing in the garden together. It sounded so natural, like they'd known each other their whole lives and Ben had just returned from some time away.

I wished I had a bit of that ease. It had taken me months to get JR to open up like that. Everything I did was shot through with an underlying seriousness; the curse of caring. Because childhood for me is a serious matter. Mine certainly was. But I felt that if I could get things right for JR, instil some core values, then whatever happened to him, he would handle it better than I did.

I thought about my father's mocking laughter, then tried to block it out.

I need to be more like him, I thought. *I wonder what Ben's secret is?* A phrase that has a couple of meanings, I soon realised.

And as we approached Korpios on the yacht, another question occurred to me: if this is a private island, then who are all those people there waiting for us?

3

Trophy wife 2.0

Sofia

The heat of the sun on the nape of my neck, the sound of golden oriole birds, that look on my treasure's face when we stepped onto the island as the locals surrounded us. He was, perhaps, a little afraid. A sudden driving beat sent my hand to my chest too, a pounding bass joined it, calling out from tall speakers amongst the trees. That's when JR's face broke into a smile and the Greek locals started to dance, to begin the show. I was sure this was Isabelle's doing, though she had kept it as a surprise. There was plate-smashing, acrobatics, a dance with hankies, even fire-breathing. I'm not sure how much of it was strictly traditional, but Isabelle knew her audience. JR's adorable eyes lit up as he watched the fire plume then collapse into air, the stilt-walking, the big finish in the human pyramid. So beautiful, so technicolour. It made for quite an arrival.

Throw in some TikTokkers and it would have been everything J loved. But then, we flew most of his favourite TikTokkers to the London house for his birthday.

We all clapped heartily as the performers bowed, JR

running up to shake each of their hands and Amelia following close behind to make sure he didn't do anything too odd. As I finished clapping, my hand smoothed down my dress and found my hip as I saw the frown on Robert's face. He was honest about the fact that little impressed him these days.

'I'm sorry, darling,' Robert said, reaching for my hand. 'I can't fake it.'

'Is it a no-dopamine day?'

'Hmm. No-dopamine day,' he said, his face an empty horizon.

His doctor had explained to us that Robert found it difficult to feel the rush of good feeling provided by dopamine that most people get at moments of joy. Someone like me, I find delight in the verbena scent of surrounding trees, the quality of light on the island that makes every moment like magic hour, I look for sensory pleasure in everything. The dark winters of a childhood in the Danish countryside make you grateful for every piece of light you get. The problem for Robert was his successes: he had had so many that he had built up a resistance to joy.

'Do you need anything?' I said to Robert. 'Anything at all?'

'Car?' he croaked, his head bowed. The question I always asked about my husband was which version I was going to get: the one I love, I love above all things. Some others, I love parts of. But there are a couple of sides to him I have to watch very carefully.

However, even in his kindlier moods he never let standards slip. That is why he always asked for spring water from the Norwegian islands of Lofoten wherever he went. It's the hardest to come by and when people provide it for him it shows he has retained his worth.

I checked my lipstick in my compact mirror then raised an eyebrow at Isabelle. She was watching Kostas jog towards the car in the distance.

'Beautiful show,' I said to the performers as they waited for a boat to take them away. 'Gorgeous, luminous, fantastic.'

I tried to look them in the eye and connect, as I believe people as lucky as us owe it to others not to seem removed, but I was understandably distracted. *Where was Ben Bowman?* Isabelle said she was resolving the matter, but time was running out. I knew from the moment Ben met JR that there was a reality to this actor. He was perfect and would be integral to everything.

When I was pregnant with JR, I would imagine him as an angelic kid, who would wait on us at tea parties. The reality is always more, well, interesting, but I still believed we could smooth out his rougher edges before he went away.

The trouble began six months ago with a silver tomcat. JR had told us frequently that he wanted a dog, but Robert said it would only dig up the garden. I shouldn't have been surprised when he became obsessed with that beautiful tomcat, who I spotted lurking around the gazebo one day. He had green eyes and a mouth that turned up at the ends, making him look like he had a permanent grin. JR spent that half term chasing him around and telling us obscure facts about cats. He identified him as a Russian blue, which cost upwards of two thousand pounds – unlikely to be a stray.

At the end of the week, Isabelle discovered the cat's head next to the limestone fountain, the body nowhere to be found. She called out to me, and the sight brought tears to my eyes. When Kostas came to take a look, it was decided that a neighbourhood fox must've carried out the butchery. But even as we settled on the idea, plausible because foxes are savages and were often spotted on the street, it was not probable because of the tidy way the head had been cut from the body and then placed away from it.

We were about to bury it when Robert came downstairs. We allowed a good number of minutes for him to stare, peering into the death of it. He agreed we should dispose of it and deny knowledge if anyone came looking. The plan fell from him so easily it was as if he was dictating an email.

It was only then that Isabelle admitted she had seen JR catch the cat that morning. Amelia added that she had found JR in the garden before their class, wiping a knife from the kitchen clean – *of mud*, so he said. But JR seemed unsure of the right answers when questioned. He finally settled on saying he had never seen the cat at all, yet when I lifted his cashmere jumper I found smears of blood on each wrist. It pained me even to think that my little boy could do something horrible, but I had to take precautions. I often stared at JR considering nature and nurture, and what secrets might be hiding in his genes. I had been watching closely for all eventualities. So, his room was searched, our serrated kitchen knife with the octagonal rosewood handle was found, there's only one of its kind. It was taken away from him and we decided he needed a role model.

I didn't want our Amelia to meet Ben back at the London house, just in case she mentioned JR's recent behaviour and frightened him away. Not that I expected Amelia to be loose-lipped, she had proved herself trustworthy, and more than that she had been specifically vetted at Robert's request. She did have one clear indiscretion against her name, but we overlooked it. Because second chances are important, I said. While Robert said he liked to employ people you had something over. I said that was a touch cynical, he said it was just practical.

Anyway, I needed Ben desperately. A single-parent child, a humble beginning, not so dissimilar to mine. I told Robert I'd handle the appointment, background checks and all, so to stand by the choice I'd made was to stand by my own independence and good mind. Childcare can be murder. Once you have the right person for the job, it's best not to let them go.

As Isabelle helped Robert into the sleek black Merc that had pulled up on the dry grass next to the dock, Kostas came over to whisper to me. It wasn't good news.

'We have another problem,' he said. 'The people carrier is out of petrol and we don't have any on the island.'

I turned to Robert to check he couldn't hear, but he clearly knew there was some problem as he was being bundled into a smaller car than he requested.

Kostas gave an apologetic smile. There wouldn't be room for all of us and despite what some people may imagine I am a people-pleaser and an utter pushover. A quick look to Isabelle and a minute later the two of us were left at the dock as the Merc pulled away.

'Nice show by the way,' I said to her once we were alone. 'Robert was touched.'

She had removed her hat to fan herself and was applying bug spray when her hand froze. 'Thought you arranged it?'

'Come on,' I said. 'It went down well. There'll be no blowback. How long did it take you to put it all together?'

'I didn't,' she said, with a bewildered smile. 'I promise you, I didn't.'

And it didn't seem likely that it was the work of Sir Anthony, Robert's favourite old boy, his CFO holding the Rathwell Company fort back in London. Wasn't quite his style.

Just then, our eyes were taken by the sight of a figure emerging from behind a tree. It loped along, so benign, but that's how terrible things begin, with small, ordinary movements. If we weren't here, the island was always empty. The shock of this presence rattled through me as the wind picked up; a cold kiss on the back of my neck. The figure was a man and he wasn't staff. He wore a black Dodgers cap, a white vest and pink shorts. Our security was currently driving Robert towards the house, leaving us exposed. My fingers reached into my bag, but my rape alarm wasn't in there and, even if it was, there was no one else around to hear it. His determined strides quickened. Until we recognised the tight blond curls, the tattoos. My muscles relaxed, if only for a moment.

'Bobby,' Isabelle said. 'How did you …'

'Did you like the show?' he said, with his transatlantic drawl and a light giggle, having stopped a couple of metres before us.

'Yes, that,' I murmured, 'that was—'

'A gift,' he said. 'From me to you. A … hello again. A … here I am. It's been so long.'

'Too long,' Isabelle said, 'too, too long.' But as she went to close down the distance and embrace him, he took a step back.

'Hope you don't mind,' he said, scratching at his arm with a sense of sudden shame.

'Mind?' I said, wondering how kind to be. 'No … no … absolutely … how did you get here?'

He smiled shyly before speaking quietly. 'Still got contacts, right? Still know the company that manages the island. Still

28

got the family name. Thought I'd get here before you. To surprise you.'

'And you did all this for us?' Isabelle said, and then she did hug him, and he waved me in for a kind of three-way embrace.

'When did you get here?' I said, patting his shoulder as I pulled back, watching him closely. 'It's very unusual for anyone to be here when … when Robert isn't—'

'I know, I know,' Bobby said, moving from too quiet to overly loud. 'But I called in favours, used the Rathwell flex like I rarely ever do. It's a birthday after all.'

'You know he hates birthday fuss,' Isabelle said, being careful not to tell him off.

'I came over last night to get it ready,' Bobby said, before swiftly adding, 'don't worry, I didn't stay in the Grand House. Not without … Robert … I was in the Aegean Rooms.'

The Aegean Rooms were where guests who hired the island for £20k a night stayed. A line of four lodges which can be made ready and stocked with luxury supplies at short notice. They were perched on the hill, and we could just about see the grass of the living roof from the dock where we were standing. Up there, you had a beautiful three-hundred-and-sixty-degree vista, including the Grand House on the other side of the island.

'I'm sure you'll be welcome to stay at the house,' Isabelle said. 'Once I've asked Robert, I mean.'

'I'll see how things go at dinner first,' Bobby said.

'Dinner … fine,' I said; he seemed to have it all planned out. 'Let us give you a call once we've spoken to Robert. Can we do that? The lines are working at the Rooms, I assume?'

There was no mobile signal on the island, but the landlines worked adequately at the Aegean Rooms.

'Everything works on the hill,' Bobby said. 'It's the Grand House where the landline is a little in and out. That's why I always preferred staying on the hill.'

He had spent a lot of time here as a child.

'There would be a few things to discuss about how exactly we introduce you,' Isabelle said.

'Why's that?' Bobby said, with an innocence that moved me, before giving us a puppyish smile.

'It has been a few years since we've seen you,' she said.

Bobby's look turned to a scowl that broke away in favour of a howl of laughter. 'I'm kidding, I know how long it's been, better than anyone. But I'm very hush-hush, you know that. I'm just Cousin Bobby, here for the celebrations.'

'Good,' Isabelle smiled, squeezing his arm as we turned to see the Merc coming in the distance, kicking up dust as it careened along. Kostas had driven back fast given he'd have had to settle Robert in his room, but he was used to the extra responsibilities, he seemed to crave them, and he was a very resourceful man. We were all seeking Robert's love in many ways. It was like starlight.

'So, we'll call, my darling,' I said, turning, but Bobby had disappeared. Into the trees where he came from, I supposed.

'We'll call,' Isabelle yelled, in case he was still within earshot.

But all we heard back, as her concerned eyes returned to mine, was her voice echoing on the wind and the somehow foreboding rumble of the Merc, glinting in the blinding sunlight in our periphery.

4

The security and the father figure

Amelia

The rare times I'd nodded to Kostas across a room he seemed too shy even to acknowledge me, as if I might cause a black mark against his name. But despite that, I always thought I sensed a smile behind his eyes.

In the early afternoon of our first day on the island, I decided we should have a proper conversation. It was ridiculous for us not to acknowledge each other when staying under the same roof. I found him willing to talk, if not so keen to do what I wanted him to. I asked to come along to pick up Ben that afternoon, who was arriving by helicopter, but some of the rules of the London house had followed us on holiday.

'But you are already in the best spot you could be,' he said, his voice both soft and firm. 'The beaches of the north are the most beautiful.'

'I'd just like to get an idea of where I am. I did a lot of exploring at Mr Rathwell's house on the British Virgin Isles last summer, and at the one in Bora Bora the summer before. Why not here?' I said, trying to come across as forthright as my mother making a complaint, but things always came out like an apology.

It was like a game of Taboo. The one word I couldn't mention was *Ben* and how curious I was about him. He had missed the jet but, typically, we hadn't been told why. Isabelle got him the next commercial flight out, then a helicopter from the mainland. I had covered for his late arrival with double lessons, so I thought surely I'd be released and free to roam at some point.

'Why,' Kostas mused, 'are the English so obsessed with jiggling around? We Greeks, we find the best place to sit, and we sit in it, for as long as possible.'

He gave a wolfish smile, the corners of him brightening further. He then chanced a quick look around and gave in with a shrug. I'd like to think it was my charm that won the day, but it's possible he just took pity on the girl with the prosthesis.

*

The car rumbled on as we headed towards the helipad, just beyond the dock. The island rose and fell at either end, like a dish, lush greenery lining the hill that led to the Aegean Rooms at one end, just as it did on the ascent to the Grand House at the other. The two dirt roads that stretched between were mostly barren. Whereas other Greek islands I'd visited had a welcoming array of tavernas and small stores selling holiday wares, Korpios had lonely cypress trees and silence. I could feel the sparseness of the place in my bones. It wasn't just that we were the only ones for miles around, but that no one had ever truly lived here, no one had been born here. I needed the low hum of constant connection and there were few signs of life on the barren rock. Until, out of nowhere, we passed what looked like a bar with a terrace made of oak boards, which had fallen into disrepair.

'The previous owner of the island,' Kostas said, 'liked to have a bar he could go to. Mr Rathwell, he likes the beaches, the house. Woosh, simple. There are six hundred islands in Greece to discover, some with more party, some with more amenity, none more quiet.'

None more eerie, I thought as I watched the blur of arid yellow. But I consoled myself with having discovered a new companion who, against the odds, was a talker.

'Mr Rathwell,' Kostas said, 'he bought Korpios for a knock-down price in the 1980s. A hundred thousand. It was the previous owner that called the main house the Grand House. Mr Rathwell rebuilt it, but kept the name out of tradition, even though he finds it a little simple. Little stupid.'

He nudged me. I laughed. He was a bit of a raconteur when he got going. I was pleased whenever a man opened up, just so I knew he wasn't one of those sullen figures who spent most of their time alone with their private grievances. I grew up with one of those men. And I promised myself I'd never let a man like that dominate me again.

'The running costs of an island such as this, they are not small,' Kostas muttered. 'The previous owner wanted out fast. An island can bleed you dry. Ha. So can a family.'

It felt like a test, so I gave no reaction, as if I had no libido for gossip at all.

Then the car came to a screeching halt. I held my breath at what I saw. Three flamingos of a dullish pink hue were crossing the road. I wanted to take a photo with my phone but, given there was no signal anywhere, I'd left the redundant thing in my room. So, instead I just watched. Their thin legs, so fragile. The longer it took them to go the more the wonder drained from me, but Kostas waited as if waiting was utter serenity. I wasn't used to this sloth-like pace, I'm a Londoner, it frightened me.

'How did they make it here?' I said, half expecting him to say Rathwell had them shipped in.

He looked at me and made a fluttering motion: 'They fly,' he said. 'They're the only guests permitted to stay for free.'

'Anyone else try and get over here?' I said. 'Sneak onto the island when no one's watching?'

'Sure,' he said. 'This is why, although we are an island, the Grand House still has security. The boat people come on the kind of boats that sink. The kind that come from Syria. But most end up on Lesvos, where there is a large camp. Don't worry, if we make a day trip there, we'll avoid all this.'

I wanted to make it clear that I didn't want to particularly avoid refugees, that I'd like to help them in some way, but I didn't know how to put it.

Then I heard a deathly drone, somewhere far away.

'It won't hit us,' he said.

'What won't?' I said.

'The cyclone,' he said, so matter-of-fact. 'It hit Crete, caused a ton of damage. But not here, here will be fine. You didn't check the weather report?'

'No,' I said, 'I didn't.'

Another crack sounded, a little closer. This time even he stared out at sea: 'It will be fine,' he said. A little less sure than the first time he said it.

*

A matter of minutes later, Kostas stopped the car and we got out into the blazing sunshine, the helipad ready in front of us. He ushered me well back with a hand as the noise of the chopper broke the air around us, putting the distant storm in its place. Dust was hoisted upwards as the silver wasp-like vehicle landed. When its rails were safely on the ground and the propeller slowed, Ben stepped out for his grand entrance. The pilot didn't even move from his seat, simply giving Kostas a thumbs up before urging the propellers back towards full pace as Ben walked towards us, hand outstretched.

'Sorry I'm late, is it Kostas?' Ben shouted, giving him a firm handshake. We hustled towards the car, Ben removing his panama hat in case he lost it in the wind.

Kostas nodded, silently throwing Ben's two cases in the boot.

'Very good of you,' Ben said as we slid inside the car. I took the front seat and Ben settled into the hot white leather behind me, staring out of the window in silence.

'Wow, what a life,' he whispered, at last. He was right, but saying it was a bit on the nose. I found my eyes lingering on his mouth, in the rearview mirror. Turning to the front, he said, 'Sorry, I'm Ben.'

'I know,' I said, damning myself for the enthusiasm. 'Your name's been mentioned,' I muttered, trying to water it down.

'I'm Amelia to meet you. Sorry, I mean, I'm Amelia, lovely to meet you.'

I smiled, resolutely ignoring my awkwardness, and with mercy, he did too. 'I'm the tutor,' I added.

'*Super*-tutor, I hear,' he said, raising his eyebrows. And I smirked as Kostas jumped into the front seat and we got going.

'It's not far to the Grand House,' I called back.

'Oh *lovely*,' he said, stretching the word out to four syllables. Seemed like he was trying to rise to meet his surroundings by playing a little posher than he was, which was kind of sweet.

I glanced into the rearview, trying to stare at him when he wasn't looking at me. I watched him playing the same game. I lingered on his eyes as the road swerved like a finger dragged lightly across fine sand for the feel of it. At last, he looked up and caught my gaze, and I held the look with a smile until it was too awkward not to speak.

'Sorry if I'm a bit elsewhere,' he said. 'D'you ever do that thing where you're replaying a moment in your mind to figure out if you've done something terrible?'

'Always,' I said.

'Ha, well, I'm sure that's not true,' he said, hesitating once more before deciding to press on: 'I had to get a plane, then a boat, then the helicopter. I have no idea how Isabelle arranged it, it was basically the most exciting thing that's ever happened, and I've done a three-episode arc on *Emmerdale*.'

I laughed, and was relieved when he did too, but he became a bit grave when he went back to the story of his trip.

'There was a young woman at the port. Syrian girl, who had fled the country and was trying to get to Lesvos where the rest of her family were, in a camp.'

'That's one of the largest camps in Greece,' I said, 'terrible. For them, I mean. It's probably the right place to come, they're treated better there than most places.'

I said it all like I was an expert. Kostas gave me a wink but didn't say a thing.

'The other people waiting to board started telling her to go back to where she came from, well, I wasn't having that, so I told them … where they could shove it, basically.' He looked uncomfortable for a moment, then continued. 'And then I … paid for her ticket,' he said, almost rearing up as he did so, as if telling the story embarrassed him.

Kostas noted all of this with a subtle slant of his head.

'Good for you,' I said. 'That's very kind. But don't mention that story to the family. They go to the Greek islands for tranquillity, and here you are, shipping more people over.'

'Oh,' he said, before he caught my eye.

'I'll put a finger up when I'm making a joke, shall I?' I said. 'Just so we're clear.'

Then I turned to catch his bare eyes in mine again. We passed the stone buildings where the maids stayed, with their typical Greek colours of white and loulaki blue, ochre and burnt oxide. Then as we approached the house the gates opened up in front of us and he let out an unintentional gasp. The house had the typical clean white aspect of Greek architecture but was wider at each side than you would expect, like a little Versailles, the left flank holding the full-sized gym, the right containing the large dining room with a bar stripped from a 1920s Parisian Art Deco bistro and shipped over. The whole place was ornamented by vines reaching like arms around a shoulder and had the appearance of being open and welcoming. But its position – low enough to sea level to require few stairs to the beach, flanked on all sides by ocean, with a subtle fence at the front – made the property a fortress. From the drive, you could just about glimpse the leaves of the tallest tree in the orchard. It was so quiet you could hear our footsteps and the water feature of stone angels pouring into the Olympic-sized pool behind the house. Isabelle emerged to greet us, and Ben physically shook with excitement as he leapt up the marble steps to press his hand between hers.

Isabelle had put her face on, arriving like a ravishing mature French actress. I often felt that if I got to know her, I'd discover she was one of those brilliant women who really had their shit together and only had to appear prickly to assert herself. I hoped we'd share a drink while here, make a breakthrough, talk about something meaningful.

When Isabelle left to find JR, I went up the spiral stairs, looking down at Ben as I circled above, glimpsing his handsome face, dark eyes, strong jawline, perfect symmetry. He was surrounded by the marble chessboard flooring before our eyes left each other.

When I reached the top of the stairs, I found my pulse was racing. I was usually able to stay so calm, despite the tensions of the Rathwells. But Ben had had an immediate effect on me.

Then I heard a noise on the top floor, coming from Sofia's room. Which was odd because she was downstairs. I trod upwards, taking each stair with silent care until I saw Kostas in there.

'Looking for something?' I called as I entered.

He stopped and turned in one swift movement, before responding: 'Ah, caught me, just as I was thinking this is not my baggage. I was told my case had been taken up here by mistake, but it must still be downstairs.'

It was a reasonable story. I doubted he would be so bold as to pry into her things, given she was his boss, so I let it go as he passed, stroking my arm gently. But as I watched him leave, I did start to wonder whether I'd scuppered his plan to analyse her underwear drawer, or if he had another motive. In the end, I decided lack of privacy is the price you pay for security. But as I watched him disappear downstairs, I made a mental note to keep what I had hidden even closer to my chest.

5

An extraordinary boy

Isabelle

'Isabelle?' JR said, in the hallway. He enjoyed the formality of saying adults' names. When I turned, he had quite a blank expression. He seemed like a boy who wanted to be happy but didn't know how. We lavished him with things, but neither that nor the weather had helped his mood by the look of him.

'I want you to know, if I seem down, you don't have to try and fix it,' he went on as if he'd read my thoughts. 'Sometimes, that's just the way I feel.'

I never knew quite what to say when he said things out of the blue. His therapist had taught him to talk like that. 'But isn't it nice Ben's here?' I said as I saw our new arrival approaching, having finished his good long look at Amelia going up the stairs.

'It's... OK,' JR said. He was only being honest. It was nice to be in his confidence. 'It's just ... Ben's not daddy.'

And with that he attempted a smile as Ben tried to give him a high five and was met with a formal handshake. Then JR began showing Ben the house like a dutiful tour guide.

He leant into one of the columns, arms folded in the grand hallway, telling Ben the exact size of it in cubic metres. Then I watched him go to the den and show Ben how he lay on the tiles with his vest off. He took him to the opulent dining room, then the kitchen–diner with the huge pink marble fireplace filled with a stack of wood we never lit.

He looked up at me as he passed, and I nodded, encouraging him to continue with the gym, the cinema, the relaxation deck, the Turkish bath and the orchard.

This would be a chance for J to enjoy real things. The manly, physical, normal side of life we hoped Ben would bring. No memes. No YouTube. No accidents.

I heard Ben and JR go up to the first floor, where both their rooms were, as well as Amelia and Kostas'. Then I saw them venture further up the spiral staircase, to where my room was, as well as Robert's and Sofia's. They had separate rooms because they required their space. Her especially, of late, I had noticed.

I met up with them again by the pool as Ben kept up a flow of exclamations, 'Wow,' 'Cool.' He was, however, a little quieter than he'd been at the London house. Perhaps he was nervous. JR seemed to notice it too. He really was very observant. That certainly wasn't one of his problems.

'You OK, Ben?' I heard JR say.

'Yes, mate,' he said after a pause. 'You?'

And after an even longer pause J said: 'I'm *in my feelings*.' It was another term his psychologist had taught him.

I watched JR invite Ben to test the temperature of the pool and soon they were both on their stomachs, leaning on the hot stones, hands in the water. JR was never allowed to have friends to the foreign houses, so this was a nice compromise. He didn't have many friends and those who did come over to play games often left upset. There was a biting incident. Though who bit who was difficult to say. They both had teeth-marks on them. And boys will be boys.

Ben turned sharply when Sofia arrived, telling her he 'wouldn't have missed this for the world.' I said nothing of course and soon we were heading down to show Ben the beach.

The view of the ocean revealed itself, but Ben was barely looking. He seemed distracted. Nervous. As if expecting Robert to jump out at any second. But there was really no need to worry about that.

Ben stepped onto the hot sand, and I saw him wince. I remember being startled by that heat at first, though you soon got used to it. But Ben was a full bag of nerves when he saw a figure sitting on the lounger, propped up on the best spot next to the wine cooler and the iced water.

We wandered over and Ben put his hand over his face because of the sun.

'It's a pleasure to meet you, Mr Rathwell,' he said.

It should've been terribly embarrassing because it was Kostas sitting there not Robert. That's why there was no need to worry about Robert appearing unannounced. Because he seldom did. He was careful about how often he appeared out in the open. That was just part and parcel of being a public figure, and one who easily got sunburn. But when he did arrive, it really was wise to keep your wits about you.

JR spared Ben's blushes by leading him over to see his sandcastles. Then he showed him something, obscured from my view. Ben's face didn't give anything away as I wondered what it was that JR kept hidden down there. JR even chanced a smile up at me, and it warmed me to know he was enjoying himself.

It was only last week he brought me breakfast in bed for my birthday. All his own idea, Amelia said. He wanted to see what it was like to be a butler, he said. It was just this kind of sentiment that got him in trouble, it seemed. If it hadn't been for the incident with the cat, I would've said he was almost completely misunderstood. But then, later conversations did lead me to question exactly what I saw that day.

*

Later on, Bobby's possible arrival still preying on my mind, JR passed with what looked like a smile on his face.

'JR, how *are* you?' I said.

His brow furrowed as he thought deeply about the question, then said, 'Good,' and I was delighted and surprised in equal measure.

'Good,' I said. I couldn't help but marvel at the alteration in him. It had previously been decided that Bobby was a far too wayward presence ever to cross JR's path. But there was a maturity and independence of thought in JR, and I wondered whether Robert may be wrong about JR not being ready for Bobby.

'Where's Amelia?' I said. Because I was anticipating needing her help.

'She's upstairs with Ben,' JR said, giving a little wink. 'Flirting.'

I nodded. I didn't know quite what to say, so simply noted

it for later, along with a thought about how naïve I'd been. There were already other elements in the house I couldn't control, I had to make sure Bobby didn't get free rein in the way he surely wished to. Bobby was a secret JR simply wasn't ready for yet.

We didn't want to disturb the balance of things, not when whatever seemed to be happening was good for JR. That was something not to be trifled with.

'Boys and girls, huh?' JR said, winking as he hurried upstairs. Such a particular humour to him, so wise beyond his years. He really was an extraordinary young boy.

I followed him upwards, realising more words with Robert were necessary.

6

The letters

Sofia

Dinner was approaching and we hadn't made the call to the Aegean Rooms. The Bobby situation really had nothing to do with me, so I absconded as the subject raged audibly between Robert and Isabelle beyond the door to Robert's bedroom.

I descended the stairs, took a quick look around as I sat, then produced a letter I had brought with me from London.

But I was soon distracted by the pleasant noise of JR and Ben, playing in JR's room. Isabelle was a wonder; Ben was only six hours late and right on time.

At first, my interactions with Ben during his few visits to the London house were brief and ordinary. If time allowed after a conference call with the foundation, I would breeze over and make a few suggestions about things they could do. We were breaking him in gently, so JR could get used to him. But on his last visit I was changing when I saw them playing, out of my dressing room window. When JR went to the bathroom, Ben quickly took out a cigarette and lit it, but after a couple of draws he looked up and, despite being on the third floor, he caught my eye. It should have been him who felt caught out, but it was strange to be so un-composed in front of him, my shirt open, though from his angle he could not see that I was in my underwear. He lifted his head and waved apologetically, before throwing the cigarette onto the grass and stamping it out. A blush coming over me that eclipsed his, I disappeared from view.

Later that afternoon, I informed Ben that Robert deplored smoking as a weakness and asked Kostas to check for cigarette butts in the garden. The task was far below the pay grade of a man who carries a gun, but he also sprayed weed-killer on the lawn and pulled out dead roots with his hands, so he just said, 'Yes, miss,' in that way of his.

Robert's puritanical attitude to smoking could be seen as hypocritical because I often smelt cigar smoke in his room. But Robert's smoking was virtually medical, for the release of stress, because we had had a few surprises through the letter box in recent times; including something lumpen Isabelle was afraid was toxic that Kostas said he would make arrangements to safely dispose of. And then there were the letters. Handwritten, just ink and paper, but words can be worse than poison. They used to come weekly, but were becoming ever more frequent, like contractions. Which, I guess, suggested something or other was about to be born. Whenever they came, they sent a bolt right through me, and Isabelle was soon at my side, rushing them away to be analysed. What was worse was that I could never let on I knew who the letters were for. The notes simply read: *How do you sleep?*

I held one of them as I sat by the pink marble fireplace in the kitchen of the Grand House. It was so warm on the island we barely used the fire, but if it had been roaring, I would have tossed the note onto it and enjoyed the scent of it burning.

Then I quickly closed my fist to hide it. I had a strange feeling I wasn't alone in the room; I looked up and there was Ben standing over me.

'Sorry,' he said, realising he'd startled me.

'No, it's …'

I watched him wander over to get a cool bottle of Norwegian water from the fridge. He seemed to have made himself at home already.

'I like that photograph of you in the hallway,' Ben said.

The one he was talking about was of me, in monochrome, about to enter the sea on the British Virgin Islands, in a Hunza G bikini.

'The photographer's talented,' I said.

'Isn't he?' Ben said, becoming very proper. He blinked and tensed various facial muscles. He seemed to be wondering whether his enthusiasm for a photo of my flesh was a little too much.

'It was a gift,' I said, to break the moment. 'But we insisted on paying the photographer something anyway.' Perhaps I said that to remind him that almost all my relationships were essentially professional, and Ben's would remain strictly the same, despite the small talk that had developed between us.

He simply nodded and took himself away.

I ran my hand along my dress, closing my eyes, reminding myself to be grateful as I felt the quality of the fabric. It was a black Alexander McQueen piece with a bolt to hold it up at the neckline. I always dressed like I was going somewhere important, because I so rarely was. I was a kept bird. But

I didn't grow up on the wealthy side of our family and I knew from my mother's disposition that I had to guard against melancholy.

I left the kitchen in a different direction to Ben.

Passing the dining room, I saw Kostas in there, checking the locks on the windows. He frequently sized them up like he was waiting for us to leave so he could redecorate. He was often there when I walked into some room I thought was empty and always made me jump. Kostas had been in Robert's employ since they'd met in Santorini, a few years before Robert and I were married. Robert values privacy – the euphemism I have come to use for his paranoia – and this meant cutting down his staff and vetting each of them rigorously. In Santorini, he had searched for a good man who could single-hand a sub-seventy-foot yacht, as he had downgraded from the superyacht so he could feel the ocean like the old days. Kostas was also something of a fixer on the islands and had the added virtues of having no family and no regular income. Robert found he couldn't let him go, bringing him to England where Kostas had nothing but the lure of a new life. He had once been a member of the police force in Santorini, so didn't need too much training to become Robert's head of security. A factotum, Robert called him, a man of many jobs.

'Anything you need, Mrs Rathwell?' Kostas said, his hands casually in his pockets.

I heard my handset vibrate as he spoke and tensed automatically.

'No, no. Thank you though,' I muttered as I wandered back upstairs. I didn't want to miss the call, but I didn't want anyone to hear me take it either. Everyone knew there was no mobile signal on the island. But there were transceivers from when Robert had more staff on the island who needed to communicate with each other. What Robert didn't know was that two of those handsets were still being used.

My pace quickened, the transceiver was set up so it would vibrate discreetly to let you know someone wished to speak, which gave me time to go somewhere private. But the caller had made it known they didn't like to be kept waiting. Once on the second floor, I took a quick scan about, then headed through the first door on the left into my room.

'Yes,' I said, answering in a whisper.

The voice came like I knew it would. I was not to disobey it or show any resistance.

'I know the rules, you don't have to remind me,' I muttered. I bit at the corner of my lip as I listened to the response. 'What do you have planned?'

But then they were gone. The voice's sudden arrivals in my life made me shiver even in the heat, but so did its departures. I smelt rich dark smoke behind me and turned, the smooth black transceiver in hand. And there was Robert, in the wheel-chair he used when exhausted. I hadn't even had time to close my bedroom door, and there he was staring at me from the edge of his room.

He looked up at me. His brown and green eyes held an accusation in them that made me feel like a bad child about to get her comeuppance. I waited for his gaze to become warm or cold, a fist in the pit of my stomach. Finally, his eyes lowered to somewhere around my hips. In time, by way of a response, I strode into his room, turned him around and closed the door. Then reached behind me and let my dress fall, allowing him to look at me in my new underwear. And though his face didn't move, I knew I had stirred something in him, and so I drew closer, knelt down so I could sit back on my heels and look up at him.

He was still a fine, beautifully structured man with an ochre-coloured tan, as he approached his ninth decade. He didn't celebrate birthdays publicly anymore, but I thought we could celebrate in our own way, before dinner. His gaze shot right through me, his pupils so small, so still, a little smoke in them, I realised, a little deadened. I tapped his thigh, realising that he was no longer there.

Just as quietly as he had arrived, he was gone. I felt especially naked as I heard the air expelled from his nostrils. He was asleep. He had a habit of doing that recently, falling asleep with his eyes open. It was more than a little creepy. I adjusted my stockings and suspender belt, which I fleetingly thought had got some recognition at last. I spent most days doing stomach crunches to create a perfect picture that only I ever saw.

Looking at him there, his plan to get some use out of the Grand House gym seemed ambitious, but his strength sometimes did come back after adequate rest. To his credit he still did his bench-presses in London, but I wondered how much his heart could take.

I had hoped my naked body might've stirred that heart a little.

Instead, I simply put my head in his lap, both of us so alone, though together. And I pondered how much of my call, if any, he had heard.

7

An uninvited guest

Amelia

JR passed on a message that Isabelle needed me downstairs. With a skip in my step, I looked for her in every room, thinking this might be the moment when we bonded, expecting to find her waiting for me with something sparkling. Eventually I saw the lighted tip of a cigarette beyond the open front door and smoke billowing from an unseen mouth. I thought I'd have one too if it meant we could talk; I hated smoking but liked the kind of conversation that came with it.

I strode out there and was shocked to see a young man leaning against the grey stone of the porch like he was holding the place up. He looked at me but kept his slouch on, greeting me with: 'Hey, baby, how are you?'

He was pretty familiar with me, but he wasn't familiar to me. This stranger was young, mid-twenties, a couple of years older than Ben, a couple younger than me. He had curly bottle-blond hair and wore a green and gold tracksuit. Somehow it looked smart like it was a high-fashion option. This was dressing for dinner for him, I guessed, whoever he was. From first impressions, he looked like he either called the shots on the island or he wasn't strictly allowed on it.

'Er, hello,' I said.

I was neither warm nor cold. It was always best to hedge your bets with the Rathwells. The stranger leant down to pick up a glass of wine he already had on the go.

'The phones working in this place?' he said.

'No mobile signal on the island. But the landline should be—'

'It was just a little joke, cos, well … you know when you feel like you're waiting for a call that'll never come?'

I didn't know what he meant by that. I mumbled in generic agreement. He offered me a swig from his glass.

'Er, no, thanks. Sorry, who are you—?'

'Cousin Bobby,' he said, kissing me on both cheeks before I knew what was happening, then placing his glass on a ledge so he could hold me by the hand. 'How're you enjoying the island?'

'Haven't seen much of it yet. What should I—?'

'See everything, man,' Bobby interrupted, twirling me around like we were dancing, his smoke ribboning around me, and I had no choice but to go with it. I stared at him closely as I rotated under his arm, his tracksuit top was zipped halfway down so I could glimpse his reddened body underneath, and the hint of his hip flexors.

He made a signal to one of the maids, who came over and topped up his glass. He was getting special service out here.

'Honey? Another glass for our friend.'

It was then I noted his voice, some transatlantic accent more like that of an old British rock star than someone of his age.

52

'Oh, I actually don't drink, sorry,' I said, finally letting his hand go.

'I never want anyone to feel they have to be *sorry*,' he said. 'And you're right to deny yourself. I need to learn to do that, it's a very good habit to get into. Here's to self-control,' he grinned, and took a long swig.

He seemed like he meant well. He was personable, like he was convinced we were already friends. It was as if he was in the middle of a big joke and I was being let in on it. I leant against the opposite wall as I noticed a presence on my left, Isabelle watching from the hall before drifting away. The stranger couldn't see her from his angle and, as soon as I turned, she disappeared. I was clearly being charged with babysitting this guest, who had arrived out of the deep blue – if things like that can happen on a private island.

'Pretty creepy place, right?' he said, taking a drag on his cigarette.

'Not really,' I said. 'It's stunning, spacious, got a hundred-and-eighty-degree view of the ocean—'

'What are you, the estate agent? Come on, creepy AF, isn't it? Dinner for eight. An old powerful man who keeps himself to himself. Suspicious glances over shoulders. Standard shit.'

'It's just a dinner, isn't it?'

'Hahaha, yeah, I know him a bit better than that,' he said. 'He'll pull something out of his ass. You're serious, you don't find anything about this … strange? We're let in by two sinister housekeepers—'

'I think you just mean attentive and over fifty,' I said low, turning to check the maids were out of earshot in a way he had flatly neglected to do. 'If you're feeling a tension in the air, it's probably just because there's a storm on the way.'

'Bingo, storm coming,' he said, winking. 'Classic. It's like old Dracula stage-managed the whole thing himself.'

'I'm not sure you can buy the weather.'

'If anyone could,' Bobby said, 'he could.' Then he let out a raucous laugh. It made me start, then turn, hoping no one was hearing us getting on like a mansion on fire.

But as the humour subsided, he said something under his breath that caught me off guard: 'You really don't remember me, do you?'

'Uh …' I fumbled, embarrassed eyes to the sky. I could've played along but felt it was better just to set him straight: 'No, I really don't. I don't remember you.'

He gave me a look that said he thought otherwise, and that level of certainty often hustles me into questioning myself. It's a weakness I've been trying to stamp out in myself, and JR.

'Are you messing with me?' I said.

'Ha,' he grinned, leaning in, taking a good look at me: 'Yes, I am. I'm fucking with you. Probably. Sounds like something I would do.'

He was a riot, but I preferred it when he wasn't rioting all over me.

A bell sounded and he stamped out his cigarette, which had burned into the tipping paper, and zipped his jacket up to the top. He looked me up and down, checking I was adequately dressed for the occasion.

'OK, you're good, I'm good,' he said. 'Let's get in there first, otherwise they'll hog all the Dom Peri. You like this look, by the way?'

I threw up my hands, unsure whether to condone what I saw before me. 'It's great.'

'Fun fact,' he said airily, 'they call him a property developer, but he's really a slum landlord. Gets as many people as possible in shoebox flats and sucks them dry. What do you think of that?'

'Well,' I said, 'people need cheap housing, right?'

'Right,' he said, tapping me on the shoulder. 'He feeds on desperation, watch out for that. You're staff so I assume you've never met him, properly?'

'I was in the back of a car while he was in the ... no, I ... actually haven't,' I said.

'And you won't today, not really. I mean, you'll be in the room and so will he, but that won't be meeting him. That's if he turns up at all.'

'We ... were all told—'

'Hmm,' he said, his hand hovering up and down. 'I'd rate it fifty–fifty at best. Right, let's go. Just remember, steer clear of the red meat. I've no idea exactly where old Dracula gets it from, but he's been known to feast on villagers from local islands, so ...'

And with that he was striding inside and I was close behind, unsure if my new friend was a good one to be seen with.

At the table, steam rose between Bobby and I, sneaking out under the lids of china serving dishes. He beamed and reached over to tap my hand, like I was cattle that needed calming, and I appreciated it.

I heard footsteps to my left and then it was dinner for three.

'Hello, darling boy,' Isabelle said.

'Izzy, there you are!' Bobby said, raising a glass to her. 'Hope I'm not too early.'

Isabelle

They must've seen me cringe. I'd never been an Izzy. Bobby lifted the champagne from its sterling silver bucket and said, 'Come on, sweetheart, won't you have—'

'Oh no, lovely boy,' I said, 'I'll hold off until we're all here. But thank you so.'

You couldn't let him take the reins in this kind of mood. He had a habit of steering the carriage in all sorts of dangerous directions.

'Wow, total shut-out,' he said. I was glad I was here to save the girl, who knows what he would've done with her. As I sat next to him, he put his elbows on the table, then his face in his hands like a sullen child as he examined me.

'Dear Izzy,' he said. 'It's been so long. Feels like I was just a kid when I last saw you.'

'That's because you were one,' I said, swiftly turning to Amelia. 'Well, a teenager anyway. Bobby's been away—'

'Travelling,' Bobby said.

'For what is it, five?' I said.

'Six years,' he said.

'That's quite a holiday,' Amelia said.

'More of a lifestyle choice at this point,' Bobby said.

The girl was intrigued. The levy was breaking, the flow of information spreading over the banks. I thought of that question in the letters. *How do you sleep?* For me, it's by keeping secrets and keeping the peace.

'And dear, dear, Izzy,' he carried on. 'How've you been holding together?'

56

He had moved from silly, to charming, to abstract in the space of one sentence. I didn't quite know what he meant.

'I'm very well, Bobby, thank you for asking ...'

'I meant, more specifically, how is your *back*?' he said.

My smile was curt. I like to keep my internal issues to myself.

'My back? *Ça ne casse pas trois pattes à un canard*, as my father would say,' I said. 'Which means, you can't break three ducks' feet. Which means, it's as well as it can be. Ha.'

'Hey, buddy,' Bobby said as he spied Ben in a sleek black shirt at the door. 'Won't you join us?'

'Course,' Ben said, taking a seat, visibly wrong-footed by our guest but trying to enter with confidence, as all actors must.

'Dom Peri?' Bobby said, standing to play the waiter.

'All right,' Ben said, looking at me for an introduction to this guest. 'Are you ... joining us for the summer?'

'We'll see,' Bobby said, leaning over and punching Ben on the arm with an intimacy Ben didn't know they had. Ben didn't flinch. But he did stare openly at Bobby's tattoos. One ran across his cheek in handwritten script, another falling down the slope of his forehead, and another at the base of his neck, surrounded by an orchid: *Baby, Wanderlust, Generation*, they read.

'And,' Ben said, 'hope you don't mind me asking, who are you?'

'This is Cousin Bobby,' Amelia said.

Bobby gestured to himself and raised a glass with a smile. They'd never heard a cousin referred to. And nor would they have. Robert even did his best to keep Bobby's name out of the gossip columns, which is a little easier when you own one of them and you've got dirt on the owners of the others. Unfortunately, even this wasn't leverage enough to stop the story currently breaking back in Britain.

I saw Bobby's gaze wander and noticed Kostas was just behind me, standing like there was an invisible force field stopping him from entering.

'Waiter, I'll have the veal,' Bobby said, with a smirk. 'No, you're one of our guests, of course, it's the wonderful, magnificent … sorry, enlighten me, what the hell is your name again?'

'I was going to ask you the same,' Kostas said, being coy, because they had met many times. But to a nineteen-year-old who was barely present or sober, Kostas was just another body in the house.

'Me? Oh,' Bobby said, speaking into the champagne flute just before taking a sip: 'Oh, I'm just Cousin Bobby.'

'I see. I've heard such … things about you,' Kostas said.

'You'll make me blush,' Bobby said having real fun, 'my deeds are known the world over. And, sorry to repeat myself, who the hell are *you* again?'

'I am Kostas,' said Kostas, with an air of pride.

'You remember,' I said. 'Kostas does a few odd jobs around the house.'

'I'm sure he does,' Bobby said, giving him a strange nod.

Sofia entered the room and immediately stopped when she saw Bobby sitting there. 'Oh,' she said, clutching at her Cartier diamond necklace.

*

Sofia

'Bobby, you look gorgeous,' I said, without breaking stride. 'I'm so delighted you could make it.' A model of composure as I swooped over to kiss him.

'Are we doing that?' He said, 'Yeah let's, both cheeks, round we go.'

Then I glided back to my seat and, when I started eating, everyone else did the same, other than Bobby. I was determined not to give him too much attention when he was in this mood.

'Please,' I said to him, 'do eat.'

'No, hang on a ...' he said. 'There are only six of us.'

'That's fortunate,' I said, 'because if there were eight there wouldn't be enough food for you. Not that we don't like unexpected guests.'

'Unexpected,' he said, with a sad little laugh. 'Really?'

What did he mean, really? I took in the oregano, laurel and thyme textures as I tried to eat mindfully to stave off my nerves.

'Shouldn't we wait for the dark lord?' he said. 'Old Dracula himself. The Old Fart.'

I could've told him off, but I knew that's what he wanted. And anyway, I was not his mother. I simply tensed my core, as I did when I wanted to put my tension elsewhere.

'You know Robert,' I said, 'comes and goes as he pleases. He said he'd be along in a moment.'

Bobby gave a knowing glance to Amelia. They seemed to be familiar with each other.

'Oh yes, I know Robert,' Bobby said, letting out a long sigh then a *pff*. He folded arms, not touching his food while the rest of us ate.

Isabelle stabbed her chicken and gave him a pointed look to behave.

'And where's my man, JR?' Bobby said, picking up his fork and rotating it between his fingers.

I looked to Isabelle for an official response.

'He ate earlier,' she said. 'He's all settled, relaxing, reading a book.'

He frowned at his drink. 'Sounds boring.'

We all sat in silence and listened to the polite sound of cutlery on crockery.

'I'd love to go say hi,' Bobby said, rising. And I saw Kostas stand to stop him gaining access to the rest of the house.

And just then, we heard slow footsteps like the sound of cavalry. The room filled with Robert's dark cologne.

The first thing Robert heard was Bobby singing a powerful version of 'Happy Birthday'. Amelia and Ben looked surprised to hear it and no one at all joined in. Robert stopped it with a hand gesture before the first mention of his name.

'Thank you, cut it,' Robert rasped.

Bobby stood in silence for a few moments before saying, 'Hello, Robert.'

Robert paced towards him and Bobby strode over to give him a kiss on both cheeks.

'Darling boy, you dressed up, you look wonderful,' Robert said.

'Hmm,' Bobby said, lifting an otherwise redundant fork to gesticulate. 'Are you patronising me?'

'Dear old thing, would I stoop so low?' Robert said, at which Bobby had to laugh, as Robert wandered to the head of the table unperturbed, and Bobby made his way to the opposite side, watching Robert all the time.

Such was Robert's star power, even a boy like Bobby was quelled. Robert's energy had a mercurial quality. He was trying to roll back the years here, walking and talking without the aches and slurs and he could do it all right, but it would cost him. He usually saved himself for photo opportunities, during which his skin would be made peerless by a make-up artist and he could give you a very vibrant hour answering questions before having to recuperate for at least a day. Little did the younger ones know it, but Robert was spending most of the vigour he had left on Bobby's appearance. The question *How do you sleep?* wasn't a hard one for Robert. Whenever he made it to his bed he slept like a baby.

'Eat, all of you, eat,' Robert implored. He would sit with us but not eat himself as he didn't like to do so in public. The food sat before him all the same, as he liked to be amongst it and deny himself, he often said. Soon even Bobby was eating as Robert surveyed the scene with a satisfied smile.

'Thank you all for being here,' Robert said. 'New friends and old. But none quite as old as me, clearly.'

It got a big laugh, full of nervous energy.

'Bobby, in particular,' Robert said. 'Thank you for coming. I'm sure your invitation will arrive in the post any time soon. Not that you've ever needed one, of course.'

When the rest of us laughed, Bobby gave one of his best deadpan responses.

'What do you mean?'

Everyone laughed again but it was drowned out by what we thought was the distant sound of thunder. Then from beneath our feet the earth moved. The table shook, the champagne spilt. Then came the screams. As I looked for something to hold onto, I heard the tap and shudder of the Art Deco bar behind us, a couple of crystal glasses martyring themselves and a bottle of forty-year-old Macallan whisky crashing onto the Rhodesian teak flooring after them, the brown ooze creeping towards us from within the shards of glass. I looked down, feeling sure that next I would see the ground open up beneath me.

*

Amelia

I'd never felt anything like it. It must've been a few seconds, but when the whole world shakes, it feels like it will go on forever. We all held our chairs with one hand and our hearts with another, except for Kostas and Robert.

'That was a firm one,' Mr Rathwell said, with strange relish.

'What was that?' I said, hands still shaking as I realised the maids had come in and were clearing up champagne, ice and broken glass from around our feet.

'Tell them, Kostas,' Mr Rathwell said, like this was his birthday treat. I watched him closely. Studied him with a blend of curiosity and suspicion.

'Earthquake,' Kostas said.

'More a tremor,' Bobby said as if he wasn't as shaken as the rest of us.

'About four on the Richter, four-point-one?' Kostas said.

'Not bad, not bad at all,' Robert said. 'You see, we are very close to the convergence of the Eurasian and African lithospheric plates. The latter sinking about five centimetres a year, causing quakes. That's what's so special about the South Aegean Sea, we're on the fault line, figuratively and literally, between the intellect and philosophy of the Eurasian world, typified by the Greeks, and the … well … the primitive savagery of Africa.'

He couldn't help himself, he glanced in my direction. The discomfort was immediate, but they didn't know how to give it words. Or were afraid to. I just watched on.

'She knows I didn't mean *that*,' Robert said, with a twinkle.

And I smiled back. 'Yes, don't worry, I know *exactly* what you mean.' I was used to dealing with not so microaggressions.

'Robert,' Sofia said, 'savagery is … not a term I'm comfortable with.'

'No,' Ben muttered, 'I don't think you can say … least not …'

'Pah, she said she knows what I mean,' Robert said, turning his sharp light blue eyes on me. 'All these white saviours around, must be a real bore for you, hmm?'

I gave a short breath, expressionless, my eyes on his. No matter what other evils might be around, I was still grappling with what to do about this one.

'Oh God, that's not …' Ben said, it seemed to fall out. 'I really don't think …'

'That's Robert Rathwell for you,' Bobby muttered. 'Always ready with a swift counterattack. Problem is, Robert, you really can't get away with things like you used to.'

And Mr Rathwell did give the slightest pause at that. 'No, I … I do apologise to our … lovely … where are you from in Africa exactly?'

I didn't even pause: 'Fulham.'

Robert laughed until he coughed, then composed himself: 'Very good. A palpable hit.' He slapped his chest like he'd received a bullet wound. 'I do make some awful mistakes, but I'm trying to be better, and I can only say you all should be thankful you didn't meet my father.'

I certainly was. But then, I was used to monstrous fathers. I even had one of my own.

'And what about you, Ben, where are you from?' Robert said.

'All over,' Ben said, just a touch combative.

'Very modern. No, no,' Robert said, wagging a finger. 'You can't fool me. You're northern. But I can see why you'd hide it.'

'I'm not hiding anything,' Ben smirked.

'Then where are your parents from?' Robert said.

'I grew up in the Midlands.'

'And your father?'

'I didn't know him so well.'

'Oh, I see,' Robert said. 'So, you're a foundling?'

'No,' Ben said, taking a sip of his champagne, unflustered, like he was used to defending himself. 'Fortunately, I'm very close with my mother.'

It felt like there was something else Ben wanted to say, but he managed not to.

'Ah, well, good,' Robert said, blowing out his lips as he eyeballed everyone, one by one. 'Don't get so tense, all of you. So sensitive, this family, and this generation. How about … a toast to mothers everywhere.'

And we all drank to that, especially me, because mother was never far from my mind. But the toast didn't help Bobby who sat staring at his uncle and, for once, didn't drink.

'Now, all of you, eat. I must visit the little octogenarian's room,' Robert mumbled as he ambled away. My eyes followed him loping down the hall and I wondered how he had managed to shamble into the room and kick up so many ugly things in such a short time. He was, in so many ways, awful, and yet there was something magnetic about his presence.

Bobby drained his glass and stood, turning his back to us all with a heavy energy.

'He's not coming back, is he?' he said, so soft.

'Robert has to save his strength,' Isabelle said. 'And he always prefers a French exit.'

It was all so bizarre. I supposed this was why I was never allowed to meet Robert. He had only been with us for a few minutes, but I had already confirmed a few suspicions I'd always had about him: bigot, charmer, fool. I recalled finding a green shard of glass on the kitchen floor as a child, and not being able to resist reaching out and touching its sharpest edge. It cut me, as I knew it would. That glass, that blood, that was Robert.

'And JR? I don't get to see him, do I?' Bobby muttered, with his back to us all.

'We don't want to unsettle him tonight,' Sofia said. 'You can see him another day.'

He repeated her words to himself, none of us brave enough to take our eyes off him. Then in a firm monotone he said: 'I want to see my cousin, JR. Any idea where he is? Anyone?'

'Darling,' Sofia purred, palms outstretched, approaching carefully. 'Not tonight.'

'Maybe tomorrow then?' Bobby said.

Sofia nodded instantly.

'Wow, so much excitement,' he said, gesticulating so wildly it put Isabelle on her guard, Kostas was half standing and the rest of us just watched, unnerved.

'Don't think I'll sleep tonight. I'm not a good sleeper anyway. What about you Sofia, how do *you* sleep?'

Her face fell. You could almost feel her blood run cold at his words. Next, he went to the table, took a sharp swig straight from the bottle, slammed it back into the bucket, then produced a gun from his inside pocket, which he placed against his temple, still keeping his back to us.

There were various shouts from around the table, Sofia swearing in her native tongue as she put her hand to her chest in shock. Kostas stood, putting his arms out to close down the distance and adopt a good position from which to take the pistol off him. But he froze when Bobby turned and pointed the thing in his direction.

'Oh, put it away,' Isabelle said, barely looking up, 'and have some food, darling.' She was trying to bluff him into believing she wasn't alarmed, but I wasn't sure that was the best way to go. This was the first time I'd seen things with the Rathwells threaten to fall into violence. My composure, which had taken years to build, was fading. I wondered whether I could make it to the door before shots were fired. I enter a room always looking for an exit. I have a sixth sense for trouble I honed during my childhood.

'Don't call me darling,' Bobby snapped, slamming his fist down on the table, then turning the gun on himself. He pressed it into his skull as he said, 'I'm not doing anything wrong.' His free hand came up to grip the back of his neck as his face contorted into a rictus frown. 'I just want to see my relatives, rather than the entourage. That's not evil, is it?'

Then he pointed the gun at Sofia across the table. We could feel he meant it, and for a second no one moved. I looked at Ben, then the door, wondering if he was judging if he could make it too.

'OK then,' Bobby said, cocking the gun. 'But remember, this was your decision. And there are witnesses.'

'Don't—' Sofia said.

But then he pulled the trigger and she was silenced. Red everywhere. Red on the tablecloth. So much red.

But Bobby just gave a single high laugh.

'Oh God,' I gasped. 'Jesus Christ.'

'Call someone quick,' Isabelle said, 'we need help in here.'

Ben raced from the room to find one of the maids.

'My God,' Sofia said, clutching her chest. 'Why did you do that?'

Bobby could only laugh, remorseless. The corn syrup was all over the tablecloth, all over the crockery, all over Sofia. It had gone off with a squirt rather than a bang.

'This is Dior,' Sofia said.

Ben arrived back in the room so the maids could clear the mess Bobby had made.

'I was just fucking with you,' Bobby said. 'It's not real.'

'That was pretty clear as soon as you pulled the trigger, darling,' Isabelle said. 'But Sofia is still covered in it, you frightened her half to death and someone has to clear it up.'

More paroxysms of laughter as we looked on stunned.

Bobby sat down, wiping his brow of sweat, inadvertently leaving a red mark there. 'Sure, but not us. Let's not pretend this family cleans up after itself. It's a ... toy gun that fires blood. It's a present, for JR.'

Sofia clenched her fists and darted out of the room to clean herself up. And as she did so Bobby placed the pistol on the table, his hands over his face, and there was a long silence. After a moment, we saw his shoulders shake and realised he was crying.

'JR's not allowed to play with guns,' Kostas said.

'Oh,' Bobby said, his voice so fragile. 'Didn't know that. Remember I used to do those pranks on my YouTube channel? Thought you'd get it, thought you'd remember.'

Kostas swooped over and gently took the gun. I'd almost forgotten our security man was there. He had reacted pretty fast, but it wasn't as if he had dived in to take a bullet for Sofia. Maybe my standards for devotion are too high. And I suppose it was Robert's security he was most interested in, rather than anyone else's.

Isabelle went to Bobby and hugged him to her chest, stroking his head as I shared a look with Ben. I was more assured than before that we were of the same mind.

Then after we watched on, hearing them whisper to each other, Isabelle drew me and Ben outside the room to ask if we wouldn't mind taking Bobby away, for a drink.

'He knows a place,' she whispered. 'I know this isn't the best advertisement for him, but he needs a friend. Maybe two. He's just a sensitive boy, as you can see.'

I could hear Bobby gathering himself in the dining room. We clearly weren't enthusiastic volunteers, but we could tell she was about to say we were being paid to be here. And I sensed he was a gentle soul. Being a Rathwell can't have been easy.

'One drink,' I said.

Isabelle placed a hand on Ben, whispering: 'We're all a little eccentric, aren't we? And that goes double for the Rathwells. This is just family all over, isn't it?'

My family was dysfunctional and I was used to certain Rathwell eccentricities, but even I hadn't seen anything like this. As for Ben, he looked nauseous. We had been witnesses to a cry for help, and it began to dawn on me that it was the kind I wished I'd have made as a child. Every so often I still pictured what difference it might have made back then, if I'd kicked open a door, made a scene. And when they were listening, told my parents that enough was enough. That I could feel things were only going one way between them.

Bobby waved to us from across the room. Such a sweet look, he had. There was something so childlike about him.

Minutes later, Kostas brushed past me and with a touch of my arm he told me to be careful. Then Ben, Bobby and I wandered outside to the driveway, climbing onto our mopeds once Bobby had retrieved them from the garage. I told them to go slow, as I hadn't ridden one of these for a while. But then the engines roared into life and we shot off into the dark, following Bobby through the night, wherever he wanted to lead us.

8

One drink

Amelia

After a fifteen-minute ride to the south of the island, the hum
of our engines cut out, and we parked up our bikes. I asked
whether we might see a landslide or even some open ground
because of the quake, but Bobby reassured us there were often
tremors on the island and tonight's one wasn't big enough to
do anything like that. He put an arm around our shoulders,
leading us towards the rundown bar I'd spotted at the roadside
that I thought was no longer in use. When he let us go, I found
Ben's arm was around me instead, lingering there. I didn't shirk
away from it and he seemed to notice I enjoyed being close.
When he finally removed it, we locked eyes.

Then Bobby pushed the door open and there was a perfectly
preserved taverna, complete with stocked fridges full of beer
and optics full of spirits. He flicked on the lights and we sat
on high stools while he played barman. I felt suddenly hot,
my face red. Looking over at Ben, I thought it was due to him
at first. But no, it was a creeping feeling about what had just
happened back at the house. It hit me, how easily I had chosen

not to speak, to give Rathwell a pass. Even after all this time I still withhold judgement, find excuses for the inexcusable. Sometimes it's as if I haven't learnt a thing.

I asked for a Coke and Bobby gave me a beer with it, which I left untouched. Someone once said that people who don't drink either had a parent who didn't drink who they didn't want to disappoint, or one who did, who they didn't want to follow in the footsteps of. For me, it's the latter.

'Listen,' Bobby said, 'sorry you had to see that. Family shit.'

'I get it,' Ben said. 'My mum didn't want me to go away at all. She did everything but hang onto my suitcase.'

'Ha,' Bobby said. 'Nice problem to have. You should be glad of a problem like that.'

'I am,' Ben said, looking up at Bobby. 'She's not a big fan of the Rathwells … no offence.'

'What's there to be a fan of?' he said. 'Seriously, Robert has a newspaper that peddles stories about rock stars with things up their asses, and half of it's not even true. Old Dracula wanted me to work there. I mean, jeez, it made me retch. I don't want to be *that* guy, with the crazed look in his eyes, like I've swallowed the family Kool-Aid. That's why I had to take a year out. And a year became two, and, you know, so on. What about you, Amelia, you speak to your family much?'

'Er … my family's a whole different thing,' I said, and they saw I wasn't ready to get into it. 'But I'm glad you said all that. Because I know Robert has his charitable foundation. But, after tonight, I'm not making any excuses for the Rathwells.'

Bobby nodded, the sensitive version of him revealing

himself. 'He really did give you both a going-over. I'm so sorry about … all of it.'

Ben gave me an easy smile and, not for the first time in our very brief relationship, his presence seemed to make strange things comfortable.

*

A little later, Bobby put on the sound system and disco lights on the terrace by the beach and we swayed as we talked outside, Italian disco playing, pink fluorescent lights illuminating our faces on the empty dancefloor.

'To be honest with you guys, I'm feeling kinda raw that you saw all that, and I'm feeling kinda like I gotta explain,' Bobby said.

'No,' Ben said.

'You're kind to say that. But it's good to get these things out, right?'

I nodded, happy to be with a Rathwell who was different.

'I'm kind of on the whole … bipolar … spectrum. Not as high up there as some, but high enough to have a decent view down on you all from where I am. Seriously, I have good days and bad days, and you just saw one of the bad ones. Can't believe you were there to see that actually.'

He looked past my shoulder at the dark sea and suddenly he seemed sober and full of a sad kind of balance.

'One of my more embarrassing moments,' he muttered. 'Anyway, accept my apology?'

I had the urge to give him a hug, so I did. And as Ben stood there, I was sure there was a glassy look in his eye that may have been a tear, and he was only one beer and some champagne down. Perhaps it was because we felt we were about to have quite some holiday together. The three of us.

Later, when Bobby disappeared to the bathroom, Ben and I sat on the edge of the terrace looking at the waves, getting stronger as the night drew on. He'd rolled up the sleeves of his black shirt and I found my eyes were lingering on his forearms. I enjoyed his gentle company, found myself agreeing to things even before he'd finished saying them. That's when I knew I was in trouble.

He complimented my green velvet dress. He laughed softly at something I said. I lingered close, noticing Bobby was still gone.

Then Ben interrupted the flow, as he said: 'I overheard something, back in the London house. That the Rathwells were coming here because a story was about to break.'

'Ah, I don't do gossip,' I said, our faces close. 'But if I did, I'd say it might be to do with the first Mrs Rathwell.'

'Oh,' he said.

'She died,' I said, 'some years ago. Suicide. But people never stopped talking about it.'

'Yes,' Ben said, 'God, yeah, I think I did hear that.'

Then Bobby burst in, instantly realising he seemed to have caught us talking about something delicate. He was far more tactful than he'd seemed on first meeting.

'Sorry, you two, sorry,' he said. 'But I've got an idea.'

*

Twenty minutes later, we were on a small speedboat heading out towards Lesvos. 'That's the one problem with this island,' Bobby called over the cry of the engine, 'there's nothing fucking here.'

We laughed as we ploughed through the darkness, the sea was rough but the drinks the boys were downing meant they weren't so afraid. Maybe we should've been. No matter how far we went we didn't seem to be getting much closer to the lights of the larger island.

'Know what,' Bobby said, cutting the engine, 'maybe here's fine.'

Ben and I looked at each other. Without the engine we were dead in the water. We felt the movement of every wave getting out here, I was sure it would be even worse when we were still, but Bobby seemed to sense a tranquil patch had come to us. And soon, we found ourselves, heads together, lying in a circle on the small deck, looking up at the bright stars against the velvet dark.

'There was one time I thought I might want to be an astronomist,' Bobby mumbled. 'I even applied to do a degree in it.'

'I think it's astronomer,' I said, wishing I could let these things lie.

'That's probably why I didn't get in,' Bobby said. 'That and my grades.'

Ben cracked first and then we were all laughing into a night that had happened so fast. Bobby simply wasn't the person he'd been back at the house.

'Can I say,' Bobby said, 'you two are the best strangers I've ever met.'

'Likewise,' Ben said, taking another swig. 'Plus, one of you is extremely exhilarating to be around and the other has an incredible figure. I'll let you decide which is which.'

'Wow,' I said. 'I know you're playing dad but easy on the dad jokes.'

I held up a finger to let him know I was joking as he squeezed my hand. Then I reached for my arms because of the breeze, and Bobby took off his hoodie and laid it across me for warmth. I kissed him on the head. It was the kind of thing I wished I could still do to JR. To let him know he was in my care.

A matter of minutes later we were heading back to Korpios. As Bobby steered, he glanced at us in the moonlight: 'You've made me feel good tonight. And people hide their feelings too much, so, I don't want the night to end without saying that. And one more thing ... you should get out while you can.'

We all cracked up again. We were on the same wavelength. But then Bobby stopped laughing, abruptly, and said, 'No. No, I'm serious. You should get out while you can.'

9

The unwanted gift

Sofia

The next morning, I sat alone at the long mahogany kitchen table. Steam rose from where the maids were creating dishes to make you salivate, the scent of which mingled with the citrus carried to me on the air from the garden. The glass doors were open, but the netted screen was closed to shelter us from pests.

Last night came back to me in a split second. After the youngsters had headed out on their bikes, Kostas went on an errand for Robert, as I made my excuses and went to bed. I drifted off to sleep, but at some point I was sure Kostas returned home and hurried into Robert's room for a postmortem of the evening.

Later, I certainly recalled being woken from my dream by a moped engine. I guessed that Ben was back. I heard the door downstairs, wondering why he came home after Amelia, who I had heard come in earlier as I lay half-awake, losing track of time.

The front door opened and closed, light appeared in the hallway then disappeared, before everything settled once more.

But when I went downstairs to get a bottle of water, there Ben was in the partial dark, as if he had never been to bed at all. I jumped in shock and he stared at me for a second before approaching. I must have looked so startled that he felt the need to comfort me, pulling me into a hug, his arms holding me for a beat too long. I stiffened at first, primed myself to jump back, but something made me pause. Maybe it was the feel of strong arms around me, or the cedar and musk scent of him. There is no substitute for human touch. It creates oxytocin in the body, I once read. I felt it filling me. It also gave me the gift of realising there were muscles in my body that had been tense perhaps for years. Slowly I relented, curving into him until my head touched his firm shoulder. A learnt move I hadn't used in a while. Then I remembered myself, pulled away and stepped back.

I hadn't been held so intimately in a long time. Artists are tactile, it seemed. Rathwells are not. I wanted to tell him that wasn't professional. But he meant no harm.

'Dinner must've been difficult,' he said. 'But it's all done now.'

I heard a noise, then turned to check it wasn't the quiet electric hum of Robert's lift. There was nothing there, but someone was moving upstairs. Neither of us spoke in the half-light. It felt strangely exciting to be down here with Ben all alone. He was handsome, that was obvious, so the look he held me with was pure flattery.

I sneaked past him, whispering a simple thank you, bare feet patting the tiles, and then I saw his shape start to move away too.

*

This memory of Ben, the bizarre feeling of being in his arms, receded as I was jolted back to the present moment. I heard a shout outside. It sliced through the pleasant morning like a knife. One of the maids in the kitchen dropped a plate. They both looked to me and froze. I felt a chill in my bones, like a premonition that whatever was out there was only going to make things worse. Then the shout came again. I dragged myself up from the table and went with haste to where the pool patio met the grass of the garden. Isabelle stood over something, hand to mouth, and Ben hovered behind her.

'What's the matter?' I said.

Their silence was infectious. I looked down at the floor. There was a small smear of red, no more than a couple of inches long. It began on the paving stones and ended when it kissed the grass.

'It's just a little blood,' I said. 'Nothing to get too excited about. Someone must have cut themselves.'

I took a look around, wondering where Kostas was.

'Sorry,' Isabelle said, giving me a meaningful look. 'It just startled me.'

'Well, let's get it cleared up before anyone sees it. Particularly JR,' I said.

'We should keep note of it,' Isabelle said, sounding apologetic but duty-bound. 'Even something as small as this. I mean, with everything going on, we really have to—'

'Go on then,' I said, allowing her to run back to the house and fetch what she needed as my eyes fell on the red smear again.

I started to think about the possibilities as I looked over at JR at the other end of the garden. He was well out of earshot, swinging from a tree on the edge of the orchard. I was certain Isabelle would be scouring the ground for an animal carcass. I'd seen the implication in her look.

'I just thought you should know,' Ben said. 'I saw it out of the corner of my eye, came over, and there it was.'

Isabelle returned, Kostas' Leica camera held to her eye. She clicked two, three times, getting a couple of good shots of it.

Isabelle finished and her eyes went to Ben. 'You were out late last night.'

'Sorry,' he said.

'Oh, don't apologise,' Isabelle said. 'It's just a statement of fact.'

But Ben was hardly listening. He crouched down by the blood, staring at it. 'Is this a threat?' he said, pointing at the smear.

I laughed, but it sounded forced. Surely this speck of red couldn't be linked to the letters we'd been receiving. I felt a rising dread inside even to think of the words, a tightness in my muscles that spread to my chest. I pushed a fingernail hard into my palm to focus and ward them away.

'It wouldn't be a very good one. I might've walked past it all day and not seen it,' I said as if amused. 'Don't worry, it's probably the same as the blood from the gun last night. Same shade, you all saw it. And I got it on my shirt, I should know.'

'But Kostas gave the gun to me, and I disposed of it myself. Threw it into the sea.' Isabelle shrugged. 'A bit drastic, yes, but whenever we hide things, he seems to find them, even in the bin. And things tend to stay hidden in the ocean.'

'OK,' Ben said. 'Then maybe Bobby did it before dinner?'

'Oh, no,' Isabelle baulked, 'I didn't let him out of my sight. The only moment I left him alone, Amelia was there to babysit.'

After a moment's silence, Isabelle went back to the house.

I moved closer to Ben, saw his breath flutter, then stopped and looked beyond him, into the garden. 'Where is JR? He shouldn't be left on his own.'

'He's just back there, in the orchard, he'll be fine,' Ben said.

I took a long look at him. He didn't seem so easy to control any more, like he was settling into his surroundings and was no longer the obedient man I had hired. For some reason I liked that. It was possible he could be even more useful now. But I couldn't let him know it.

'Then clean this up, will you? You'll need bleach.'

It was not in his job description, but he was not about to tell me no. I sat on a sunlounger and watched him fetch chemicals and a mop from the house and do it, a feeling about him like he'd been demoted to manual labourer. It was just the kind of dejection I was looking for.

He rolled his T-shirt sleeves up above his firm shoulders and scrubbed, as I watched on in silence, wondering what he, Amelia and Bobby had got up to last night.

It was just as he was finishing, sweating as the last spots of red disappeared, that my eyes studied the orchard and realised I couldn't see JR anywhere. I stood up and concern must have shown on my face. Because when I started to wander across the garden towards the trees, Ben laid down his mop on the wet stones and followed.

'I'm sure he's here somewhere,' he said as we entered the orchard. The light dappled on his face. But when he said it, he became less sure. We wandered deeper in, within the pines and branches, but JR was nowhere to be seen.

I turned back to Ben, breath heavy. 'You shouldn't have left him,' I said.

'You asked me to clean up,' he said.

That's when I saw it, behind him, through the trees. I thought it was an optical illusion at first. Something about the light or the way the branches hung. But it wasn't that. It sagged like something empty. I reached out for Ben as I'd searched for my alarm at the dock, but quickly withdrew my hand. I stared at the lifeless body leant up against the apple tree. As my eyes widened, Ben turned, seeing it immediately. It was only five or so metres away.

10

The orchard

Sofia

Bobby sat there on a patch of reddened earth. Red stroked the grass, was baked into his clothes, his lap, all of it the same light red shade as the fleck on the patio.

Ben stumbled towards Bobby's body, his shaking hand reaching out for him.

'Don't,' I said. 'Don't touch him.'

Ben was close enough to see the details. He turned and gave a shake of his head to confirm there was no life in him. This was no game. Each of my manicured nails dug into my palm as I went closer. His wrists were cut deep and wide from just above the palm right up to his forearm, the skin curled open like the pages of a well-worn book. My eyes studied those arms. I shook my head. Had that poor troubled boy done this to himself?

'What do we—' Ben started to say.

'Mum?' JR called from behind us. I turned to see him smiling as he jumped down from a tree at the edge of the orchard. He must've been up there a while. Then all the air left me at once as he started to jog towards us.

Ben began to run, run to cut him off before he saw the body and his childhood was over forever.

'Mum, is daddy still resting or can I—'

JR entered the orchard as Ben intercepted him. I followed too, trying to steady my breath so JR wouldn't know something was up. But I couldn't stop thinking of the black fissures on each of Bobby's arms, the darkness peeled open underneath, the delicacy of the light citrus scent from the trees surrounding us. Flies and mosquitoes buzzing around him.

'We're going back to the house,' Ben said, cutting him off.

'You're not my daddy,' JR said, pushing past him.

'J, please,' Ben said, grabbing his hand and spinning him back the way he had come.

'No one tells me what to do except daddy,' JR shouted, turning again, but Ben held him from the waist and lifted him roughly, as I reached the two of them.

'Ow. You're hurting me,' J screamed as he beat Ben's back.

'Darling, when Ben says go back to the house, you do as you're told,' I choked out.

'Don't you turn, mate,' Ben said as J continued to struggle. 'Don't you turn, not for a second.'

'Get off me, I'm warning you,' J said, his voice fading.

I couldn't speak any more. The paleness of the body had infected me, all the horror in that poor boy's form, his empty eyes just visible where his chin rested on his chest, head bowed. The image would never leave me.

We hustled J into the house. Isabelle took him to Amelia while Ben told the maids to stay in the house and I ran to find Kostas, who swiftly emerged from Robert's room. I stood in the hallway and told him Bobby was out there, dead, and he took it all in trying not to show how much it affected him. It was his job to be the calmest amongst us. I watched him rouse himself before wandering towards the orchard like a condemned man.

*

After Isabelle had spoken to Kostas about what he'd seen out there, she joined Ben and I in the black Merc on the drive. She'd asked us to wait there for her as it was a safe place to talk. She slammed the door, composing herself as she sat in the front. Ben and I had been waiting in the back.

She was calmer than us, maybe because she hadn't seen the body. Meanwhile, Ben and I fought knots in our stomachs in the back seat.

'Never seen a dead body?' Isabelle said.

'Not even a picture,' Ben said. 'I feel ...'

She exhaled heavily and said, 'You shouldn't have had to see that. I, perhaps, knew Bobby better than anyone. I knew about his troubles. His relationship with Sofia was more complicated.'

She said all of this without even glancing my way. Like I was some ghost under a sheet. I thought of Bobby hunched over, wrists so open they resembled a smile.

'I wouldn't say complicated,' I said.

'Either way,' she said, 'I had more dealings with him before he took himself away. I was very fond of him. That's why you'll have to forgive the strength of my reaction.'

She gestured to her eyes, as if tears lay there. This level of control was Isabelle all over. But just because she wasn't making a show of it, it didn't mean there wasn't a lot going on inside.

'I hope you don't mind us addressing this straight away,' I said, from behind him. 'Seems like you got to know him well, in one short night. He can have that effect on people. He was really a very loving boy. Did he say anything ... unusual?'

'No,' Ben shook his head, eyes so wide. 'God, no.'

I pressed my hands into my face. I wondered if I could have done something to prevent all this.

'Did ... Mr Rathwell know that Bobby was coming?' Ben said.

'No,' Isabelle said. 'But we'd never turn him away. We all wanted to prevent a scandal, you understand. I suppose we're far beyond that now.'

This was something of an understatement.

The one consequence I knew for sure, as I listened to the air conditioning whir away, was that things were about to change. I felt the suffocating grip of a death in the family, though he wasn't my blood. Nor was he Isabelle's. And yet, here we were, the mourners. I'd heard that some people employ professional actors as mourners for people who don't have sufficient living friends and relatives. I suppose it felt fitting that we had one with us.

'Where's his mother?' Ben said.

I stayed quiet.

'Oh,' Isabelle said, opening her eyes. 'His mother's dead. She died. A fair time ago.'

Ben said nothing. He had mentioned his own mother briefly a few days before we left for the island, saying it was a shame he wouldn't be able to contact her while away. But that was what the island was for. To sever us from the constant flow of information.

'His mother is Robert's sister?' Ben asked. When neither of us said a thing, the air changed a little. 'My mother thought I shouldn't come here,' he said.

Perhaps she was right, I thought.

Ben went to speak, then held it back.

'What is it?' I said.

'It's just,' Ben said, 'it wasn't suicide. I could tell.'

Isabelle looked to me, showing her scepticism even before she asked, 'How?'

'Well,' Ben said, trying to find the words. 'He didn't seem suicidal last night. He was excited, talked about wanting to get to know me and Amelia this vacation. And, then there's his wrists. Once, I had to wear plasticuffs for a play. After a couple of hours, if they're tight, you get indentations around your wrists. I could see them ... on Bobby's wrist. The cut started just above them. And ... you can't slit your own wrists while your hands are tied.'

Isabelle glanced at me.

'Yes,' I said, after a long intake of breath. He had a good eye. First that fleck of blood and now this. 'I think ... I think I saw them too.'

11

The heat

Amelia

I had been trying to relax in the Turkish steam room when Isabelle marched JR down to me as if it was a matter of emergency. J quickly changed into a towel and joined me in the wet heat, staying silent as he watched his fingertips prune. He looked like he didn't want to talk but I always found a way in.

'I heard,' I whispered, with a knowing look, 'you lost your temper.'

He looked down, pressing finger and thumb together. 'Don't you ever feel that way?' he asked. 'When you get so angry, and you tell yourself not to be, but you just can't?'

'Of course, sometimes,' I said.

'I'm sorry. I wish I could be different,' he said. And I hated it when he talked like that, so I gave him a hug, and he hugged back like he needed it.

'Can I see daddy?' he mumbled against my arm.

But I had been told in no uncertain terms that his father was not to be disturbed, not today.

'J,' I soothed, 'your daddy's resting.'

87

'No,' he said, pulling back, his fists tensing. 'I really want to see my daddy.'

That's when I saw a figure approaching through the steamed glass, swelling until they opened the door. It was Ben, staying on the precipice as he was clothed. I saw his eyes were riven, but he hid it well.

'J?' he called out. 'Mum wants to see your crawl, up at the pool.'

JR glowered at Ben like he was out of favour.

I watched Ben decide to play repentant. 'Sorry about earlier, mate. I made a mistake.'

JR examined the words, as Ben waited for his judgement.

'Never heard mummy or daddy say that,' JR said as if that was particularly interesting to him. I had heard drivers apologise to him for being late. I'd seen him greet the words with a nod or a worldly 'Not to worry.' But a sorry was different when it came from someone you felt close to. Especially if you needed to hear it.

'It's OK to be wrong. And to admit it,' Ben said. 'You deserve an apology.'

J's sour look faded. 'OK, yes,' he said, a faint smile appearing. In the presence of Ben, JR wanted to be won over, it was a fresh feeling I hadn't seen in him before. He seemed to be learning what he would and wouldn't put up with from others, which was exactly what I wanted for him.

As he dragged his sodden form away, I stood and went to follow, but Ben stopped me. JR pattered along the hall, in the direction of his mother, and disappeared around the corner. Ben stepped into the steam, a strange figure in his clothes, onto the handmade blue and white ceramic tiling, and closed the door behind him.

'Don't you want to change?' I said, steam rising between us.

Ben held a finger to his lips, his eyes wide with fear. 'Don't say a word,' he said, hushed, and I felt an energy move between us. 'You're going to get some questions fired at you, say as little as possible.'

'About what?' I said, smiling, my voice echoing against the sound of slow drips.

'Bobby,' he said, his hand touching my hot forearm as he did. I couldn't tell whether he was worried someone was coming, or if he just had the urge to touch me.

'What's Bobby done now?' I said, a mist between us.

He leant in closer, his voice gentle. 'I'm so sorry. Bobby's dead,' he said. 'He's dead.'

My heartbeat took over in my ears. I felt the blood draining from my face. I found myself sitting before I knew what was happening. I had so many questions fighting each other to be heard that nothing came out at all.

'So, who would want him dead?' he said, his eyes staying fixed on mine as I realised that was a question that required an answer. 'I'm asking you, because you must know more than I do.'

I didn't answer. I understood him, but the shock was still working its way through me.

'He was murdered?' I asked. And Ben told me everything he knew and all the things he suspected. I closed my eyes, wished I could blank out the images he had put into my mind, then silently wished I had cut things off with the Rathwells sooner, hadn't agreed to this one last summer.

'They could look at us for this, you know,' he said, and I felt it cut through me. 'I can already feel it. And if it doesn't fit, they may be tempted to, you know, make it fit.'

He sounded paranoid. But with the Rathwells, no extremities were out of the question, that much was true. I was told so by the agency. It felt like a heavy euphemism, but I was desperate.

Then Ben said, 'We need to make sure our stories match.'

I nodded, my breathing unsteady, tears stinging my cheeks.

'Last night,' Ben said, 'Bobby told me something about you. He said you two had met before,' his deep voice felt like it was all around me as it echoed against the tiles. 'He thought you were just playing with him when you denied it, or you were worried someone was listening in.'

'That's ... ridiculous,' I said, standing and fighting the shuddering breath in my throat. 'I like him ... liked him ... but he was hardly the most reliable—'

'Good, that's good. Don't tell them you knew him. It might make things more complicated,' he said. 'Be sad, as anyone would be, for a young man who's died. But I think it's important we don't look guilty, either of us.'

'But we aren't guilty. Are we?'

Ben hesitated, then said: 'No, but we are disposable. So, be firm. Try not to look weak.' Did he think I was naturally weak? He came closer, his breath touching my ear, the bass notes of his voice sending a shiver through me. 'I don't know you that well,' he said. 'You don't know me. But things are about to get rough, and I don't think we're safe, so let's stay together, whatever happens, until the end. Sometimes with powerful people, whatever they decide is true becomes true. Don't even give them a chance to make you something you're not.'

He opened the door, letting the heat out. I was gripping myself tight, an old coping mechanism. I felt so light-headed

I thought I might faint. He brought his other hand to my opposing forearm to support me, his linen shirt wet with condensation. He had me completely.

I saw a figure over his shoulder, coming down the hallway, lit by metal-latticed lamps and candlelight.

'And there's more—' Ben said.

I held my composure and squeezed the bone on his wrists to save him from spilling more than he should.

'You come now,' Kostas called. And with a nod we followed him in silence. I noticed how much Ben was dripping with moisture.

And as I went, I thought about Bobby telling us to get out while we could. About how we had laughed it off, imagined he was joking. Now I wondered what truths he knew that we didn't. And if it was those truths that killed him.

*

Isabelle

After I let Ben leave the car, Sofia tried to follow, and I quickly put the child lock on. She pulled at it a couple of times, frustrated, maybe a little scared. Of me, of all people. When it was her who held all the power.

'Forgive me, my love. Just a second, please,' I said.

'Go on then,' Sofia said. 'What is it?'

I merely wanted her to be privy to what Kostas had told me just before we got Ben in the car.

'Kostas says he's spoken to the police on the landline,' I said. 'Knows someone at the station. They're on their way to pick up the body, but it'll be a few hours. They're underfunded, understaffed, underpaid. In short, they're not much use. Until they come, Kostas said to tell JR they've doused the orchard with weed-killer and it's not safe to go in there. Will that work?'

Sofia took a moment to apply her lipstick, but her veneer of calm was betrayed by her shaking hand. 'JR will do as I say,' she said, ever confident in her methods of persuasion. There were some ways in which she had ceded control of the house to me, but she generally regarded my side of things as the 'dirty work'. Admin, anything she didn't wish to know, like that news story breaking back in England, as if she thought lack of knowledge would help keep her hands clean.

'We're going to find out how this happened,' I said. 'Kostas is going to contain it.'

'Contain it?'

'There'll be no scandal, but there'll be no doubt either. Most stations are like leaking ships, so he says we'll tell the police as little as possible to stop it from going public.'

'All right,' she said, processing it. But it didn't take long, as it was standard practice for the wealthy to think themselves above the law. 'And what did Kostas find last night?'

He had followed not far behind the three mopeds, which were not hard to track down, given the one bar on the island.

'Ben and Amelia certainly seemed to be getting on well.'

I watched a flicker of something cross Sofia's face in the rearview. Keeping relationships professional is paramount to her; she's very prim in her own way.

'They went out on a boat and then Amelia went home early,' I said. 'Then Bobby and Ben stayed drinking. They had a particularly in-depth chat on the beach, apparently.'

'Any idea what about?'

'None at all,' I said. 'But it ended with them playfighting.'

'Did it turn nasty?'

'Difficult to tell from a distance, so Kostas said. Bobby's tracksuit got ripped. But it seemed like drunken roughhousing. Ben soon left to follow Amelia home. Bobby went to the Aegean Rooms. Kostas reported back to Robert and me, then went to bed, I believe.'

'So, what now?' she said, sinking deep into her leather seat, the sun creeping up above her forehead. She stroked the base of her neck, a frown shrouding her face.

'Ordinarily, we might want to get Robert off the island. But given that the story will be hitting right around now, the papers would love to snap him scurrying off his little safe haven. We can't give them a column inch more than they've already got. So that's another reason to contain things here.'

She gave a reluctant nod.

'Look, could Ben be right?' Sofia said, breathing deep, her palm coming to her forehead. 'I know the way last night went wasn't good. But could you believe Bobby would do this? Doesn't seem very him.'

I took a moment. 'I think he was a troubled boy, so yes. And Kostas thinks the simplest answer is the most likely too. But he also said he would be looking into every eventuality. He's already found the knife he did it with. It was resting there on his lap. Did you see it?'

'No,' she said, staring into space. 'I was too shocked to look at the details.'

'But ...' I said, 'did you see indentation marks on the wrists?'

'I don't know,' she said. I wasn't trying to challenge her,

I knew how that would go, I just wanted to get things straight. She blinked suddenly. Her hands gripped each other in her lap. 'No,' she said. 'I did. I know I did. And I know everyone would prefer it if that wasn't the case ... even Kostas. It'd certainly make his job simpler, but I know what I saw ...'

I let out a sigh. 'I thought as much. There was something else strange about it too, apparently. The knife. Kostas said he'll explain more when we go inside. Then he'll deal with all this and make a reasonable solution. We don't want any more scandal than what's going on back home.'

I wasn't trying to torture her with what I knew about the story, it just kept coming up. I had to be careful with my language; even locking the doors was, what would they call it these days, a microaggression. But not knowing was all her choice. It was a lawyer's instinct: she didn't want to hear anything that she couldn't defend. I understood the feeling, but I didn't have such luxuries.

She made an open gesture with her hands that told me she considered the conversation to be over and she wished to leave.

'Oh, sorry,' I said, releasing the locks with a touch. She didn't hesitate to open her door, but before she disappeared from earshot, I quickly spoke again.

'You can always come to me if you need anything. Let's be really careful—'

The door slammed.

As I watched her go, I wished for a second we could be closer. But, given our proximity to Robert, I knew that would never be the case. Robert was one of those people who swore by the value of competition in the workplace, and in every other aspect of his life. I just hoped she realised what I'd sacrificed to get here, what I did every day to make the man she loved happy. Because my work brought risk with it. Recently, I had had the sense I was being followed. A figure hustling away in my periphery when I turn suddenly in a department store, a photo being taken of a landmark just over the road that I just happen to be in the way of, a car that's careful to be the second vehicle back, following my every turn for miles. An association to him was a dangerous business indeed. I knew that, just as well as Sofia did.

12

Notes on an interrogation

Amelia

Having dressed and returned to the house, I followed Ben and Kostas into the den, my body feeling weaker than an innocent woman's should.

Just as we were entering, Kostas stopped me at the door and said: 'One at a time, please.' And next I was back in charge of JR in the house, both of us wondering what exactly they were saying behind the doors of that small room. I tried to act like everything was fine, but suddenly I felt like my mother, bluffing that all was well when I was close to tears.

I wouldn't have to wait long to speak to Kostas. I was soon called into the den myself, passing Ben on the way who gave me a nondescript look, aware he was being watched, sweat dripping from him and anxious to change his clothes. And in no time, I took his place in the uncomfortable leather club chair in the den.

'You're a musician, I hear?' Kostas said.

'That's right,' I said.

'Then how did you come to work for the Rathwells?' he asked.

'Times got tough, I suppose, and I wanted to pay my mortgage, so here I am.' I didn't like the sense I was being lulled with small talk. 'You'll know all this, I'm sure,' I continued, 'you probably looked into me yourself when I applied for the job. But what you may not know is how many well-to-do families wouldn't give me a second glance. Degree from Cambridge or not. Though they wouldn't say it, the mixed-race girl with the prosthesis didn't fit the picture. And I was getting desperate. So, I'd say I'm particularly indebted to the Rathwells, for not being so… traditional.'

A grin briefly passed across Kostas' face, before he moved things on.

'You like this Ben?' Kostas replied.

'I suppose,' I said.

'You have your doubts?' he smiled.

'No, I mean, I barely know him,' I said. 'Yesterday was the first time we'd met.'

'Not before? Not at the house?' Kostas said.

'Things are strictly professional at the house. You know that.'

He nodded.

'You see, when I sat Ben down here,' Kostas said, 'I threw him a piece of cord and asked him if he could make a Prusik knot.'

I blinked, unsure what to say.

'It's a knot sometimes used for restraint,' he continued. 'I thought Ben might be able to help out on the boat, because, see, in his interview, he'd said he was a good sailor. But he took one look at the cord and gave up his whole story with a laugh. He raises his palms like he is surrendering. "Never sailed in my

97

life," he says, "sorry." Would you start to wonder, Amelia, if a man lies so easily, what else he lies about?'

I shook my head, a lift of my shoulders. 'You say what you need to, to get the job. If you need the job badly enough. To be totally open, the Rathwells pay well, well over the odds, and he probably needs the money as much as I do.'

He watched me smile nervously, the power dynamic having vastly changed since we were in the car together.

'I'll be *totally open*, as you say. No one gets onto Korpios without me knowing. I'm in contact with police and the coast-guard. And, given the height of the walls, the position of the house, the gated system, an intruder is ... unlikely.'

I looked up as he continued.

'If they'd let me install security cameras,' Kostas said, 'they'd know for sure how all this happened. Mr Richard Branson, I hear, has them all over his island. But Sofia, she says cameras make her uncomfortable. And yet there are photos of her all over the house, black and white ones, taken by some incredible, of-the-moment, hotshot photographer. Right?'

'Yes. Quite striking,' I said. But I wasn't about to agree that the lady of the house was vain, especially not at a time like this.

'No cameras,' he sighed. 'This presents a professional problem for me. But still, I agree to it, and now this. I guess I should be more forthright, bolder with my opinions, don't you think?'

'Guess so,' I said.

'Anything strange happen last night?' he said, with that searching quality of his. 'Any arguments? Anything said?'

'No,' I said, quickly trying to find some details so as not to be evasive: 'Bobby apologised for what happened over dinner. He told us he was bipolar—'

'You and Ben come home at the same time?' he cut me off, not blinking at Bobby's admission, his pace quickening.

'… Er,' I said. I instantly had the urge to lie, to stick by Ben as we had agreed. But Ben hadn't done anything wrong, he didn't need an alibi, I told myself, and if I lied it might not tally with what he said. 'No, sorry. Ben came home a little after me. I was tired and the boys still had all this energy, I mean, I wasn't drinking so … what did Ben say?'

Kostas raised his eyebrows and breathed in slowly before he spoke: 'Ben told me exactly that, just a few minutes ago, sitting exactly where you're sitting.'

I stayed quiet and nodded.

'Did you stay in your bed when you got home?' Kostas said. 'Or did you get up for any reason?'

'No, I didn't get up.' I shook my head.

'That's what Ben said too,' Kostas muttered. Just as he predicted, Ben and I seemed to be the only ones under the microscope.

'Sorry,' I said, sudden palpitations coming on that I had kept at bay until then: 'but do you think this was suicide?'

Kostas paused. 'It could be. But then Ben starts telling everyone it's murder. I imagine he told you too?'

I opened my mouth to speak but he got there first.

'Yes, I see that he did,' he said. 'Ben seems very free with his opinions. We don't know enough yet to be sure if it was murder or suicide. Now, I promise this is my last question: had you ever met Bobby before?'

I folded my arms tight to my ribcage. The room got colder.

'It's my understanding that Bobby thought you had met?' he said.

'Yes,' I said, 'yes, I'm sorry. I was a little nervous to mention him saying that. Because I still have no idea what Bobby was talking about.'

'Or maybe,' Kostas said, 'you do? Because Isabelle overheard your conversation before dinner.'

'No,' I said. 'He was wrong.'

'Or you are,' he said. 'A boy took himself to the orchard, cut his wrists deep and sat himself down at the base of a tree. We need to know why. So, think on, think back. It's OK to forget. Come and find me if you remember. Now, I'm sorry to keep you.'

He made a gesture to make clear he was granting me my release from the room. I stood, keeping my eyes on him.

Then he got up and I must've flinched because all of sudden he became very gentle.

'Can I see your arms?' he said.

'My arms?'

He nodded, his eyes firm.

I was draped in a cream-coloured cover-up, something chic I'd ordered to attempt to fit in with my surroundings. I gave a slow nod. Submitting to it seemed to be an admittance that things were now beyond serious. Slowly, I turned my arms over and revealed my skin. He looked them up and down before running his middle finger smoothly along each one. It didn't feel intrusive, he had a light touch. And I'd never been so relieved my skin was so smooth. Until I remembered the tiny bruises on each arm below the bicep.

'What is this?' he said.

'Oh,' I said. 'Sometimes when I'm anxious, I tend to fold my arms, push my thumbs into the muscle, because of the tension. See? I'm doing it now.'

I thought of my childhood bedroom and those raised voices again.

'A little act of self-harm?' he said.

'No, I wouldn't say that,' I said. 'I've done it ever since … ever since I was a girl.'

'OK,' Kostas said, running a hand across his face in thought. 'If you do remember anything about knowing Bobby?'

I met his steely gaze, trying to remain as friendly as I could.

'You'll be the first to know,' I said.

*

Isabelle

'I have examined the body again, and spoken to Amelia and Ben,' Kostas said, 'and I have talked to Robert about all of this.' Sofia and I were sitting around the black marble kitchen island. The others were out on the beach. 'And I think Ben is right,' Kostas continued. 'I don't think this is suicide.'

I saw Sofia look at him meaningfully as he confirmed it. She pressed a hand into her forehead, a gesture she did when trying to keep hold of her emotions, fixing her eyes on Kostas as he spoke on.

'You and Ben both saw those indentations,' he said, before a pause. 'I too believe they were made by plastic ties,' Kostas said, gripping Sofia's shoulder, which hardly seemed to make her feel any better. 'You were right. The marks can't be easily explained away. We have two options, we let the police investigate this as a murder. Or we give them a reason for the wrist marks and treat it as a suicide.'

There was a long silence. Sofia looked to me, running through all sorts of possibilities in her mind, as was I.

'Robert and I are in agreement,' Kostas said eventually. 'We do not trust the police. We think they would come in and make a mistake, leak this to the press,' he continued. 'Jump to the wrong conclusion, make a circus of this. Murder is a headline, but suicide can go away in time. Robert's health is not so good, a scandal is the last thing he needs, given what is happening back home. So, I would like, with your permission, to tell them Bobby wore a bracelet on one hand and a watch on the other. This is Robert's wish. I hope you understand this. But if you disagree, Miss Sofia, we can go back to Robert?'

I watched the fear ripple through Sofia as she took it in.

'I need to speak to Robert,' Sofia said eventually, standing up.

'I have only just finished talking to him,' Kostas said, moving himself between her and the door. 'He needs time alone. It is your choice too, madam. If you want us to trust the police to get this right, we can do it. I can only offer my advice as one who knows their limitations. Someone tried to make this look simple for the police. I say let them. The local police aren't going to turn a suicide into a murder and make their clearance rate look any worse. But, say they do, say they throw resources behind it and we become the stars of the next true crime series. Whenever anyone hears Robert's name, this is what they will think of. And for all that, in the end, chances are there'll still be no satisfactory verdict.'

Sofia shook her head. 'The burden of proof is always on the police and prosecution. Despite what people believe, murder is very hard to prove without a witness.'

'So, let's avoid their intrusion. Let me look at these mistakes the killer made, I'll solve this, and when I do, I'll bring it to the police tied up in a bow. Or I'll resolve the matter internally. As you please.'

There was an ambiguity of sentiment but a surety that whatever dark conclusion he was suggesting he was more than willing to carry it out.

'Robert must have what he wants,' Sofia said, in a great exhale. 'So, you've spoken to the boy and the girl? What's your theory? How would Bobby have got into the house?'

Kostas pursed his lips, like he was about to name some unnamable thing, and was determined to put it as tenderly as he could. 'There is one flaw in the security. If you walk along the cliffside, there's a place where the fence ends, that no one else may know about, except perhaps a boy that has been coming here all these years. I had missed this small opening, until I saw it this morning.' A ripple of shame passed through him that he failed to hide. 'It still means an outside intruder is almost impossible, but I believe Bobby may have made his way in. And we all heard Bobby use the words from those letters last night, so he can be the only author. But why is he dead? What if there is a co-conspirator within the house? Maybe once they let him inside there was an accident.'

'So we're looking at the help,' Sofia said and I felt myself included in that. I couldn't let her extricate herself so easily.

'Or, someone who was being blackmailed wanted to put a stop to it,' I said. 'That's possible too, isn't it?'

Sofia gave me one of her stares. She didn't like it but couldn't disagree.

Kostas nodded at me. 'Of course, this is also true.'

And in a matter of words, we were all suspects.

'But we don't even know if it was Bobby that sent those letters, not for sure,' Sofia said.

'Oh, come on,' I said. 'Robert has a horde of enemies but not a single one of them would lower themselves to write a letter by hand.'

Sofia opened her purse and pulled one of the crumpled letters she had brought with her. Just four little words. The problem for the author was Robert didn't negotiate.

'Is there anything else someone could gain from the letters?' Kostas said.

'The letters have one aim. Money,' Sofia said. 'Next would've come some instructions for payment involving an unmarked hold-all inside in a roadside bin.'

'But Bobby,' I said, 'has decent access to money.'

'Everyone could stand a little more money,' Kostas said. 'In uncertain times. Particularly if he doesn't have a good cut of the will.'

'Yes,' Sofia said. 'But the will is simple, practical, an even split between living family members.'

I decided not to touch that topic. Instead, I said, 'So, this *someone*, who did this, they felt the note was specifically for them and they didn't want to pay, or they couldn't. But why do it like this? Why bring the crime inside the house?'

Kostas shrugged. 'Maybe that wasn't part of the plan. I believe this is the work of a first-time killer. For the investigator, a novice makes things harder. Because good sense goes out of the window.'

'And what about the staff?' Sofia said, her eyes bright, her ring finger playing with her diamond earring.

'Hold up your hands,' Kostas said to Sofia and after a curious look between them she did so, smooth limbs high like she was protesting her innocence. 'Another complexity is that we know Ben and Bobby fought that night. And as for Amelia,' Kostas gripped Sofia around her biceps, staring into her eyes. 'She has new bruises here, exactly where someone may hold her if they were protecting themselves against her.'

Marry that to another secret we knew of Amelia, and it created a distinct possibility. Sofia was clearly thinking on it as she withdrew from Kostas towards the sink.

'And I'm afraid,' Kostas said, bearing the weight of having one more revelation on him. 'There's something else. You see, the knife on Bobby's lap, the police have no reason to believe it is not his. But this knife, I recognised it, and you would too. It was the one we confiscated from JR back home with the rosewood handle. I could tell he had designs on getting it back.'

I thought of that cat's head back in London, sensed we all were thinking of it. I'd found it myself, so odd in its perfect loneliness that I thought it was a waxwork at first glance. Sofia had always wanted to keep an option open that JR didn't do it and I knew well who her other option was. But I saw JR trying to conceal the head by digging it a little grave.

'The cat back in London was killed by human hand,' Kostas muttered. 'The problem we have is that, it is said, people who do this kind of thing eventually graduate to bigger things.'

Sofia dropped her glass into the hard enamel of the sink and the shards fired back like sparks. The noise echoed from floor to stucco ceiling. She composed herself and spoke, pushing away as much of the tension as she could, as if she hadn't just lost all control in front of us. 'He's a boy, he's not a monster.'

*

Amelia

I knocked on JR's room, escaping the noise downstairs. The maids had been sent back to their lodgings and an eerie stillness had settled over the house. Ben let me in with a grave look before putting on a brave face for J.

We heard a smash downstairs and I closed the door with a shaking hand. It was like being a child again, back with my parents, as I shut out what was really going on in the rest of the house.

JR asked what all the noise was about and Ben said it was just 'adult nonsense'.

I looked between the two of them, unnerved. They snickered like there had been some secret joke between them before I came in. My shoulders tensed.

JR stared at me, so innocent, but they had the look of naughty boys together. That was the thing with JR's tantrums, they never lasted long.

'Want to hear a joke?' JR said.

'Did you know JR was good at jokes?' Ben said, hiding all his fears very well, circling behind me to make sure the door was closed.

'I didn't,' I said. JR used to find jokes 'childish'. I must've seemed distracted.

'Why did the monkey fall out of the tree?' J said.

'I don't know,' Ben said, behind me.

'Cos it was dead,' J said. Ben laughed, but I couldn't find one in me.

'Why did the second monkey fall out of the tree?' JR said.

'Dunno,' Ben said.

'Cos he was stapled to the first monkey,' JR said.

Ben indulged J with an even bigger laugh. We were both looking at JR very closely by that point.

'Why did the third monkey fall out of the tree?' JR said.

'Don't know,' I said.

JR was delighted. I hadn't seen that in him for a long time.

'The third monkey fell out of the tree cos he thought it was a game,' J said.

And Ben really laughed at that. I tried to do the same. Perhaps it was the attention that had brought out something in JR. I had tried my best, but there was no substitute for a big brother. And the novelty of something new to play with.

'Brilliant,' Ben said, throwing himself on the bed and lying down. He looked up at me. Away from JR's gaze, Ben's eyes were as tense as mine.

We heard more voices downstairs. A door slammed.

Ben patted the mattress next to him and soon we were all sitting on J's bed.

'Buddy,' he said, giving a quick glance to me. 'Where's that knife of yours you showed me at the beach? You bury it down there?'

'No,' JR said. We both watched him as he twisted his middle finger over his ring finger and looked through the little gap in between the two fingers.

'Then where do you keep it?' Ben said.

'Closer than that,' JR said. Putting his thumb on the skin between his index and middle fingers then looking down the line of it at me like his hand was the sight of a sniper.

Then his eyes flicked to his desk drawer where he's supposed to do his work. Ben stood straight away with a smile on his face and pulled open the first drawer. Then the second. But JR just sniggered. 'Some people are so easy to fool,' he said.

Perhaps he was more independent of mind than I thought. Nothing like me as a child at all.

'Come on, bud,' Ben said.

And after a while he let his eyes drag along the wall to his *Post Malone* poster. And we watched him look for a second before Ben slowly went to it, J nodding as he did so. Ben undid the Blu Tack at the bottom and lifted it to reveal a little shelf scooped out of the wall.

Ben looked at me.

'Hey, bud. Come on,' Ben said.

I adjusted my position and saw the shelf was empty. I folded my arms tight.

'Now that is *weird*,' JR said.

I gave him the look I use when he's up to his tricks: avoiding his homework because it's 'too easy' or telling lies. He was the picture of innocence. Ben's eyes went a little hollow. JR's were much the same. Ben didn't believe him. Neither did I.

'It should be there,' JR said, his eyes widening as they did when he was stimulated. 'I promise. Bible promise.'

*

Sofia

'Of course, he's just a boy,' Kostas said as I glanced at my dark reflection in the kitchen island. 'A child does not even fit our assumptions, a child cannot be blackmailed, a child is not often driven to such extreme solutions, cannot plan something so meticulously that, but for a tiny indentation on a wrist, would've appeared entirely like suicide.'

'Only it wasn't that meticulous, was it?' Isabelle said. 'The blood on the paving stones tells us there was a real struggle getting that restraint on him, a struggle in which Bobby was cut, one that, whoever did this, didn't have time to clean up in the dark after they'd finally got him over to that tree and slit his wrists.'

Kostas paused, perhaps noting, as I did, how coldly she had mapped it all out. 'Maybe so.'

'This is conjecture,' I said. I thought I should bring back some sense of legalese before we got carried away.

'No, we have no absolute proof, as yet,' Kostas said. 'But this is the beginning of the process. And it leads me to ask, Mrs Rathwell, why you were keen to clean up that blood? You said at the time it was fake, but then I found it in the trash, and you can smell the iron.'

I pressed my fingers into the diamond on my ear for the sharp feel of it. This was a question I knew was coming, but I had used the length of the conversation to assemble my armour, piece by piece. Still, I didn't like the way the two of them were rounding on me.

'I suppose,' I said, 'when I thought this was a smaller matter, an animal for instance, as you suggested, I was concerned it would fall back on JR. I wanted to protect him. I certainly didn't mean to destroy evidence. But can I ask, what about Ben? He was closer to the substance than me. He must've realised it was real, so why did he clean it up without mentioning it?'

'Perhaps,' Kostas said. 'He's ... frightened of you?'

I couldn't help but smile at this inside. I wouldn't say it was fear, but there was a connection between us, that I knew for sure.

Then Kostas spoke low, with a simple flick of his head towards the door. 'Oh, come in, please.'

He had spotted Ben and Amelia skulking in the corridor. Nothing got past him when he was on his game. They wandered in, looking at us like children in pyjamas.

'Don't try to go anywhere by boat, you won't make it out. It wouldn't look good,' Kostas said.

'I ...' Amelia said.

'We won't,' Ben said.

'I know the pressure might be a lot to take,' Kostas said. 'But I would be forced to catch up with you, and you won't like that. That goes for all of you.'

His words made me feel as unsteady as if I were on a boat in the middle of the ocean. I acted quickly. Maybe I was flustered and wanted to shift the attention away from me. But I beckoned Ben and Amelia further inside.

'Oh, close the door, will you?' I said, with a brief look to Isabelle. And they did so, creeping further along the terracotta tiles. 'I have something to tell you.'

Isabelle went to pour herself a glass of water. I was certain that it was meant as a distraction, to break the moment and give me a chance to reconsider what she had realised I was about to do. When Robert wasn't here, Isabelle felt she was his presence in the room. But unfortunately for her, sometimes when he wasn't in the room I did as I pleased. I was about to disregard the sanctity of the flow of information. Because it wasn't fair on them not to know any more.

'Is JR upstairs?'

I spoke it softly and Ben nodded. 'He's reading a Shakespeare play.'

'This whole episode has to be kept from him at all costs,' I said. 'Because, you should know, just so we're all clear, Bobby wasn't a cousin of the family.' Everyone stared at me. Some because they knew what was coming next, others because they didn't. 'He was Robert's son.'

I saw it land heavy with them both, the image of Bobby's pale body coming back to me as I said it. Ben shook his head like he was trying to solve an insurmountably complex puzzle. Amelia put her hand to her mouth, gripped herself in a tight embrace.

Isabelle took a long sip from her glass. Kostas reached under his jacket as the room fell silent. 'We're going to find out who is responsible for this,' he said, taking his gun out of his holster and laying it on the marble sideboard. 'And we'll do it as a family.'

PART 2:

We'd be delighted to have you

13

An escape

Amelia

As evening closed in, the air turning a darker blue, I began to wonder where Robert Rathwell was. He was at the centre of this, yet he was nowhere to be seen. Resting, I guessed. I had seen bodies go in and out of his room, but no heart-wrenching sounds or tears through the wall. It didn't seem normal. Not that anything about this was normal.

When my mother died, I woke crying for her arms for months that became years, but then I was a child and had been next to her when she died. This death returned that same tightness to my chest.

The fact that I had no reasonable expectation of how this family would react to a tragedy was part of the problem. The Rathwells' rules had left us far from normality for a long time. When reality shifts until you can't place what is normal any more, they call it gaslighting. I didn't want to be gaslit so, while the family had dinner, I asked if Ben and I could get some air. Kostas had asked on our behalf and got us an hour, telling us not to go far.

When we passed through the grand wrought-iron gates, the tremors in my hands began to die away. I breathed deep as I did while tuning up in a concert hall, surrounded by the chaos of so many rising strings. But fresh air wasn't the only reason I was here; I had something to share. Before I could say anything, Ben spoke.

'I need to tell you something,' he said, glancing behind him when we were far enough from the house.

It sounded ominous. My stomach churned as I thought about how I'd bound myself to a stranger. And I couldn't help thinking about the resonance of how Bobby was found that no one was talking about.

'I didn't make the plane because I told Isabelle I was backing out, because of an acting job,' he continued in a whisper.

'So ...' I said.

'So, Isabelle called ... offered to pay me the twelve grand I would've earnt on the acting job. Which is ... not what I intended. But I couldn't turn it down. I had to come when I knew how desperate they really were.'

'And . . .' I said.

'And, there wasn't an acting job. And if there was, it wouldn't have paid that much. It was cos of my mother, you see. She ...' he didn't know how to explain it at first '... she mentioned the Rathwells to me as a kid. If there was anything on the news about them, she'd say they were dangerous, and that she knew it for a fact. So, when she heard I was working for them of all people, she begged me not to come. But I came. And then suddenly I was twelve grand richer.'

I looked at him. He seemed so self-conscious all of a sudden. Then I leant in and whispered: 'I'll keep your secret. But you're a sneak, you know that?'

'I'm not, promise,' he whispered back. His hand brushed my wrist, and I felt a moment could've happened between us if things weren't what they were. I looked behind me, careful in case someone had wandered from the house and found themselves in earshot. If I was going to say what I needed to, we didn't have long.

'Since we're sharing,' I said as we got walking again. 'I figured out where I knew Bobby from. It was innocent. Didn't even know he was a Rathwell at the time.'

The moon lit our path on the side of the makeshift road beside the ocean. 'We just met once or twice, at Boujis,' I added, but that meant nothing to Ben. 'That's a club. People like William and Harry used to go there.'

'Who are they?' he said.

'The Princes?' I said. 'Don't look at me like that, I didn't go often, but I remember meeting Bobby. This was before the tattoos, that's why I didn't recognise him. I try not to admit to the Rathwells that I used to move in those circles anyway. I'm just *the help* and it's good to remain that way. Our family used to have money, but it got up and left a long time ago.'

'Your secret's safe with me,' he said, just as I had said to him. His hand brushed mine once more as we went. Our eyes met for a second. Our gazes stayed connected as I breathed deep. Then I opened my mouth to say what I really needed to, but heard a sound in the undergrowth, something snapping. I stopped, turned, but no one was there. On the other side of us, the ground ebbed away before a sheer drop to the sea.

'Did you wonder if the twelve grand was a down-payment on your trust?' I asked him. 'A way of implicating you in something.'

'No,' he said without pause. 'They couldn't have known my job didn't exist'.

'Maybe they want you to feel lucky, indebted, a little afraid.'

He shook his head and I saw the thought land even though he fought against it. 'Maybe you're right, maybe that was when this all started. But whatever someone's trying to do, I won't let them. I came here with my eyes wide open.'

But I wasn't so sure about that. 'Let's not get caught out again. Remember, the thing that costs the Rathwells least is money.'

Suddenly, I started running on impulse, and he followed until we reached a large tree behind which we definitely wouldn't be seen. Leaning against it, we caught our breath. It took longer for him to calm himself. Despite his protests, he seemed more afraid than when we last spoke, like reality had finally crept up on him. I moved close to him and leant my head against his shoulder as we stared at the orange sunset. I wanted to tell him what I knew, explain why we were in even more trouble than he thought. But I also saw a possible glimpse of myself through his eyes: a rubbernecker, that lame-footed girl post-tragedy, her face pressed up against the glass of a better life she could only stare at. But when I thought about the manner of Bobby's death, I found I had to talk.

'You should know,' I said, 'about the first Mrs Rathwell. Bobby's mother. Her name was Isa Marnell.'

I sensed a recognition in him when I mentioned the name.

'She …' I murmured. 'She committed suicide too, apparently.' His trembling hands came up to cover his face. 'Just like Bobby, I mean, exactly like Bobby,' I intoned. 'She was found with slit wrists leaning up against a tree, at the house on Billionaires' Row.'

He swallowed hard and looked out to sea as if he'd find a way of processing it there.

'I think that's what the story breaking back in England is about,' I said.

'How do you know?'

'I don't,' I said, 'not for sure. But it's always been hanging over Mr Rathwell, and when I saw him at dinner, there was something not right about him. Didn't you think?'

'That doesn't mean he did this. He's from a bygone age,' Ben said. 'What he said to you was idiotic, he's the savage, but that doesn't mean he's capable of …'

'That's just it,' I said. 'Savage. He has no remorse. A classic narcissist, I've met them before. He has all sorts of tricks, but in the end he's just another version of my father.'

Ben was silent for a moment. 'Then maybe you're project-ing.' He watched my hands ball into fists. 'I don't know. I just think we both need to keep a clear head.'

I moved away from him a fraction. Sounded to me like he was taking Robert's side. 'No, I'm thinking clearer than ever. Bobby warned us about something, and we took it all as another joke. But it was more than that. What else did your mother tell you about the Rathwells?'

Then, sensing something a few metres behind us, I stopped and turned. Headlights appeared and slowly we stepped out from under the tree. I held up a hand as the lights made us dark silhouettes. Kostas had left the Merc in the garage and opted for the electric Porsche, which made it easier to sneak up on us. His shadowed form behind the windscreen shifted and the doors clicked open. We stepped a little further apart. I felt marks of guilt all over both of us.

'Get in,' he called. 'Storm's coming.'

The hushed sound of a breeze quickened on the trees. But the sky was utterly clear. There didn't seem any immediate danger, that promised storm seemed far away, but we couldn't deny him. This, we realised in a glance to each other, was how things were going to be.

We remained wordless on the journey back to the house. Only yesterday we arrived on the island with such hope. Now we were bound for our silent beds where we would lie, eyes open, barricaded in, waiting for sleep to anaesthetise the fear.

14

Authorities

Isabelle

Amelia and Ben arrived home ten minutes past the one-hour window I'd allotted them. Kostas brought them in, sat them down, and asked them to recite where they were when the body was discovered, the order of events. It felt like every other feat of organisation I had performed for the Rathwells. But this wasn't a charity mail out. This was about what we would be telling the police. It all had to be precise. Once we had agreed on our story, the two of them were allowed to go to bed.

Kostas had informed me we were about to get a late evening visit from the local police and medical team. The police to talk to us about suicide, medics to take the body away. It felt so callous to leave Bobby in the orchard, but we were told not to move him.

Kostas agreed their first contact would come from me and no one else should be there to kick sand in the water. I made sure every door was closed, everyone inside with the fear of God in them about the night to come. I composed myself and put on a public face as I watched the authorities coming up the lane. They had reached the island on a boat carrying the ambulance and a battered Peugeot, the ambulance containing two white-uniformed medics, the Peugeot holding a plain-clothed policeman, named Georgios.

I pressed a button to open the gates. A torch was about to be shone into the house so we could be examined in the dark. As I waited by the door, I had the feeling someone was watching me, or listening to my breathing through the wall. I shook my meds into my hand from the little white bottle and swallowed them down with water.

Georgios came to the door and introduced himself with a smile, flanked by two silent medics. I walked them through the house and out into the garden, then stood watching as they disappeared into the trees. I saw a flash of photography that looked like localised lightning, which served to remind me that the storm seemed to have missed us. Eventually Georgios emerged from the orchard, removing his plastic gloves, as we stepped back inside the house.

There were so many more ordinary ways he could have done this. Instead, he leant casually against the wall in the hallway, holding my gaze. It was as if he was waiting for a prompt from me on how we should begin.

Then he gave me a crumpled, apologetic look and reached out to touch my wrist. 'I am so deeply troubled by your loss,' he said. Kostas had said they would be gentle with me.

He turned back, sensing the others coming, and suggested we go in the den so that I didn't have to see the body carried through the hallway. He was dressed in a polo shirt under a navy blue suit. He lurked along in white sneakers, examining the expensive monochrome expressionist art on the walls, before we sat down.

'Thank you for having me in your home, I just wanted to address a couple of things with yourself. But please, miss, Kostas has told me what a wonderful, loving family you are.'

What disappointed me was how good his English was. I was hoping to stick to smiles, shrugs and yes or no answers if I could. Georgios, however, was athletic of mind and body, and he didn't miss a beat.

'Kostas told me Bobby wore a watch on his right hand?' Georgios said.

'Er, yes, I think so,' I said, breathing deep and keeping things simple. 'Gift from his father,' I added for realism's sake.

He noted it down. 'I would like,' he said, standing, 'to pass on my condolences to Mr Rathwell himself.'

I saw where he was going, a little feint of the shoulder and he must've thought he was in. Down the line, or something, as they say in football, probably. No, Robert wasn't in any shape to be seen and, even if he were, he wouldn't react well, and by that I mean appropriately.

'I'm afraid he's sleeping,' I said. 'And I'm afraid, he was in the midst of one of his troubled periods even before this terrible tragedy. Putting into words the depth of his grief would be far too much for him.'

'Ah,' Georgios said, with understanding, leaning against the doorjamb. There was something feline about him. 'I will say, madam, I am practised in talking to seniors, this job often entails it. We revere the elderly much on the islands. And I myself nursed my grandmother in her late days.'

I bet he could crack a nut by whispering to it. There was a kind of glow around him; or perhaps I'd taken one too many of my pills.

'I'm sure,' I said, staying even. 'And how kind you are to offer to visit him in his time of need. But you wouldn't want me to wake him, would you?'

'As you wish,' he said. He wasn't conceding any ground. He looked around him in a way that unnerved me, as if silently judging us for everything we had. 'I may have to wake him, in future,' he said. 'I may have to make my presence felt, depending on how the examination of the body goes.' Then he smiled, like there was nothing in the threat he'd just dropped at my feet.

I was struggling, my thoughts sluggish. Sir Anthony, Robert's right-hand man, always had the right words on his silver tongue. Not too robust, not too permissive. He was composure in a pinstripe suit. I suppose confidence comes with a seven-figure bonus.

'You're quite instrumental in Robert's company, is this correct?' Georgios said.

'Oh, I'm a lifestyle assistant. The Rathwell Company? I don't go there so often, it's not my place.'

He looked surprised. 'Oh, then it is unfortunate that your name made the papers.'

So, the story was out. The disadvantage of being here to hide from it was that we were the last to know. Sir Anthony knows not to call the Grand House; ordinarily I might have phoned London for the state of play, but other things had taken over.

'That's understandable. I am with Robert almost everywhere he goes. Even I sometimes forget where my remit ends.'

It was an idiotic thing to say. He blinked by way of answer and fixed me with his olive-coloured eyes.

The medics escorted the body through the hall and we sat for a while longer. Georgios asked me a few more questions, but nothing about where I had been last night, as if he already knew exactly what had happened.

'OK,' he said at last. 'I would like to speak to the others.'

The medics had finished and were waiting in the van. They would travel back with Georgios on the boat once he was finished.

I set him up by the pool with a glass of water and a chair, then brought them to him one by one. As each of them answered his questions, I watched from the kitchen window. His face was illuminated by the glow from the underwater lights built into a mosaic of Aegeus the goatish man, father of Athens, who gave his name to the sea. I've never liked it. Horrible. But though they all looked a little ghoulish in that lighting too, their subtle nods assured me that all had gone to plan.

I was pouring myself a glass of pineapple and turmeric juice when Georgios hurried in, no longer relaxed.

'You've been so hospitable, but I'm afraid I must leave you,' he said.

In England that would have passed for good sarcasm. I hadn't offered him a thing. Even my account of where I was last night. Did that mean I was less under suspicion? Or something worse?

'I have another urgent matter to attend to in Lesvos,' he said, but I wondered if one of the others had said something against me. Something he needed to corroborate right away. Of course, I was overly anxious, but that was understandable, given all this and having recently been followed. I had not long ago shaken off the shackles of that figure in London and now I had something else to worry about.

'So soon?' I said. 'No more questions?'

He turned and looked me up and down. This wasn't the gentle man Kostas had promised.

'I have spoken to all but Robert, who you say is too unwell,' he said. 'I have searched the body and the surrounding area for a note of some kind. There doesn't seem to be one. Did you find a note at all?'

I shook my head. 'Do they normally leave a note? By which I mean, when people …'

'Not always,' he said, a hand on my elbow. 'Are there any other questions you would *like* me to ask?' It was somehow neither passive nor aggressive, though out of any other mouth it would've been both. I really couldn't read him.

'No, no questions, but …' I said. 'I can't tempt you to a cup of English tea? It's Fortnum and Mason.'

'No, no,' Georgios said. 'The rest of Europe, no matter how hard we tell them we work, they say the Greeks spend too much time on their butts, that's why we're bankrupt. What would they think if they heard I was lounging drinking English tea when I should be—'

'Solving crimes?'

'Doing paperwork.' He paused, his bare forearm against the cool white wall.

'I do have one question that it might be uncomfortable to answer,' he said, continuing. 'What did Robert say when he saw this estranged son of his?'

'Estranged is a strong word in England.'

'Six years is a long time. It can be no small thing that keeps a father and son apart for such a time. How did Robert greet him, when they were finally reunited?'

'Oh, Robert was just delighted,' I said, my voice breaking

with emotion, which took me unawares. I felt weakened by all this, and I had remembered a glimpse of a younger, cherubic Bobby hugging my waist.

'He held him in his arms,' I said, 'all his prayers answered, and they would've stayed like that for the rest of the trip if circumstances … had allowed.'

His hand came to my shoulder. 'Please pass my condolences to Robert. I see now that to speak to you is to speak to Robert himself.'

His face paused in sympathy and then with the words 'I go now,' he left.

I let them out of the gates and watched the chipped ambulance taking Bobby away. Once it had gone, I closed the front door and put my forehead against it for a second. Then I walked down to the beach and stared at the dark horizon. My eyes suddenly alighted on something down on the sand. I walked forward and reached down to pick it up. This black mass. It was the gun I thought I'd disposed of by tossing it into the ocean. I stared at it.

Chacun voit midi à sa porte, means everyone sees noon at their door.

Robert taught me that himself.

I tossed the gun further this time, far into the deep, so far it would never come back to haunt us. And I braced myself for what lay ahead.

15

3 a.m.

Sofia

I sat bolt upright when the transceiver under my pillow vibrated, answering before the sound became any more conspicuous.

The voice spoke fast, leaving me little to do but listen as my face fell. On it went until I was left shivering in the dark.

'If things get tough,' the voice said by way of ending. 'Remember *Adam Sands*.'

That was all they had for me and all they needed to say. I got up and went to my en-suite, dabbing cool water on the back of my neck to calm myself. I had done something before bed to try to alter the course of things. Something decisive that I thought no one else would discover. But after that call I worried it wouldn't be enough.

Then I heard the crack of wood against stone downstairs. The noise continued, turning into a swing and a bang, and eventually I decided it was better to know what it was. I took a deep breath as I left my room, my feet padding silently along the Rhodesian teak floor. And that knocking just kept going, drawing me downstairs with its siren song into the tall reception hall.

All was quiet down there, but the front door was open. The fresh blue light of Greece that could seep in through every nook in the house had no problems with an open door. I wet my lip, deciding to tread heavier as I stepped out onto the porch, so if anyone was out there they knew I was coming.

No sign of an intruder. Someone must have left the door open by accident, I concluded. I had thought perhaps the voice on the line had decided it was time to speak in person.

'Hello?' my voice shivered on the porch, disappearing into the blue, the hills staring me down from far away across the sea. I spoke to the vista and my voice came back. I had started to scare myself, so I took the girl inside me into the house, thinking of the conversation I had with Georgios by the pool. Isabelle didn't seek me out to confirm what I had said. Maybe she should've been more thorough.

As I walked up the stairs to my room, I saw a figure at the top of them. Something glinting in his hand, half obscured by a darkness.

I stopped.

'What's the noise down there?' he said.

'Nothing,' I said, swallowing. 'I checked.'

Ben and I looked at each other. His bare torso was lit by the invading blue light from the high windows. He stood there like he was the man of the house, and I enjoyed the roleplay. Because, in truth, I owned everything around him.

'Well, I can't sleep,' Ben said. I took in the curve of his bicep as he rubbed the back of his neck.

'Is everyone else ...' I heard myself say.

'Asleep?' he said. 'Think so.'

I had hoped to talk to him privately, and here was my opportunity. I halved the distance between us. At this proximity I could see the darkness separating itself from his form. He stared at me, taking in my hair resting on my shoulders.

'This is what I would call a fucking nightmare,' I said in a casual tone I hadn't tried with him before. 'It's like we are thousands of feet in the air. I can feel the cabin pressure.'

He paused to assess this new level of intimacy. Then said, 'I'm sure we're safe now.' He sounded like one of those men who is so afraid of life that he is determined to rationalise everything into oblivion, even this. 'Whatever is going on, it'll be simpler than we think.' I wondered how he thought he knew that. 'The shock and grief will lift, we just have to wait it out.' He lost his surety and went looking for mine somewhere near the end of his speech.

'Hmm,' I murmured. There was so much he didn't know. My foot flattened against the white wall.

'But until it blows over,' he said. 'We're stuck.' His hushed voice all consonants, tongue tapping behind his teeth. I imagine he practised such delicacy in speech class.

'You and me?' I said after a moment.

Slowly, his eyes met mine and they stayed there. I could see that keen mind of his racing to keep up.

'Well, all of us,' he said, giving a short exhale and shaking his head. Then he gave the quietest laugh I had ever heard. 'I better at least try and sleep,' he said. His body brushed mine as he walked away. But just as he got his hand to the door handle, he spoke. 'You look great, by the way, you dress for bed like you're dressing for dinner.'

'Thank you,' I said. I didn't want him to go. I took a few steps towards him, thought about placing my hand on his shoulder but felt that would be too much. 'What did the police ask you?' I asked. He turned and I remained close so I could keep my voice low and because I wanted him where I could see him.

'It felt casual. He just wanted me to run him through the night Bobby died. I did what we agreed, told him I went to bed straight after dinner. That's right, isn't it?'

'Yes,' I said.

'The police said the time of death was around three a.m. About now,' he said, glancing at the grandfather clock on the stairs. 'I'd have long been in bed. Which was true anyway.'

'Depends on your definition of long,' I said. 'I was downstairs getting a glass of water and saw you there about half two.'

'More like half one,' he said.

'Were you scared?' I said, cutting in. 'To say you didn't go for that drink? To tell a white lie like that?'

'Guess I just don't see it as much to do with me, I did what was asked of me. He wanted to know if there were any disagreements in the house. Or if it seemed … strangely quiet.'

'Didn't ask me that,' I said. 'It's starting to sound like you're his prime suspect. Those are the sort of questions he might ask when he brings you in, puts you on tape.'

I nudged his shoulder, teasing him. It was good to release some tension.

He ignored me and went on, 'I told him everything was good, with everyone, except for Robert, obviously.'

But that stung. 'Why did you say that?'

He paused. 'Because I hadn't seen him since the death. And I've only met him once, so it's not up for me to say—'

'Do not be petulant,' I whispered. 'I know Robert was playful over dinner, with you and Amelia, but you implied that there was something odd about his behaviour? Why do that?'

'I told them Robert didn't seem well because I don't know the man and I assumed you didn't want me to tell Georgios he seemed absolutely fine, the night after his son's death. Isabelle told me to impress on Georgios that Robert wasn't fit for visitors. Which doesn't seem far off to me. He doesn't look good.'

'This is my husband you're talking about.' I felt like cuffing him. 'And I love him very much.' I looked at the flat, taut silhouette of him. 'No matter what sort of man people think he is. No matter what sort of man he really is.'

I wandered away and didn't stop when he whispered, 'Wait.' Only when I was out of sight on the stairs did I hear his door close.

He had riled me, but even I didn't fully know why. My husband was a tender subject. He was *suspicious* because he had learnt to be. *Exacting*, because his position required it. *Cutting*, because that's what his childhood was. But unlike others his age he was capable of change. If anyone said they knew for sure who Robert was, they were lying. Even me.

I thought about what Georgios had asked me. He wanted to know who had seen Bobby last, rephrasing the question, doubling back to it a couple of times. The longer he left that thread dangling there, the more I was tempted to pull on it. Eventually, I made a decision to unravel what we'd made together, spoil the version of events we had agreed on. I told him Amelia and Ben had been out drinking with Bobby, contradicting everyone else completely. While they wanted this case closed, I needed it open. Given what had been set in motion, I realised this might be my only chance. So, I decided to take control, entice Georgios to dig a little deeper. I thought a few inconsistencies might help. Help me out of the great machine I'd found myself in, before the cogs started to really turn, and I was trapped within it.

16

The day came

Isabelle

The next day I rose from a thin sleep, only knowing I achieved sleep at all because of the dreams I had of Robert. He was digging in the garden with his hands, covered in dirt, so black it stained every nook of him. The image was lodged in my head because he often said it's a dream he was haunted by, but in his dreams it's not him but everyone else who's digging desperately on their hands and knees. Silly to reflect on dreams, the height of self-obsession.

When I awoke, Robert was standing over me. The day had barely begun and I was already shaken. He hadn't respected my privacy for a long time, but I was happy for him to have all of me.

'Sorry, it couldn't wait,' he muttered, flushed from having dressed, Sofia having clearly helped him don a sheer black designer tracksuit and burgundy trainers. It was a strange circumstance with Robert, you never knew what level of health you were going to get. His current state was better than it had been on the plane, nearly as good as at dinner and certainly better than I had led the policeman to believe.

'I need to speak to everyone on the beach, my darling. Make it happen, would you?' he said. But as well as he was in body, I could see behind his eyes that Bobby's death had taken its toll, had worked its way into his corners, like that dirt of my dream. He couldn't hide anything from me.

'Kostas will handle all of that, Robert,' I said, sitting up, wondering whether he required a pill. 'You should save your strength.'

'No, I would like to do it myself,' he said, his voice so spirited.

'You shouldn't be—'

'Come on, darling, don't play should and shouldn't with me,' he muttered through a smile, eyes lowered. He was in a mercurial mood.

'But a man in your state—'

'Isabelle,' he shouted, so loud it shook me again, but then he placed his hand to his chest, with a breath that felt like he was ascending a great mountain. 'I apologise for my emotions. You know how they are. But please, my son is dead. I must say a few things. And get a good look at that boy.'

*

I asked Amelia and Ben to gather on the beach so Robert could say a few words to them. I had long felt that Robert didn't quite trust Sofia's judgement on staff or her ability to run a thorough check on their pasts. Ben, apparently, had one single family member, Celia Bowman, a one-time model, and a father that even Sofia's tracer – a specialist who works on the Strand – couldn't find.

This was why Robert was determined to get a look at him and attempt to pull apart his sparse family history, a process he had started at dinner. I watched from the balcony as Robert kissed a watchful-looking Amelia on the cheek and sat down with her on the sand in the glaring sun. Ben and Sofia left them alone, wandering along the beach, as Robert said something that sneaked under Amelia's defences and made her laugh.

Not knowing quite how that would play out, I took JR away. We had been trying to get him out in sunshine, be a little less in his head, but I allowed him to use the movie theatre in the basement as he was always asking to. I even got the maids to make us some popcorn. As I turned the lights down, I thought about that cat's head and wondered what this small boy I was alone with was capable of.

'What we watching?' JR said as he settled into the red velvet seating and noticed that the opening credits didn't look modern.

'*North by Northwest*,' I said. 'You love the classics.'

'That's because I watch them with daddy,' he said. His voice when displeased was ominous.

'I thought you'd like it, because you love *Vertigo*,' I said, avoiding mention of his father.

'OK. I did. I'll try it,' he said, his face sullen.

'Tell me something honestly, will you? I won't tell your mum,' I whispered as the sound kicked in. 'Did you take your knife back?'

I heard the popcorn crunch in his mouth. 'Yes, I'm sorry. I shoulda said. Cos it's gone now. Someone must've taken it.'

'Right,' I said. 'And who do we think did that?'

'Hmm,' he said as I stared at the dust in the projector beam, wary he was going to miss the beginning. 'If I had to guess I'd say … Ben. I showed it him earlier and I had a feeling he wanted to get it.' It came out reluctantly and ended with a shrug.

I looked at him by the light of the Technicolor images in front of us, trying to figure out if he was telling the truth.

Despite all that had happened, it did feel good not to be the one under the microscope. It was a relief to be far from London and the shadows that seemed to follow me everywhere.

Then I noticed Kostas at the door. He beckoned to me. I left my popcorn on my seat and stood up, told JR to start without me and then wandered into the corridor. He was waiting for me with a very male expression; the harassed look of a man determined to get through something. I felt myself begin to perspire.

'Two hundred thousand,' he said, when the door to the cinema was closed and he was well out of earshot.

'Have we received another letter somehow? Is it blackmail?' I said, but my naïvety sounded forced, even to me.

'No,' he said. 'Something unusual got flagged on Robert's account from this quarter.'

'Impossible, I would've caught it.'

'Correct, you would have. Yet, you said nothing. But then, of course you would say nothing, if …'

'If, say … the payment went to me?' I said. 'I see.'

'Isabelle, I am not playing games,' he said, pulling back his jacket to reveal his small revolver. My heart started to pound. The pressure and suspicions of London had returned to me after such a short holiday. 'Two hundred thousand. And who knows if it wasn't the first time. How much were you planning to siphon off? Maybe you thought you would get an even bigger cut when Robert passed away if Bobby wasn't around.'

'For that to be a logical accusation,' I whispered, my throat suddenly dry. 'I'd need to be in the will.'

'Yes, you would.'

There was a long pause. What an insinuation. It seemed deeply unfair to be under such pressure after all I've done for this family. I was already looking behind me, seeing passing shadows everywhere, people in cars whose gazes lasted longer than they should.

As he stared at me, my natural reaction to feeling under threat came as it always did. The anger my father gave me rising.

'Don't corner me here and bait me, because I'll come back at you and you won't like it at all,' I said. 'It was a single payment Robert knew all about. I'm not explaining the maths of it to you, I don't have the time or energy. Ask Robert.'

Kostas leant over me, his arm on the wall in the narrow corridor. He was quite a presence when he wanted to be. Right now, there's a killer on this island and I'm the only one who can keep you safe. You need to trust me. When Robert has finished with Amelia and Ben, I will ask him. For now, put me at my ease. Explain to me why you needed the money?'

I didn't like to give ground at the best of times, but certainly not in these circumstances. I swallowed, my mouth dry, but I would not be dominated. I smiled as I spoke low. 'I don't have to tell you shit.'

He frowned. 'Our lives are under threat, and every lie you tell helps our killer.'

138

I let out a sigh and told him what I had to.

'It was a gambling debt,' I said, looking into his eyes.

'Didn't see you as a sports fan,' he said.

'Not mine,' I said. 'My father's. He bet the farm, literally. My parents were about to lose everything, including the farmhouse in La Rochelle where they lived, and I couldn't let it happen to my mother. Robert offered to dig them out of the hole and there was nothing else I could do but accept.'

Kostas thought about it for a long moment. The sound of the film reached us through the closed door. Eventually he gave me a long look and then turned to leave.

'Happy?' I said.

'Sure,' Kostas said.

I grabbed his arm before he could go. He flinched at first, then stared at me as the string music bled from the cinema.

'I need a favour,' I said, realising this might be my only chance to speak to him alone. Back in London I thought this might make me seem like I had something to hide. But here I saw an opportunity to move things away from me and into a more useful direction. 'I'd like you to look into something for me. Make some calls even. It could be important.'

His face was blank.

'Someone's been following me,' I said. 'I see them every so often, wandering eyes in coffee shops.'

'A woman such as you must have many admirers,' he said.

'This person clearly didn't want to leave me alone for a second. It was just before we went away, but it might have something to do with Bobby's death, and those letters.'

Kostas stayed silent. But I had a feeling he wouldn't let something like this go without taking a look at it.

'I'll leave that with you, I'm sure you have your ways.'

And without another word, he was gone.

When I opened the door to the cinema, I heard JR snicker as he threw some popcorn into his mouth. Cary Grant was getting marched along with a gun pressed into his back. I watched the flickering images before me and considered what my next move would be. I felt like I had only postponed the inevitable. Because when Kostas talked to Robert he would inevitably discover what I had long been trying to hide.

17

Mr Rathwell

Sofia

'He's not as intimidating as people think,' I said to Ben as we walked back towards Robert, lying on a sunlounger surrounded by bottles of Lofoten water as he spoke with Amelia, in the very spot Kostas loved to sit when Robert wasn't around. I had to say this sort of thing. I had been downplaying Robert so often it had started to become natural. 'What he's fond of most in people is honesty.'

I took Ben's arm, and I could tell he didn't like it. He didn't want Robert to see him so close to his wife, but then, I was starting to pluck up the courage to rebel in all sorts of ways. Having both Ben and Amelia here with us was starting to make me believe there were new ways to live my life. Words were being said that were helping me realise how stultifying things had been for so long. Robert could appear different on whatever day of the week you caught him, but I'd never truly known if this was his illness, his temperament, or something else. Only now was I finally feeling able to peel back the layers of my denial and get to the bottom of who my husband really was.

'Amelia and I had been wondering about Robert,' Ben said, and hadn't we all. 'Gotta be honest, I've seen him on the news so much that when I saw him at dinner it didn't seem real.'

'He's as real as it gets,' I said. We were close enough to hear Robert and Amelia talking. Robert had some work to do given how he'd been with her at dinner, but he was not shy of work.

'I give a lot of money to the Royal Philharmonic and know a couple of high-ups there,' Robert was saying, with a twinkle. 'Remind me to put in a good word for Amelia,' he whispered to me as I sat, and he gave me a peck on the cheek.

'Of course,' I said. Amelia didn't seem to believe him, but when Robert wanted something, he tended to get it.

'Thank you,' Amelia said. She seemed to have enjoyed her private audience. Robert nodded as he held my hand tight. It was to stop his hand shaking, as it did more often than not these days.

Then Robert's gaze went to Ben, backed by the sun glare. Robert grabbed Ben's outstretched hand and moved him, so he could use Ben to shade his eyes. I sensed him stifle the urge to shake him off. Robert gave a crotchety sigh.

'Sorry, dear thing,' he said to Ben, 'the sun makes strange things of me. If I'm not strange enough already.' He turned to the rest of us. 'Now, I know you must all be terribly worried, but do understand no one is more concerned than me. It's an unimaginable loss, that I know for sure I will never truly recover from, but ...' he sighed heavily, his eyes red. I held him tighter '... but if we stick together,' he rallied, 'then that gives us the best chance of staying safe.'

We were all startled into silence. When Robert showed you his better side it made you wonder if he was just misunderstood. Ben sat, his eyes never leaving Robert.

'Pleased to meet you, my boy, I'm sorry about the circumstances. All the cash in the world can't turn back the tides of time. Last night, my whole life changed, and now I see everything I could have done to be a better father.'

I wasn't expecting self-reflection from Robert. He was adept in many fields. He would go into a kitchen to tell the Michelin-starred chef how to make a clam chowder, he would instruct lawyers on how to get through to a jury, he even got on stage on our second date to show a tenor in *The Barber of Seville* the proper way for a man playing a barber to stand, and though people grimaced through it you could see something in them concede he was right. And he still wished to learn, that was what saved him every time he was nearly lost to me. Suddenly, that part of him that would listen to me for hours would return. But I didn't know he was capable of this, and Ben certainly didn't.

Ben spoke falteringly. 'Bobby said he loved his family, he said that. He just said families were difficult.'

Robert's head cocked, the cogs working away. 'Then he was very shrewd. And very kind. The problems in our relationship are for me to reflect on. It's so important your children are cleverer than you are. They're certainly better educated than I ever was.'

He fell silent, lost in a reverie of sadness. After a moment he shook his head, as if trying to gather up the pieces of himself.

'Look, I want to say that none of this will affect JR. We're here to make sure of it,' Ben said, with a look to Amelia. 'As you say, education is important.'

'No, it isn't,' Robert said, cutting him off.

'No?' Ben said, startled at how easily he was willing to contradict himself.

'Dismantle it, I say,' Robert proclaimed. 'I gleaned everything I know from life. Dropped out of Oxford, learnt it all in the army and business. Learn in the field, use your contacts, use what capital you have, make a name for yourself. Kill the institutions, waste of money. You've probably already been infected by one. Take my advice, start forgetting everything you've been told, and you'll be on the right track.'

Robert looked up at Ben with a devilish expression; another part of him had arrived. Ben smiled back and then seemed to regret it. Robert was a pioneer of sarcasm and was so good at it you never knew whether he was serious or not. MPs had motions virtually ready to put before the House of Commons before Robert admitted he was joking.

'What if you don't have any capital?' Ben said. 'Or contacts?'

'In that case,' Robert cried, 'you're *completely* fucked. And that is the perfect place to start from. I envy you. Nothing else for you to do but take them on, on your own.'

'And how do I do that?' Ben said.

'In *acting*?' Robert cried. 'Damned if I know. Interrupt producers over dinner, tell them who you bloody are. I did some acting at Oxford, but never again, filthy habit.'

Ben smiled. Then said, in a more natural, regional voice, 'Yes, I heard you'd be a bastard. That's what people say, isn't it?'

I don't recall the shape my face made.

'Yes, I think that *is* what they say, isn't it?' Robert said. We laughed, as we watched him move to charming. I knew how much every breath was costing him.

'What's your mother do? Mind me asking?' he said. I'd told him all this, having done the vetting myself, but he couldn't help the urge to get the measure of them himself.

'I do mind, a little.'

'Yes, but I've asked now, best to say something,' Robert croaked, with a slow wink. 'You see, always better to be rude than ask permission. I used to ...'

Robert seemed to lose his way. He squeezed my hand. I kissed it.

'I never used to ask permission at school. One day at prep I was thinking about what it was like to bite through my water glass, then I did. Little bits of ...' Robert flailed his hand, as we looked on. 'Shards of ... glass ... in my mouth. I spat them out, I wasn't cut. But I felt them on my ... tongue. They probably would have said I *had problems*, but they didn't exist back then, and my parents wouldn't have had any of that, they ... what were we ...'

He turned to look out at the sea, and we waited.

'Was school tough?' Robert said, turning back to Ben.

'I made out fine,' Ben said, with a subtle kind of dignity. 'Kept my head down, tried to be funny. And always threw the first punch if it seemed like there was going to be a fight.'

Robert reached for an empty bottle of Lofoten. I handed him a full one and he smiled. He was determined to do things on his own. That was part of his problem.

'Boxer, eh? Good boy,' Robert smiled at Ben. 'Think JR has the old ADHD?'

Ben thought about it. 'No, I really don't.'

'Think he's a good boy?'

'Yes, I do.'

'*Do you?*' Robert said, like it was a strange proposition, then he laughed at himself, pulled at his trousers. It was time to go inside. He stood with great effort, holding my arm for support. It hurt a little.

'And your mother?' Robert said. 'What does she—'

'She's a nurse,' Ben said. 'On a labour ward. Loves little babies.'

Robert nodded, pleased to have got his answer. Then he became very still. 'Intelligent woman. Do what you like, as much as possible. Give her my love?'

Ben sniggered. 'Ha.'

As we all stood up to leave, Robert spoke, his voice suddenly loud. 'And one thing before you go.' They started, the volume surprising them, and it would have shocked me too if I wasn't used to such surprises. 'I will find out, you know?' he said, taking in each of us in turn, a dangerous air suddenly rippling through him. 'About everything. All of it. In fact, I've already begun to. And when I do ...'

No one said a word. The doctors had warned me about changes in him. I had chosen to stand by him.

He rounded on Ben. '... You, you've got a temper, I saw it. Dragged it out of you.'

'No,' Ben said, but he wasn't being defensive, he just seemed to disagree. 'I'm sorry, I don't.'

'Don't lie to me, fighter. It's OK to fight, but don't lie.' Robert had gone red, a line of spittle ran down his chin, he jabbed a finger into Ben's chest. 'I would have boxed you all right, man to man, because I like you.' He sucked in breaths, hands trembling. 'You remind me of myself,' he continued, his voice weaker, 'and sometimes I'd like to ...'

Robert clenched his fist. He fell to one knee and his eyes

bulged. The emotion, the heat, the tension. He was flushed, and I started fanning him and making room. Amelia grabbed some water and Ben ran towards the house to find Isabelle. My heart was in my mouth, breath high in my throat. I wondered whether this little show may have been his last trick. Ben returned with Isabelle and knelt down beside us. I held Robert's hand and he groaned, closed one eye, then his lip twitched, an eyelid drooped. But through it all, he looked up at Ben, gritting his teeth, to show him there was nothing in this world that he couldn't stare down.

18

The silence of evening
Amelia

After Robert was taken away, staring at us as he went, we wandered back to a quiet house. He was quivering in such an unnatural way when we last saw him that I couldn't help but be disturbed. But the soft signal as always was that we shouldn't ask, that he was just fine and the episode was nothing, given what else was going on.

I had stared at Robert with a smile, certain of what he was. And the enablers around him were just as unremitting, I knew the kind well. But that didn't stop the tingle of curiosity, in fact it made it sharper. He was so accommodating that it was all I could do to stop myself tactfully mentioning his first wife. Her name was on the tip of my tongue, but I had to wait, to not give myself away.

I tried to find Ben, to place some jigsaw pieces together while the Rathwells were too stretched to keep an eye on our movements.

I saw him by the pool and, when it was clear everyone else was occupied, we didn't waste time.

'Still think Robert could kill his own son?' Ben said as we wandered away from the house and towards the pool.

'Yes, actually. Despite that performance.'

'What?' Ben said, looking around. 'I didn't enjoy the going-over he gave me, but you think the whole thing was an act? And if he wanted his son gone, why do it like this?'

'Maybe he needed independent witnesses who would verify there was nothing untoward in it. In fact, I think that's exactly what we were asked to do.'

'But,' Ben said, 'just practically. He's frailer than I thought. You think that was an act too?'

I took a breath. It could have been.

'To do what someone did,' Ben went on, 'they'd have to be quick, a little strong, and have thought the whole thing out. I'm not sure he's up to it.'

'Maybe,' I said. I saw the way he held onto Sofia for comfort, his shakes. Those cuts on Bobby's wrists Ben had described to me required a steady hand and, when we were alone, he didn't seem quite as savage as he would need to be, it was true. 'There's just something that doesn't feel—'

Sofia quickly came around the corner with JR and we stopped talking. She gestured for me to take JR, then asked Ben if she could talk to him privately on the beach, separating us once again. I was left by the pool, to continue JR's lessons. As I watched Sofia and Ben walk away, I noticed their body language. They crossed the beach and then stopped on the sand. She sat, he stood, so servant and master. So much so that it seemed like roleplay, like they were holding themselves back from something. I pictured her reaching out and unbuttoning his shirt. It was a ridiculous thought, and I wasn't a jealous person. Anyway, jealousy is about losing something, but I barely knew Ben. Were they closer than anyone knew, or was I just imagining it? I had a feeling I was being naïve about something, I just didn't know what.

*

It wasn't until the evening, after JR had put himself to bed, that Kostas gathered all of us together, except for a resting Robert, to tell us what he had found out. He asked us to follow him down to the basement. I held onto Ben as we descended the narrow stairs and he flicked on the lights down there, a single lane illuminated with ten gleaming white pins at the end. I didn't even realise that next to the movie theatre was a bowling alley.

In front of us was a leather booth of fifties Americana style, which allowed you to watch bowler and pins from behind a small Formica table.

'Please,' Kostas said, gesturing us to sit, surrounded by pink and turquoise balls patterned in swirls, all of various weights in one long rack. The mirror-covered hideaway was oblong with low fluorescent lights sunk into its corners. It had a seedy, adult feel, despite the games around us. Sofia and Isabelle sat on one side of the table. I slid into the booth on the other side, taking a spot next to the wall, then came Ben, then Kostas took his place on the end. We would have to get past him if we wanted to leave.

Ben and I glanced at each other as Kostas began to speak:

'I wish to tell you that I carried out a search of each of your rooms. Even Mr Rathwell's wardrobe was inspected.'

Isabelle spoke first, more nervily than I expected: 'I thought the police took the weapon away with the body?'

My face twitched.

'They did,' Kostas said, 'but I think the killer is too smart to leave fingerprints on the knife.' He applied plastic gloves as he reached into a small leather hold-all. 'However, given how much blood comes from the radial artery, and how much was on the grass next to him, if someone was present while he was cut open then there should be marks on their clothes.'

Kostas had taken on the tone of a man about to let us in on something rather than accuse us of anything. And that felt good for a moment.

'Sofia,' he said and I watched her heart knot, 'you have barely unpacked. But don't worry, I put everything back where I found it. OK?'

'Yes,' she said, her face pale and grave.

'Ben?' Kostas said. 'I'm going to have to keep your trainers.'

The sickness hit us both when Kostas lifted them up for us to see. Underneath, against the white sole, there was the tiniest tick of red.

'Doesn't seem like much to me,' Ben said, flatly. He glanced at Sofia. 'Must've got it while I was cleaning it up.'

He was remarkably calm. I supposed actors must be good under pressure.

'And if he did it,' Sofia said. 'Wouldn't he have checked them over, or got rid of them?'

'Not if he got careless,' Isabelle said.

'Please,' Kostas said, 'I'm not suggesting anything, just

showing what I find. And it's true, it doesn't look like much.' He lifted the trainer out of the bag in his gloved hand until it was closer to the purple wall light: 'That's why I came here to check.'

The UV light turned everything purple nearby, apart from a large black lake on the bottom of Ben's trainer. I let out a stifled gasp.

'Of course, this is a rudimentary form of forensics,' Kostas said. 'I would have to check whose blood it was before I went any further.'

Ben silently shook his head, his fists clenching. He closed his eyes. 'I need some air, let me out.'

'Hold on,' Kostas said, 'We'll talk calmly.'

'If the trace is that subtle,' I said, 'then it may be something he stepped in?'

'Maybe,' Kostas said, by far the calmest man in the room. 'But normally what the blacklight shows us is blood that has been cleaned. That is generally the way of things. So ...'

'Let me out of here,' Ben said.

'Just stay calm,' Kostas said. 'Let's not do anything stupid.'

'I haven't done anything,' Ben said, standing up and trying to get out of the booth, but with a table in front of him, me on one side and Kostas not budging on the end, he was hemmed in. When Kostas didn't move, Ben elbowed then slammed Kostas in the chest with his palm, Kostas standing up and stepping back, holding his ribs.

He stared down at Ben, who was gripping onto the table hard. Ben looked pale under the light. We all did, our skin transparent, our eyes cruelly exposed.

'Get a hold of yourself,' Isabelle said. It took Ben a moment to realise what he had done.

Ben got out of the booth and put some distance between us and him, standing on the lacquered lane floor as Kostas leant against the wall, watching close.

'I didn't do it,' Ben said. 'I wasn't there when he died.'

'We understand,' Sofia said, attempting to soothe.

'My friend,' Kostas said, a little winded. 'Well done. I am used to taking blows. That was a decent one.'

I was about to speak up in Ben's defence but, as I sat there, I started to question who was to blame. Kostas certainly seemed calm and Ben's fury got up very quickly.

'You do have a temper,' Isabelle said. 'And there was blood on your trainers.'

Ben looked between us all, a hand gripping his head. 'Maybe when Bobby and I fought on the beach, he got cut,' his voice quivered. 'Yes, I think he did, I think he got a bloody nose.'

'Oh. What did you fight about?' Isabelle said.

'It was a joke, we were messing around,' Ben said through gritted teeth.

'But he got a bloody nose?' Kostas said.

'We rolled over, he hit a rock, I think,' Ben said. 'He came on a lot stronger than I thought.'

'A little like you're doing now,' Isabelle said, tapping a fingernail against the Formica table.

Ben held back his reaction to that comment.

'I'm glad you told us this,' Sofia said. 'Sounds like it could be important.'

'It wasn't, but you know how manic he could get,' Ben said. 'We just got to talking, and … Bobby mentioned a story breaking about the Rathwells back in England. I was interested, but when I asked him what it was, he got suspicious, thought

I would report back on him to the family. I just laughed, made fun of him, and then we were fighting. I … think I remember cleaning the sand off my shoes when I got back. I guess I might have cleaned blood off without realising.'

I remembered how Ben had said the Rathwells would try to control what was true, move us into the firing line. He had been warning me of this all along, and I hadn't been listening. Unless Ben really did have something to hide about that night. I couldn't deny it was possible.

'This story in the papers,' Kostas said, glancing at Sofia and Isabelle. 'You shouldn't be so very interested. We're handling it. As for our confrontation, I'm sorry for my part in it.'

Ben nodded, calmer now.

'Your words have illuminated many things to me,' Kostas said. 'I hope you understand I have to keep the evidence. But please know, I am a mediator not an aggressor. The last thing I would do is jump to conclusions.'

The rest of us were watching on in silence. Ben suddenly had three strikes against him: his rage, the blood, and the fight.

'Almost time for bed, I think,' Kostas said, flicking off the light reflecting onto the long clean bowling lane and ushering the others up the stairs, until it was just me and him.

'Let's keep in close contact,' he whispered. 'You, Ben and I.'

He seemed very alive in that moment. As if what he had just discovered required a fresh adjustment, a calculated decision. His eyes darted around in thought. He seemed to want to confide in me. It told me perhaps the blood on the trainers wasn't what it appeared to be, and that he knew something that could help us.

Perhaps I just wanted to believe I could trust him.

19

2 a.m.

Sofia

I was woken by footsteps in the hallway that night. Grabbing the heavy brass lamp I'd set aside for my protection, having unscrewed the bulb, I carefully opened the door to see a pair of eyes glinting at me in the darkness. I was sure that next they would mention *'Adam Sands'* and I would crumble.

Ben's face loomed out of the shadow and, before I could ask what he wanted, he was glancing around and then motioning me to follow him down the stairs. I placed the brass lamp back inside and gently padded my way after him. Once we were alone on his floor, he glared at me like he hadn't slept and there was some deep dread on him. I couldn't deny this heavy energy thrilled me in some perverse way.

'Was it true?' I said, before he could speak. 'What you said about the playfight with Bobby?'

'Yes, I think so,' he whispered, his dark eyes capturing mine. 'I was drunk, I can't be sure of every little detail. All I know is I didn't kill him. I didn't bind his hands. I didn't slit his wrists.'

He was passionate about his defence, perhaps a little too much. If this was his testimony, I wouldn't like his chances on the stand. But he had a symmetrical face and that always helped with juries.

'The police called before bed, didn't they? They needed to talk to you,' I said, smoothing my hand onto my hip just under my shorts. 'What did they ask?'

He sighed, looking up at me again. 'They said someone from the house had contradicted what I said about where I was that night. Someone told them I went for a drink at the beach.'

I gasped, looked exasperated. I was truly sorry the fallout seemed to be landing on his shoulders, but I didn't regret what I had done. It was my only option. I put my hand on his elbow and he pulled away, like it pained him.

'There's too many people talking,' I said. 'The police were always going to find gaps in our stories, it's what they do. What did you say?'

'I told him I'd been scared to say I was the last one who saw him alive. I may have broken down a little.'

Looking at him, I wondered if he meant that he'd really broken down or had acted it. The energy between us was thick enough to touch. Then and there, I had a choice to make.

'I believe you,' I whispered, close to his ear. 'I really do, I'm on your side.'

He stayed close. Close enough to do anything he wanted. 'How is Robert?'

His fit was both debilitating and nowhere near enough to kill a man like him. I decided to play it down. 'Nothing too untoward. These fits happen.'

He nodded, reached for my hand. 'It's nice to be able to talk to you, I feel so anxious, I …'

'Don't be,' I said, taking his hand, stroking it then letting it go. 'Get some rest. Goodnight.' I touched his arm near the bicep, he nodded again as if there was something else on his mind. He left reluctantly, like he couldn't stand to be alone, and I knew how he felt. He disappeared into his room and the door closed behind him.

I stayed. The air shivering all around me, static in my throat, on my skin. Pins, needles. I clenched my fists and found my palms damp. I wanted this feeling to cling to me and never leave. I felt like waiting here for him until morning came.

I turned to go, but something stopped me. I was thinking about what he really wanted when he came calling on me. He had surely made a noise to wake me. Was it just reassurance, to tell his side of the story, to have the lady of the house listen and understand? I wanted it to be more than that.

As I admitted it to myself in the silence, I heard a noise behind me. I turned. Ben's door opened and, before I knew it, I had stepped inside and closed the door behind me. I placed my hand over his eyes. He stood there, accepting it. Not a move, not a smile, just the warmth of my hand on his face by instinct. Then I slid my palm over his features until it rested on his mouth. All I could see of him was his hollow eyes, wet and gleaming, above the gag that was my hand. Then his hands were on me. His pupils were as dark as black opals. My forehead was against his and I felt the heat of his breath, a little desperate. I glanced around, but he brought my face back his way. The fear of getting caught made my heart thump so hard, it was impossible to stop.

He shook with adrenaline as my mouth met his and he explored every angle of me.

A glimpse of his arm, of his lips, his tongue.

He turned me, my chest and cheek touching the smooth cool wall, hands on my hips.

I turned around, pushed him back hard.

He lifted me up, gained control again.

The sound of my nightclothes against the wall.

I held him by the throat as he pushed inside.

He struggled to control his breath, I stared at him, far calmer.

I squeezed his neck.

My breath fluttered as I looked to the door, the shush getting faster, until everything was white light.

It took all my willpower not to call out as I quaked and he put me down. I blew the hair from my face, unsteady on my feet.

'I've been terribly lonely,' I whispered, 'and scared.'

He held me for a moment in silence and then I pushed away. Replacing the strap of my nightdress, I slipped past him and through the door, leaving him there wanting more.

Upstairs, I fell back onto my bed, assured that the whole episode had the architecture of a dream, but with the unequivocal knowledge that it had not been. Perhaps it was foolish, but I felt safer after that.

I heard his door open sometime later, once my breath had returned to absolute rest.

*

2.45 a.m.

Amelia

Once everyone was asleep, I crept, quiet as I could, past JR's door.

Having been left in the dark, his mood seemed fine while we all wilted in secret. This was the meaning of adulthood. To handle every new gut punch in silence, keeping the sheen alive for the ones who don't know any better.

Then I stood looking at the closed mouth of Ben's door and considered tapping on it.

I heard heavy footsteps above. They seemed to reach the stairs and I didn't want to be caught in the hallway. Didn't want to run into the wrong person on my own. I gripped my mace spray in the blackness of the corridor. It was something I always carried for self-preservation, only now I felt I might actually need to use it.

I'd heard Ben's door closing not long ago, so at least I wouldn't be waking him, I thought. I saw a form descending the stairs, so I pushed Ben's door open and found him there, legs dragged up to his chest, in bed.

I tried to quiet my prosthesis as I got close enough to him so I could whisper unheard from the hallway. 'Are you OK?' I said.

'I'm fine,' he said, 'I just wasn't expecting guests.'

'I heard you get up. What were you doing out of bed?'

He exhaled. 'I assume I'm still allowed to go to the bathroom.'

I held a finger to my mouth, he went quiet, and we listened to footsteps outside. They soon moved away.

'I think it's just Kostas,' I whispered, 'checking on things.'

'And that makes you feel better?' he said.

I wanted to believe it did, that he was someone we could trust, but I couldn't be sure. I sat on the bed as it felt safer to be close.

'Sofia,' I said, and saw his eyes widen. 'Has she ever talked about Kostas?'

'To me? Not really.' And then he stared at me like he wanted to give me something for the trouble of asking. 'You know those photos of her around the London house? She mentioned that he took them. He's a good photographer.'

'Ha,' I said. 'He told me they were by an incredible hotshot photographer. Strange. And a little full of himself, don't you think? And have you noticed the way he looks at her?'

He gave an empty shrug. I didn't like his reticence. We seemed to have subtly drifted apart and I wanted to feel closer to him again. I felt the urge to reach out and touch his skin, but, at the same time, I too felt non-committal. I was just a little nervous being alone with him. After tonight he looked the guiltiest of us all.

But he was good at knowing how people felt around him. He saw my stillness and knew I needed more.

'Look, I'm sorry if I seem ...' he said. 'It's, see, my mum's very ill, I should tell you that. She'd been cancer-free for ten years. Then it came back. She said she wanted to go through it alone. She's always said that she didn't want me to see her go through it all again, and I agreed, but I never meant it, never. It was an understanding between us that I said I'd go when of course I'd stay. But now I'm here. She's objectively the best person I've ever known. And if she … well … where do I go if the worst happens? What does Christmas look like? Maybe that's why I wanted to be near a family, if only for a while, a full house. It's kind of pathetic …'

'I'm so sorry,' I said, hugging him. 'I'm not close to my family.' I pulled back from our embrace, my hand on his thigh, below the covers. 'Maybe that's why I'm here too.'

I felt I had to bring up an inconsistency in what he'd just said about his mother: 'But you said at the bar your mum was desperate for you not to go.'

He looked at me and took a breath. 'She was desperate for me not to go anywhere with the Rathwells. When she found out it was them … well, she used to mix in certain circles in London and …'

I held my breath. 'And what?' My whisper shimmered like a cymbal, lightly stroked. This was the story I was desperate to hear.

'I can't,' he said. 'I don't want to stir things up, make more trouble.'

I shook my head. 'We couldn't be in any more trouble,' I whispered as my forearm pressed into his leg.

'I'm not sure it's the same for both of us,' he muttered, biting his lip. 'Georgios called this evening, wanted to talk about me and Bobby on the beach. He wanted to know if we took any drugs. Said traces of opioids were found in Bobby's bloodstream. Wondered if I knew anything about that.'

'Did you?'

'Of course not, you were there virtually the whole time,' he said. *But not the whole time*, I thought. 'But Bobby did tell us about his mental health,' Ben continued. 'Don't they prescribe OxyContin for what he had? Maybe suicide is more likely than we think.'

'You ever tried Oxy? Fentanyl? I have,' I said, and although I faltered, I found the courage to keep talking, because I wanted to confide in him. 'Taking too many was the closest I came to a cry for help. I remember seeing my mum after I'd had my stomach pumped, and when she asked me why I did it, I said there was no reason at all. Then it was back home to listen through the wall to my father telling her what she could and couldn't do.'

'God,' he said, with a look I read as pitying, and I instantly wished I hadn't tried to force sharing back into our relationship.

Shaking it off, I continued. 'Anyway, it's not an upper, it tends to chill you out. Is that what you thought his behaviour was like at dinner? Chilled out? And if he'd been taking Oxy for depression, he'd know his limits.'

'But take a lot and it does the opposite. Maybe he double-dosed because he was nervous?' Ben said. 'I certainly was at dinner, and there was less at stake for me.'

'Or someone made sure those drugs were in his bloodstream when he died?' I said.

'So,' Ben said, 'you think he was spiked?'

'I think we have to be proactive,' I said. 'Go to the Aegean Rooms where Bobby was staying, see if he left anything behind that can help us figure this out.'

He winced. The attention of the police, the way the Rathwell grasp had tightened around him, it all made him reticent to disobey, I could see that. My hand brushed the bare skin of his shoulder to soothe him. He let me. He laid his hand on mine.

'If you want to be proactive,' he said, 'tell Georgios you're being made to keep things quiet, and you want protection. It wouldn't be wise for me at this point, but you could.'

I took a long look at him, wondering how to explain that a man in uniform hardly represents safety for me.

'I remember hoping my posh voice would stop me from being followed around shops. My white friends always looked offended when it happened, but I just came to accept it. Someone like me, throwing myself to the mercy of a foreign police officer and hoping he'll believe me over the Rathwells and his friend who works for them ...'

A creak whined along the landing but it could've been the old house reordering its limbs.

'If you want to play things subtler, talk to Sofia,' I said. 'Prove she's not guilty.'

'Last time you were telling me it was Robert, now Sofia. It can't be her ...' he said, 'she wasn't around when Isa died, was she?'

We'd finally arrived where we needed to be.

'I'm not so sure,' I said. 'I was curious how long they'd been together when I first started working at the house and I didn't want to ask. But you can find all sorts of photos on an image search. There were shots of Sofia and Robert dining out together before Isa died. Now, do you really think Sofia was keen on sharing her cut of the will with someone else's kid?'

Ben exhaled, the suggestion seemed to weigh heavy on him. 'Do you think she would kill for all this?' he said.

'Depends how much she wanted it. She likes you. Talk to her. See what you can find out.'

Ben frowned at the floor for a moment. Even though he had sensed one of us could be thrown under the bus, he seemed to have decided making nice with his enemies was his only way out. But he was wrong, and I had to make him realise it.

'There's no such thing as a bystander, you know that, right?' I said. 'You have to pick a side.'

We heard a door close and I knew I had stayed there too long. I had to take my chance to get back to bed without being seen.

'We're lying about a murder, so we're implicated,' I said, my voice sharp and hushed. 'We're being paid, so we're implicated. As things stand, you're playing it exactly like they want you to. All that evidence they have against you. What if someone decides to use it? And if there's another body? What if it's one of us?'

I saw all these thoughts working on him. His hands knit behind his head as he crumbled, starting to nod.

'You're right,' he said at last. 'I've been scared and stupid. I'll do it.'

A rush went through me. I promised myself I'd never be an enabler, least of all to something as serious as this. I had desperately needed to know he felt the same.

I made my way towards the door. 'You speak to Sofia, I'll try Isabelle.'

'And we'll get to the Aegean Rooms tomorrow,' he said, 'I'll find a way.'

'Good,' I said, turning and catching his dark eyes in mine once more. 'Because it's not safe to stay in the dark.'

Which is exactly where I left him.

20

The fascination

Isabelle

When morning came, I knocked on Ben's door. Robert had requested the opportunity to speak with him again. Whether this meant Ben had made a good impression, or Robert had noticed something untoward, I didn't know.

Ben almost looked like he wanted to turn down the offer when I told him, but twenty minutes later he was washed and dressed, hair still wet, and I was knocking on Robert's door. Before entering, I considered that Ben mightn't ever have seen anyone in such a state, so I instructed him like he was a prole about to meet the queen:

'He's far from beaten. Give him space. Try not to stare.' Then I simply opened the door and let Ben see what was left of Robert.

We walked slowly along the marble floor of the grand bedroom, seeing Robert and Sofia sitting in a clinch before the four-poster bed as we approached. It halted us both. They were kissing like newly-weds. Sofia had seemed to want to keep her distance from him lately. I hadn't expected to find them like that. Nor had Ben, who blushed as Sofia whispered in Robert's ear before making her excuses, giving Ben a professional smile, and me a long, prideful look.

I heard her pull the door behind her, not quite closed, the imprecision maddening to me. Robert was still, his eyes rolled back, his sallow skin had seen better days even recently. His mouth was slack, his lips falling to one side and hanging there.

I wouldn't call it a stroke, not to anyone in the house. But that's the dreaded word the doctor had used when we called so he could be examined over the phone. They went through a series of tests that I helped carry out: could he touch his nose? Just about. Could he swallow? With some difficulty. Was he aware of where he was? In truth things had been falling away for some time. A mini-stroke, was what the doctor called it and said he could come straight over if I would charter a boat or a helicopter and pay his usual fee. But Robert said doctors only made him feel ill and that, given I had nursed him after a full-blown stroke, I should be able to deal with the effects of this one.

Yes? came Robert's voice, using his word board. His real voice was so tired, his hands curled. He peered up at Ben. He generally used one of three buttons on it, *Yes*, *No* or *Fuck you*. But just a lift of the inflection button was all he needed to turn the *Yes* at his disposal into a curt *Hello*.

Ben gave an uneasy exhale. I suddenly had the feeling I was intruding. It's not a sense I often get, Robert and I have shared as much as it is possible to share. We have dressed as if one being, washed as one. When Sofia is not there, I'm the first face he sees when he wakes. I have been closer than a wife, as close as a mirror. It pained me to see him like this.

'Mr Rathwell, sir,' Ben forced out, like he was addressing some dictator. 'How … how are you this morning?'

Ben took a few steps closer. Robert's wet eyes rolled upwards, working hard to take him in. I had told him to give him room. But I remained silent.

Robert's hand quivered, summoning all the energy he had, lifting it to a point where Ben thought he was about to receive a handshake. Robert appeared to be as stimulated by the boy as he was yesterday. He beckoned Ben closer still, with a shivering finger.

The whisper came, not more than a shush for a second, which brought me forward.

'Robert, save your strength,' I said.

The hand came up swifter than I thought it could. His lips made a puckering motion, trying three, four times, to find the right shape for speech.

'Like I've known you … always,' Robert gasped. And something about it moved me.

Then the other hand came up and he reached for Ben's face, who acquiesced and brought it nearer. For some reason I recalled John the Baptist's head on a platter, as ordered by King Herod. The popular story was that Herod was encouraged to behead John by his mistress and her daughter, but others believe he feared John's charisma.

'They said. . .' I could almost hear his lungs working like bellows. 'They said, you were a handsome boy. But … I don't quite see it.'

He grinned. After a second, Ben's did the same. I watched them challenge each other with a similar look.

'I'd heard you were training for the Olympics,' Ben said, 'but I don't like your chances.'

I turned my head away, not knowing what would come next, but all that arrived was Robert's staccato laugh. Ben sniggered too when he was sure the joke had landed.

'You're doing the swimming, aren't you?'

More air, more laughter. *Yes*, said the electric voice.

'Cigarette?' Ben said. I blinked, took a step forward then paused. I couldn't believe Ben would smoke around Robert, let alone ask a man in this state to join him. I started thinking of how best to remove him.

But Robert's eyes lit up, then rolled towards me. I could try and deny him the pleasure, but he'd only overrule me. Soon, Ben had lit one and then put it in Robert's quivering mouth. And Robert's hand managed to keep it there as Ben lit one for himself and they took a drag at the same time, smoke streaming from them both.

I felt a pain shoot along my spine, I glanced back and saw Sofia lingering in the hall.

'Bobby told me something interesting,' Ben said. Robert and I leant closer. 'When we were alone together. He said that when an aluminium mine of yours collapsed in Africa, he went out there to help, give aid. You hadn't seen him for many years, he told me. That's the sort of thing he was up to. Did you know that?'

I wanted to interrupt but couldn't locate the words. After a long pause, Robert answered: *No*.

'I thought it'd be weird if you never found out,' Ben said. 'Thought it might make you proud.'

Bold words. I knew Bobby was a better boy than some

thought, but I didn't know this. Yet, I could believe it. I could tell Robert believed it too.

Fuck you, the voice said, breaking my concentration.

For all Ben's confidence, I noticed the hand he held the cigarette with quivering at his side, a shudder of smoke rising from the burning tip towards the chandelier. I'd heard Robert say this to a stranger before but not often, and it always signalled the same thing. That was when I knew for sure: Robert liked him.

21

On the other side

Amelia

Ben and I closed the front door gently as we headed towards the Porsche. We didn't have long, but Kostas was busy, Sofia having pulled him into the den for a chat. We were done asking permission. We took our chance.

Georgios had apparently assured Isabelle there would be another visit to the house before any verdict was returned. It was difficult to know whether to hope for an arrest, for local police to drag a culprit out of the house. Or to fear Georgios' presence in case it was Ben or me who was taken away, as useful culprits for the authorities. We were expected to stay put and wait. That's what the family wanted but, once the bloody trainers had arrived, Ben realised we needed to act.

'How did you even get the keys?' I whispered to Ben as JR dragged his feet behind us.

'Asked Sofia,' he said with an innocent look. 'Told her I was going to take JR to the beach, on the back of my moped. But said I didn't mind taking the Porsche, if she felt that was safer.' Ben had clearly made headway with Sofia.

'And I'm guessing,' I said, 'another meeting with Robert made you even more curious.'

He nodded. 'We can't let someone kill Bobby and get away with it. We knew what he was really like. He didn't deserve this.'

We went quiet as JR caught up with us and insisted on sitting in the front, his finger and thumb tapping each other, something playing on his lively mind.

I spied a long pink plaster on the back of JR's hand I didn't remember seeing first thing that morning. I opened my mouth to ask about it, then remembered little boys are never out of the wars.

We parked at the black sand beach located not far from the dock, then made a detour up a dirt road, around a copse of trees, towards the Aegean Rooms over the brow of the hill. The island wasn't big, but we still wouldn't have found it if Bobby hadn't told us where it was. No one in the house was keen to enlighten us on anything.

I distracted JR with conversation, telling him Ben had been asked to pick something up, while Ben ran ahead, knowing we might not have long. We needed to know if Bobby had left any clues behind.

As we approached, I could see Ben struggling with the first of the four doors. It wouldn't open. JR was telling me the world was running out of sand, but his eyes wandered over to Ben. I checked my watch. We had left the house fifteen minutes ago. Ben's adrenaline was up, and I could see he was considering trying to force the door with a kick. The second door didn't open either and neither did the third. Was there any need to lock your doors on a private island, I wondered. Maybe, if there was something there you were keeping hidden.

Then JR let go of my hand and I couldn't catch him, my carbon-fibre foot not faring well against the uneven dust and pebbles on the ground. And though Ben called out too, it was JR who made it to the last door first and, whether you consider it luck or misfortune, that door did open. Ben, JR and I stared in at the contents.

I didn't expect what we found. A pristine hotel room, bespoke raw wood fittings, an outdoor shower in the back, a free-standing bathtub flanked by a wood burner and a bottle of champagne in a bucket. The king-sized bed was as perfect as a birthday cake, it had not been slept in recently.

Ben and I couldn't help ourselves, we opened drawers that turned out to be full of cookies and herbal teas. Cupboards that hid plasma screens. I could see nothing Bobby had left behind, but I did catch sight of Ben palming something into his pocket that I would ask him about later.

JR stood at the door wearing an accusing look. Had he seen it too?

'Can you blame us, buddy?' Ben said. 'Just wanted to see what these rooms looked like. Can you keep this a secret?'

He didn't look so sure, making some quiet judgement. At that moment, we heard a sound approaching. It was the roar of a car, carried on the wind; it couldn't be far away. And we couldn't be caught here.

We scrambled down through the trees, JR sliding next to us and shouting when he caught his plastered hand on a ridged stone on the ground.

'You OK?' I said, grabbing his hand, which he quickly pulled away.

'It's nothing,' he said.

'Come on, mate,' Ben said.

We could hear the engine nearer, almost on top of us it seemed, so much more audible than the electric car. Ben had asked for the Porsche on purpose. We thought the other engine might give us an early warning, given how quiet the island was.

'Why are we running anyway?' JR said as we emerged from the trees. We were behind the Porsche, its wheels on black basalt sand, which kept us out of sight but also obscured our view of the road.

'It's a game,' I said. 'Now, let's see how quickly you can get in your swim shorts.'

Our view of the road became clear as we ventured further down the beach towards the gleaming water, and I was relieved to find that Kostas wasn't anywhere to be seen. We sat on the sand, catching our breath, grabbing our books and sun cream. The sound of a car grew nearer, Kostas' vehicle soon arriving around the bend. He spotted us and pulled up on the road, giving us a terse wave before getting out of the vehicle and approaching.

I rose, wandering towards him with my hands out, part hello, part surrender, getting to him before he got to us.

'I'm sorry,' I said as we walked together along the beach, away from the others.

'For what?' he fired back, keeping his voice low, so JR, who was arm-wrestling Ben, couldn't hear.

'I suppose we should have told you before we left?'

'Darling,' he said, an odd phrase in his mouth, one borrowed from Robert, 'it's a small island, you're never far away. And, of course, we don't mind. Sofia thought it best to give you some freedom.'

There was a tone in his voice that made it clear they'd wanted us out of the house anyway.

'But remember,' Kostas said, looking back at the trees. 'It's very important to leave any suspicions you have to me. You, as the English say, should mind your own business. Let me handle this, for the three of us. I hope I don't speak out of turn?'

Somehow, he remained a model of politeness. But I wondered whether he'd seen our footmarks in the sand leading from woods to beach. It was possible, the beach was smooth other than our presence.

I nodded carefully and assured him we would do as he said. Then I returned to JR and Ben, feeling Kostas' eyes on me as I went. Ben raised a hand and Kostas returned the gesture.

Normality was key. I had prepared a lesson for JR, intended to support a cruise to the volcanic islands, which the whole group were to set sail on today, had all things been well. I sat JR down and began the lesson, aware all the time of Kostas leaning against his car, keeping watch. He was used to being present but distant, as any good security man is, yet ordinarily he would fade into the background. With just the three of us on the beach his presence was conspicuous.

'The sand we're sitting on is part of the fallout from a volcano. The Thera eruption that occurred on nearby Anafi over three thousand six hundred years ago,' I said, 'was one of the biggest recorded in history. It caused a tsunami that destroyed the entire Minoan civilisation on Crete. Do you know what a tsunami is?'

'Course. I've watched one on YouTube,' JR said.

I nodded, wiped sweat from my forehead, paused to apply sun cream and then continued. 'Some people have suggested that this is what created the myth of the lost city of Atlantis.'

'What's Atlantis again?' he said with a yawn.

'It's a story by Plato. *GII*,' I said to him.

'What's GII?' Ben said.

'Google If Interested,' I said.

'I remember,' JR said, 'you said thousands were burnt alive, their bodies encased in molten ash.'

With previous kids I'd tutored it was about getting them to catch up, with JR his parents just wondered how far ahead he could get. I glanced at Ben as he unfurled a piece of paper from his pocket and read, behind J's back, staying out of Kostas' eyeline.

'So,' I said, 'what's the difference between lava and magma?'

'Lava flows,' he said, 'above ground.'

'Correct,' I said, tapping him on the nose. 'Lava above ground, magma below. Magma, the dark pressure below, is the molten rock that can't wait to force its way to the surface where it can do the real damage. But until then it's all just potential.'

'Rumbling underneath,' he said.

Ben and I looked at each other, judging the distance from Kostas to us. I took my chance: 'Does the name Bobby mean anything to you, J?'

'Well, yeah,' JR said. 'Duh.'

Ben looked around casually. 'What do you mean, mate?'

'It's my name,' he said.

It was news to me. I had only ever heard him called JR in all my time at the house.

'But you're JR, aren't you?' I said.

'Robert was my christened name, like dad's.' I thought about what sort of person names their son after themselves, twice. 'Dad called me Robbie for a while, but mummy doesn't like it, so …'

'Does it mean anything else though?' I said. 'Anything at all?'

This time even J turned back to see how close Kostas was before he spoke: 'My half-brother. I think that's what you mean. Isn't it?'

I nodded. 'You've never mentioned him?'

'That's because,' J said, looking at the horizon, 'I've never met him. He could be anywhere. Daddy says he's a bad influence. That he wanted him to take over from him one day, but he was lazy, tricksy and untrustworthy. He didn't want me to catch any of that.'

I could tell Ben wanted to shut this conversation down, but I didn't.

'And your mum,' I said, 'has she ever mentioned him?'

'Nah,' he said. 'He's just a name on dad's Wikipedia. Dad says Bobby didn't want to get to know me. But that was for the best. They said. Cos he was a bad boy.'

And after that, Ben decided to take him away and out towards the water, turning back and palming me the note before he went, my hand tense as I took it. I watched them kick up black sand on their way to the sea. Then, stealing a glance at Kostas, I pulled my little bible from my bag like it was a holiday book, stretched out on my side and placed the note within it.

The handwriting was wild, but the words were firm, considered:

*

I told you to get out. I knew you wouldn't. If you find this, something went wrong. Think about that point when strangers become friends.

22

The view from here

Sofia

Isabelle and I sat on Robert's broad stone balcony, holding one of his hands each. It was at moments like this, on his lesser days, when fatigued and distant, that the charming man receded into the background. This fit had seemed to set him back further than I'd ever thought. From this distance the waves on the great expanse of sea moved in slow motion, which unnerved me. The horizon appeared level with our eyeline, or even higher, like the view could drown us.

'You have to be more careful,' I said as gently as I could manage, given the feelings broiling inside me. I no longer saw Robert's illness as an excuse for his behaviour, and Kostas had woken me this morning with news about the woman sitting next to him that had lit a fire inside me too.

'I'm sorry, I don't know ... why I did it,' Robert murmured. His attention came and went like a blinking light. 'The boy doesn't listen, I just wanted him to hear me. We don't have long to save him.'

Earlier, I had caught Robert squeezing JR's hand as he

spoke and, when J pulled away, he had scratched him and drawn blood.

'You didn't mean it,' Isabelle said.

'He didn't say that,' I said. I had been scared about chastising Robert for some time, but I could no longer keep quiet.

'I did say sorry, I thought I did. I was, I am. Tell him,' Robert urged, voice cracking.

'Your energy is low,' Isabelle said, 'use your screen.'

But I saw his fingers had clawed a little. Speaking was clearly easier for him. 'I'm scared,' he whispered.

Isabelle adjusted her position, pushing her shoulders back as she often did. It was like she wanted to find a route out of her own skin.

'Now, Robert,' Isabelle said. 'No time for fear—'

'Bobby was a good boy, at first,' Robert said. 'Sat on my lap.'

'Yes,' she said. 'A beautiful boy. But he had terrible trouble and that wasn't your fault. God knows you tried—'

'I murmured poems and songs to your perfect … soft … belly,' he said, squeezing my hand.

'Robert,' I said, 'that was with JR. You're confused.'

His mind was lost again.

'I massaged your legs … when you had … cramps.' His will to talk continued though it was a struggle, he looked up to find the words in the air. 'I took you on the jet to Marrakesh, Tuscany, Côte D'Azur.' I remembered it well. 'I bought you a black opal on a silver chain.'

He didn't. His memory was betraying him again.

'JR could read so early, I was never like that,' Robert went on. 'Astounded me. He used to point at words he didn't know

179

in books. He's … not like other boys. He's still finding his way …'

'Yes,' I said.

Robert was so determined to have another child that he had me write one into our prenup. These things aren't so unusual with royalty, so I had heard of such under-the-table arrangements. Powerful dynasties depend on natural heirs, but he needn't have bothered putting it in writing. I needed Robert, but I wanted him too, wanted a child that looked just like me and him. But wealthy people prefer contractual arrangements. They want what's coming to them and don't like to leave it up to chance.

'Bobby,' Robert croaked, raising a finger. 'Was a disappointment, I know you don't like to hear me say it. But he was photographed … falling out of clubs with girls … and boys. Yes, a bohemian. Which was fine, but that's for public school not for public life—'

'Robert—' Isabelle said.

'We have a reputation. It's your name … that will live on. I couldn't trust him to do even the fundamentals after I was gone. You can't let any son of yours … ruin you.'

I looked to Isabelle. 'Robert, what are you saying?'

'He's rambling,' she said.

'Robert?' I said. 'What do you mean, you couldn't let any son ruin your name?'

'What?' he said. 'No. That's what they said. And they're right. But I'm scared. They talk and talk and talk.'

Isabelle and I shared another look.

'Who talks and talks? People?' Isabelle said. 'The papers? Or someone in particular?'

But I stayed quiet on the matter and Robert was lost for words again, so she was forced to plough on. 'We're still looking at Amelia. Because of her family connection. We'd always wondered whether that would be a problem.'

Robert's eyes were alight. 'She seems ...'

And we watched him take a long pause. His breathing became heavier. We would be waiting a good deal longer for an answer. Robert was far, far away. His breath grew heavy. He was asleep.

Isabelle adjusted herself. 'He's grieving,' she said, throwing her hands up. 'I don't want us, any of us, to take advantage of this situation.'

'Nice sentiment,' I said, I could hold back no longer given what Kostas had told me. 'Because I was interested to hear about Robert helping you with your father's debts. Very interested. And surprised, particularly because your father died a number of years ago. Isn't that right?'

A horizontal smile came across her face. She shook her head, smoothed her hands across her skirt. 'I can't talk about this, I'm sorry. It's not fair.'

'To who?' I said. 'You? I'm sorry, it's starting to look very much like you've extorted money from my husband, so at least tell me why you did it with such a half-arsed lie?'

'I didn't tell the lie to Robert,' she said, shifting uncomfortably again, 'just to Kostas.'

'And you were willing to sell bullshit to a man like that. I am impressed—'

'OK, look. I told him whatever would make him go away. The money isn't something I'm at liberty to talk about—'

'So, you lied, but you can't say why. This is one of the

weaker excuses for defrauding a rich man I've ever heard. I'm sure the police would be interested to hear about this. You see, they might wonder how desperately you needed the money, if someone was close to finding out you'd been—'

'Please,' she said. 'It was one payment, and it's—'

'It's for her,' Robert whispered, back in the room, his ice-cold eyes on me. 'She's in pain. Darling, you see how she sits. Collapsed disc in her back. Didn't have the money to go private, so I ... forced her hand, put money in her account. Couldn't stand to see her in such ... such—'

'Thank you,' Isabelle said. I expected a look of triumph after the omission but all that came from her was shame. She clearly didn't want to be thought of as physically weak and in need. 'Thank you, Robert. Sorry, the whole thing is quite embarrassing.'

'No, it's not.' I let out a breath. 'I apologise ...' I said.

We shared a gaze and her look said she didn't forgive me.

'You have to have suspicions,' Robert said, 'whoever has money has fear. I've suspected you all, not ashamed of it—'

'Robert,' I said.

'I've killed two sons,' he said.

His words seemed to stop the clock. A sick feeling bloomed in the pit of my stomach. Isabelle moved first, standing to close the door to the balcony. She must've felt like this was a confession we had to close the world to.

'Robert, what do you mean?' I said, my hand on his arm.

'What?' Robert said. 'What did I ... ?' His mind had moved on, you could see it in his eyes. But the words would not be forgotten.

'You said you killed two sons?' I said. 'One ... might be Bobby.'

He looked at me, saying nothing either way, just taking it in.

'No, no,' Isabelle said, standing over me as she winced in pain. 'I see what you're doing, I won't let it happen. You've made him say something and—'

'I didn't make him do anything,' I said, quite calm. 'Robert, who is the other?'

He shrugged. Another name came into my head at that moment. It really was striking how much he looked like Adam Sands. But I told myself not even to think it in Robert's presence.

'It was just a scratch, Robert,' Isabelle said, leaning over him. 'JR is fine, he's not hurt. He put a plaster on it, and it was good as new.'

'But Bobby won't. Let him speak,' I said. She had been trying to protect him for too long. I had too. But though he was there in front of us, and his image made me ache for another time, it was just that, an image. It was time to accept there was no part of him that was the Robert I knew.

'The boy needed toughening up,' Robert said, in quite another voice. One I'd barely heard. 'My father was an … authoritarian. I thanked him for it.'

I looked at him there, a hardened shell. If it wasn't for the lift in his room he couldn't even get downstairs.

'You said you killed two sons,' I repeated, 'what did you mean?'

'I'm afraid …' he whispered, but his eyes said he wasn't sure what to say next. He broke into an apologetic smile, '… I really have no idea.'

23

The first Mrs Rathwell

Amelia

At the beach, Ben returned to where I lay and Kostas watched from the car. Ben called to JR, reminding him to stay in the shallows as he showed us his crawl.

'So, what did Bobby mean?' I said, still chilled in the hot sun at seeing Bobby's writing. '*Think about that point when strangers become friends?*'

Ben shook his head, lost in thought. I wondered whether he had charmed Rathwell as much as he had me. My eyes landed on the handsome curve of his mouth. I was so taken with his face from the moment I saw it. That careful, studied manner.

'Is it about us?' Ben said. 'Or someone else? Someone close to Rathwell who forced their way from stranger to friend?'

'I'm not sure Rathwell is who you should be worried for.'

'Maybe. But I had a feeling he wanted to tell me something when no one else was around.'

I nodded. 'How did he seem to you?'

'Stable. Sofia says he's beaten worse,' Ben said, with odd conviction, and I wondered why he had been charmed by the older man. 'He's a fighter.'

The phrase always seemed so naïve. As if other people who aren't so tough can disable their own immune system through cowardice. I thought of my own mother and all of those tubes going into her. And my dad nowhere to be seen. I cursed myself for even thinking of him here. I had kept who my father was from the Rathwells for long enough. There were times I felt sure they knew, but they never let on.

'I think Rathwell has us right where he wants us. If you ask me, that's what Bobby was trying to warn us about,' I said.

He gave me a look. Our relationship had moved across the line of flirtation, as if we were destined either to marry or to murder each other.

'Not sure Robert even knows what's in front of him, but his body's hanging in there,' Ben said. 'My mother's the other way, she's totally aware of how her body's failing her.'

'Gosh,' I said.

'God, you really are posh,' he said, like it was an insult.

'And you're not,' I laughed. 'I'm glad you've stopped putting it on.'

'I wasn't *putting anything on*,' he said, suddenly defensive. 'We were encouraged to speak properly at drama school. We were told to get a pocket mirror so we could do tongue-tip exercises. You have to adapt when you move around a lot, so I was used to it. But still, I'm neither northern enough nor posh enough. I do some regional accent I'm told I'm not as *real* as the others with it. But, as you can tell, I haven't perfected *well-spoken* either to the natives. *Neither upstairs nor downstairs*, one casting assistant said.'

He didn't see any irony in explaining being stuck between two worlds to a young mixed-race woman. But I didn't mention it.

'I think you're perfect as you are,' I said, with a smile. It was so strange, a holiday feeling had returned for a second, like nothing had happened. 'I mean, there are worse people to summer with.'

'I'm trapped on an island with someone who uses summer as a verb. Mum will never believe it.'

'This isn't a holiday. It never was,' I said, leaning over and gripping his hand. 'You do see that. Don't you? Someone got us here so they could kill Bobby. And it's going exactly to plan. But he suspected it, so we need to figure out where he's leading us next.'

'Listen,' he said, breathing deep. 'When you mentioned the name Isa Marnell it wasn't the first time I'd heard it. This is what my mum told me.' He had spoken to Sofia and now here was his mother's story at last. He was keeping all sorts of promises. 'She grew up in London and so did I till I was, like, eleven. She always had a story about this or that celebrity or rich bloke. You can act like one of them, but you'll never be one of them, mum said. Which was rich coming from her, because she's always been enamoured with the wealthy. I, however, have always been naturally mistrustful of ponces.'

I hoped I wasn't implicated in that.

'Well, I wanted to tell you about Isa. This may all be nonsense anyway, fake news or whatever, but mum heard there were doubts over whether Isa's death was suicide. The papers would've loved to print it, the other red tops, just to sink

Rathwell, but he had his super-injunction so they weren't allowed anywhere near it.' Despite his reluctance, once he got into the story, he told it vividly. 'Mum had a friend in fashion who was dating a criminal barrister. It wasn't his case, but this guy knew all about it. This Isa Marnell, she was a classic beauty—'

'Right,' I said. I remember someone saying that when my mother died. As if death is much worse when the woman is particularly attractive.

'The rumour was that the coroner's report said there were bruises on her arms like someone had held her down, but Rathwell employed an independent coroner who said something quite different, and there were no cameras, Isa didn't like them.'

Sofia doesn't either, we had been told. And Bobby had marks on his wrists too. We took it all in.

'What we know for sure,' he continued, 'was that divorce proceedings had started and Isa wanted half of everything. Rathwell would have had to sell assets, liquidate companies ...'

'I didn't know any of this,' I said.

'It's not the sort of thing you could google,' he said. I could tell he knew this because he'd tried. 'I'm telling you because I trust you.'

It felt a lot like he'd said I love you.

'I trust you too,' I said.

There was a long silence.

'How long ago was this?' I said.

'Oh ... twelve years?'

'Could Rathwell have done it at that age?' I said.

'It wasn't necessarily Rathwell,' he said. 'Was Isabelle around then?'

'Yes, and though you don't want to hear it, Sofia was too.'

'Yes,' Ben said, 'but why would she—'

He broke off mid-sentence and stared out to sea. I was so carried away by all this, I didn't see the problem at first.

'What can you see?' I said.

'Nothing,' he said, so disturbed.

'Then what's the problem?' I said.

But soon he was running, and then I knew. His feet slapped the water. JR was nowhere to be found.

I was slow to follow, it took time to fix my foot in place. We'd been negligent, and now JR had been taken away somewhere. I was flushed and my adrenaline was up. Then we heard a voice that hardly made things better.

'Over here,' Kostas said, running down towards the rocks, where a small body lay amongst them, occasionally being beaten by the tide.

We were shocked, shamed, and JR appeared to be out cold. In seconds, we were behind Kostas as he waded in to get him out. I called J's name again and again. No answer, so we called again, until my voice was raw and hot tears were in my eyes. Everything slowed, I'd come here to protect little JR and now this had happened on my watch. I raised my eyes to the sky.

And then came the laughter.

Shrieks of it, sending a shiver down my spine.

'Fooled you,' JR said, as he stood brushing himself down amongst the rocks. It was quite shallow and the tide was gentle once you got close.

Kostas put his hands on his hips and turned to us, all the blame our way. And I couldn't contain myself.

'You wicked, wicked boy,' I said. All plans of tact with him had fallen away. I was shouting.

And that just made him laugh even more. I turned away, took deep breaths, tried to stay calm. And through it all, my thoughts went to that note, and Isa Marnell.

24

Disclosures

Sofia

That night I rose from bed, rifled through my jacket then lit a cigarette. Ben had given me one from a packet of Rex. I enjoyed the drag so much Ben said I could keep the rest. I smoked out of the window and wondered whether to ask Ben about his thoughts on Amelia, but that seemed too intimate. We barely knew each other.

His body stirred in my bed.

Cigarette in mouth, I pushed smoke towards the soundless dark.

'Come back from the window,' Ben said, sitting up, draped in a thin bedsheet. It was my room, I was entitled to smoke there, but I suppose I looked significantly post-coitus to cause him some kind of anxiety. It was strange because he seemed so different with each of us. Isabelle saw him as some tough customer. Amelia protected him like he was a wounded soul. He reminded me of how as a child I used to think of the moon and the sea. I once thought moonlight shone on one particular patch of water for everyone, until I realised it was all about the angle between moon, sea and your perspective. Where the light rests on the water for you depends on where you're standing.

I wondered which one of us was using the other. I knew I had brought the situation about. It had started the day of the interview in some ways, but I didn't think of him as powerless. It was because of his strength that I got such a thrill scaring him by standing so close to the window.

He solved the problem by gesturing that he wanted a drag and I returned to place it in his hand. We had been discreet this time, hands over lips, faces pressed into pillows, slow moves. There was a lock on my door just in case Kostas decided to burst in and search the rooms.

Ben passed me back the cigarette, looking up at me, thinking.

'Bobby wasn't an ordinary guy, was he? Did you like him?'

'I hardly knew him,' I said. I didn't like the suggestion. 'I liked to think we were friends.'

He was staring at my antique gold chain, which made me touch it. One of Robert's gifts. I liked to feel it twisting over and over indefinitely.

'Did Kostas tell you about what happened with JR at the beach today?'

'He did.'

Bringing JR's name in here felt incestuous in a way Ben instantly wasn't comfortable with, but it presented no such problems for me. A woman can't simply be known as a mother.

Ben was silent. 'Does JR worry you, sometimes?' he said. Eventually, he added, 'I mean, unnerve you?'

It had been said before, but I didn't expect it from him. 'What a strange thing to say.'

'I don't mean ...' he tried to backtrack. 'It's just, like, his mind works differently,' he said, before going quiet again.

I wondered how much to tell him about little JR. I had watched over his shoulder as he viewed videos of other people hurting themselves and wondered if this was evidence of the first sign of sociopathy. It may seem extreme because when he let you in, a light shone on you, just like with Robert. But then, another marker of a young sociopath was superficial charm. None of this was my assessment, it was those school reports that had red flags all over them. An inability to say sorry or to judge between right and wrong, they said. Wasn't that boys all over, I said to his headmistress. Her dark look said not. Perhaps he had learnt all this by imitating Robert. Or it was in the genes, from a man I was realising it was dangerous not ever to have fully known.

'No,' I said finally. 'I really don't know what you mean.'

Ben took a breath. 'I've heard him wake in the night, wander around. By the time I go out into the hall he's always back in bed.'

'So, what?' I said, my voice rising. 'What's wrong with waking in the night?'

'I work for you,' he said. 'I just thought you'd want to—'

'You sound like his teachers, all these concerns about mental health. Everyone's diagnosed with something these days. He's just a boy, he's not disturbed—'

'I don't think he is,' Ben said, quietly now. 'I think he's gifted and restless.'

That calmed me, felt better. His quirks were just restlessness. I suppose I must've reacted so strongly because of my own doubts.

'Of course,' he said, 'he doesn't have anything to do with

what happened to Bobby. I'm saying put that out of your mind. Surely this was all planned well in advance.'

I took a drag and breathed out curls of smoke. 'But how would this person, who planned it all, even know Bobby would be on the island?' I said.

He grabbed the cigarette, took a long drag, stubbed it out, looking animated. 'What if they asked him to come? And if they did, no wonder he was upset when you all greeted him like he wasn't invited. He thought he was being let back in the fold. But it wasn't that at all. He was being manoeuvred into position.'

That triggered a memory. 'At dinner,' I said. 'Robert said I'm sure your invitation is in the post. And Bobby looked at him so strangely, said he didn't know what Robert meant. But Bobby would only be confused if he *had* been invited?'

'That would fit,' he said.

I thought on it. 'There are only so many people who could send a letter as if from Robert.'

He rubbed his hand across his face. 'What about Kostas? Amelia once told me he knew whenever anyone even came near the island. He must've known Bobby was coming before anyone else.'

I drew a sharp breath. 'Not Kostas,' I said. 'Bobby would recognise his father's writing style, it's like a fingerprint. Kostas couldn't replicate that, no matter how hard he might try.'

'Then who—'

'I've been thinking about bad fortune. I was so afraid people would look at JR that I had you clean up that blood and accidentally implicated us both. Well, this is exactly what JR said happened to him: he found the cat dead. He loves little creatures, so he dug out a little hole, strange to do it with that beautiful rosewood knife but he was trying to bury the cat so no one would find it. Unfortunately, Isabelle found the head and the blood was on his wrists from handling it. That's what JR told me and, foolishly, I didn't wholly believe him until just today, when I realised something similar had happened to me.'

I placed my hand on his hip. The smoke from the kitsch ashtray rose towards the curved glass light fitting with the image of an angel on it.

'How did Robert seem to you, physically?' I said.

I didn't like the fact Robert and he had met, eye to eye. But I'm not sure whether that was because he and I were cheating on him, or because that meeting felt like Robert and Ben cheating on me. I moved towards the window.

'Sick,' Ben said, with remorse.

'Yes, he's sick,' I said. 'Robert's very sick.'

'What is it, exactly?' he said, staying right where he was like one of those fake tourist ornaments on the windowsill.

'Lungs, kidneys, nerves, brain,' I said. 'Mostly the brain.'

He looked up at me in sympathy. But earlier today on that balcony I had decided not to be sad any more.

'You were charmed by him,' I said. 'Weren't you?'

Ben shrugged as he looked for the right words. 'I can see what you see in him. When you get close enough.'

'Ha,' I laughed. 'We first met at a charity event Al-Fayed was holding. I had come to London to be a ballerina. Can you imagine that?'

I knew he could. His eyes were still on me in my nightdress, analysing what he saw. I moved back towards him as I spoke.

'I swore I wouldn't come home until I had achieved my

dreams, but I tore the tendon in my hip. A couple of years of recovery went by, I finished my training at the Royal Ballet School, and then I got an ankle injury. A couple more years went by and time defeated me. But I couldn't go home. So, I stayed, my means dwindling. In the end I started working for a kind of agency. Classier than most. I would meet wealthy men who had flown in from Dubai, and I would escort them around Mayfair for a few days. They liked my royal connection, it was my selling point, meant I was flown to Moscow to spend time with oligarchs. They wanted to pay for more time with me, but I never stayed with one person long. I did it as little as possible in the end, I hated the expectant looks in their eyes, it wasn't worth the money to pay for the studio flat in Chelsea. Things got very dark for a while, I barely left my one little room. Then Sir Anthony Clement calls about accompanying Robert Rathwell to a function. And he was so different to the others.'

'He was also still married to Isa, wasn't he?'

It seemed to be important to Ben, how desperate I was, and that Isa was still alive at the time.

'They were in the process of separating. And believe it or not, the whole thing had hurt him deeply. He's more sensitive than people know. He wept that night when he spoke of it. After she died, he didn't call for a long time. We didn't see each other again until nearly a year after she passed, and when we did it was clear he was distraught. We both were in a pit of depression of differing causes. He spoke so beautifully about her. Then listened attentively to my troubles. And was gentle above all things, but ...'

Just talking about him then opened the wellspring. I wiped

a tear from my cheek and took a breath. I needed to tell him how things really were now.

'Go on,' Ben said, a hand on my arm.

'After we were married, he supported me studying law, while the papers mocked me, saying glamorous women only wanted to become lawyers because Kim Kardashian did it first. When I passed the bar exam first time, he was so proud,' I said, my voice dying a little. 'But in the last year, he's disappeared and something else has taken his place. He's turned into one of those other men, he says terrible things. Before we left, he whispered in my ear, told me I wouldn't get away with leaving him, that he'd rather I was dead.'

All words left Ben and I pulled away from his weak grip to sit on the bed.

'On other days it would be back to normal, and I would pretend it had been a dream. Because it's right, isn't it? To stick by someone no matter what happens to them. I knew what people said about us, and I wanted to prove them wrong. But I couldn't have known it'd be like this.'

My head was throbbing, I was giving away more than I intended. I had started speaking after all this time and now I couldn't stop.

'I thought I was with a person the whole world was wrong about, that they only saw a mask.' I said. 'But now it appears that the mask was what he was showing me and, as it slips, it's looking like the whole world was right. Do you understand?'

He blinked. 'I'm starting to.'

'He barely knows who we are any more. When Isabelle left the room today, he whispered to me, said JR was digging around, trying to incriminate him. I said JR only loves him.

As for me, I'm seeing a glimpse into the life of the first Mrs Rathwell, I think something terrible happened to her. I'm worried it'll happen to me too.'

Ben seemed disturbed, struck dumb, like he had forgotten where he was. Finally he said, 'You think it's possible he killed Bobby?'

In truth, there were many things I didn't know. And others I really couldn't say. There was a creak on the landing. Then shadows underneath the door. We quietened.

'Today he said he'd killed two sons. I worry he means he would like to.'

I saw Ben harden at the threat to JR, just as he did after Bobby's death. He had come to be a defender of him in such a short time.

I watched Ben struggle with everything I had told him as the night wound itself into the late hours, as the light blue of morning started to show. I looked at him for a long time, my hand playing with his hair. Then, in that small pocket of night-time, Ben offered to tell me what he'd heard about the super-injunction and Isa's demise. If the details had even made their way to someone like Ben, it seemed ridiculous for me to still be hiding from them. I was finally ready. I told him it may seem strange that I'd always sheltered myself from it, but why start listening to the case for the prosecution unless you're putting your husband on trial? All these years I kept a candle burning for him, a hope that he was a good man after all. Today, I blew it out.

All Robert had said about his first wife was that he didn't completely crush the rumour because it gave him a ruthless afterglow. Sharks don't bury their dead, they keep the blood in the water, he once said; the words seemed so unnatural in his mouth. But when he spoke to me, thinking I was Isa, I saw the brutal side of him come out. I told Ben all of it.

'So, who's helping him do it?' Ben said. 'He's not strong enough to kill Bobby himself.'

I took a few long breaths, wondering whether to let him follow this line of thinking.

'Some days he's stronger than others. He may be stronger than you think,' I said. 'When I kissed him goodbye, when you came into his bedroom today, I felt his body tense, that old strength has been there the whole time.'

But it was a long shot, given all I knew. The truth was, accepting Robert was lost to me just meant I was under an even greater threat. The primary one I couldn't talk to anyone about, not even Ben. I wouldn't dare to reveal my other keeper. Some truths were far too dangerous to tell, there would be consequences beyond even death. I had been warned.

'What do you want me to do?' he said.

I looked at him hard. 'I don't want anything from you, except for you to believe me. And if they try to frame this on me, don't let them do it. If I turn up dead, don't believe a word they say.' My shoulders began to shake. 'I don't feel safe, not any more. I think I might be next, it would make sense. I don't want to be left alone with Robert, or anyone else.'

And he put his arms around me and told me the thing I needed to hear. 'I won't let anything happen to you.'

25

A verdict

Isabelle

'Miss,' Georgios said on the phone that morning, 'I have something to discuss with you.'

'Yes?' I said, breath held. This was the moment. 'With me alone?'

'Yes ... difficult ... circumstances ... present yourself ... serious matter.'

The line was breaking up. The tremors must've played havoc with the line, which was shaky at the best of times. The single connection we had to the outside world, that seemed to come and go as it pleased, had never been so important.

'I can't hear you,' I said. 'Can you ... hear me?'

'Isabelle ... miss ... hear you ...'

I didn't want him to think I was being evasive. I knew, whenever it did this, I had seconds before the line went.

'Let me give you another number. It's of the Aegean Rooms, where the line will be better ...'

'Miss ... miss ...'

I found the slip of paper and repeated the number hurriedly

down the line as his voice started to disappear. 'Can you hear me?' I begged. 'Must know what you've decided ... what you've found ... I ... can you hear me?'

'Yes ... I will call ... ten minutes? Is this ... ten ...'

And the line finally gave out. I didn't have time to tell the rest of the house and that was probably for the best. Instead, I ascended the stairs, calling out.

'Amelia? I need your assistance.'

'Yes?' she said.

'You *can* drive, can't you?' I said. It was important, because I couldn't. It wasn't that I doubted her foot's role in the matter, I just wanted to make absolutely sure. I hoped I wasn't being politically incorrect, but it was so hard to tell these days.

'... Yes,' she said, after a pause. I got the distinct feeling that if she could've found a way to say no, she would have. 'Is it important?'

I almost laughed. I make it a rule never to beg, but this was as close as I'd ever get. 'Yes. I need you. It's an emergency.'

*

I struggled to relax as the Merc shook and we aquaplaned out of the gates, powering down the long uneven road. I had planned for the two of us to take an idle trip together at some point, to get Amelia to talk outside the confines of the house. Now the trip was anything but idle.

Her hands gripped the wheel hard, I could see the tension in her bones. She was clearly nervous at handling the six-figure vehicle. But I couldn't have cared less if she'd scraped the entire car along the metal barriers beside the cliff edge, my mind was on what Georgios was planning. The authorities like to pretend they can reconstruct events in one perfect aerial shot. But, in reality, they just play games of your word against mine, like everyone else. Robert said once, there's no such thing as morality. All there is, is a godless chaos and the stories people tell about it.

Whispers of clouds lumbered ahead, dragged across the sky. I needed some biblical downpour to wash away everything I'd done.

The things I'd done for Robert.

I thought of those notes: *How do you sleep?* The ones I knew were meant for me. And now, having given me no chance to tell my story, Georgios wanted to speak to me. I felt sure someone was setting me up. It had to be Ben or Amelia, I reasoned. It was all so unfair after all I'd sacrificed for this family. My tension must've been obvious, so I decided to shift the focus.

'Do you know much about Ben's family?' I said.

She turned to me, then remembered to keep her eyes on the road. 'Not much,' she said. 'Other than that his mother isn't very well.'

'Terribly sad,' I said, 'the pancreas, hope she'll pull through, but it's one of the nastier ones. She used to be a model, you know, a real model, I mean.'

Amelia didn't appear to understand the distinction, but I meant one of those who walked the catwalks, rather than the kind found up some stairs in Soho.

'Really? Didn't know,' she said, like it was good news.

'We couldn't find any photos,' I said. 'Seems like a fledgling career that was stopped in its tracks. But there was a record that she modelled for Vivienne Westwood. And her IMDB page lists one credit, a Bond movie, *The Living Daylights*, that was the one. But she seems to have been cut. Unfortunately, people get bored of It Girls quite quickly. And as soon as you're not *it*, that's it.'

Amelia had put her foot down, speeding up as she listened. I wasn't sure if she was aware of it. Lush colours of summer flashed past in a blur of freesia and lilac. Her knuckles were white on the wheel.

'You've had far more conversations with him than I have,' she said.

'Oh no,' I said. 'I've never mentioned it to him. That was from a background check Sofia ordered. When you were interviewed at the house, I had one done on you myself. You go by your mother's maiden name, don't you?'

'I do,' she said, eyes fixed on the road.

'You'd mentioned your father lost his job. A trader gone rogue. But you'd never know from your name that it was Simon Langrish. Is that why you don't use his name? Or was your mother some sort of feminist?'

'Not quite,' she said. 'My brother took his name, and I took my mother's. Not the usual solution but a decent one. It's not as if I was hiding who I was – I mean, if that's what—'

'Oh,' I said, 'well, I would've hidden it, if my father was such a renowned … However, I might have felt it important to be more open with the Rathwells, and I know you'll know where I'm going next, my darling, because of the connection.'

'It wasn't a vendetta,' she said as the car raced along. 'Dad barely talked about Robert, and nor did we.'

'But you can imagine how it looks.'

'The papers said he named Robert at one point—'

'The papers,' I said with great self-possession, 'reported that your father repeatedly said Robert had given him insider information about impending takeovers, mergers and acquisitions, which did not come to pass. Your father claimed that he discovered Robert was feeding him false information to influence the market in ways that benefited Robert himself, but were catastrophic to your father. And it is *my* belief that this *might* be the sort of thing it would be best to disclose at, say, the interview stage at Robert Rathwell's household. Otherwise, such a revelation *might* force me to think you are a saboteur, a fly in the ointment, the first person I should look at if anything untoward were to happen.'

I had her. She knew Bobby before this holiday, that was what I believed. How far back their relationship went, I didn't know.

'So, you've known all this time?' she said.

'Yes,' I said. 'But we liked you. Robert is a great champion of second chances and people rising above their past.'

'If you suspected me,' she said, her voice calm, 'why leave me alone with JR?'

She gave as good as she got and, while I can't say I liked it, I had a grudging respect for it. I had no idea she could be so robust.

'OK then, full disclosure, another word for Robert's love of second chances is that he believes people he has potential leverage over tend to be more obedient. But then sometimes things happen to challenge that theory. When asking someone to rise above their history, you have to always be aware that they may fail, then you are left to deal with the consequences. And here we are.'

I saw her seething, her hands sweating on the wheel. It would be understandable if she had issues with driving, given her history. She was clearly going through something, but I couldn't stop, not now we were here.

'I knew what the papers said, and I knew what my father was,' she choked out, voice quivering. 'If we kept grudges against everyone dad was mad at from that time there'd barely be enough time in the day to write all the poison-pen letters. And I'm sure you know my mother died in a car crash but let me fill in some details of my life that may not have made it onto the email attachment. She was driving in a rage after another row that had ended in my father striking her with a closed fist. I was in the back. We were finally making our escape. Then she went through a red light and was hit from the side. She died when the car flipped, I lost the lower part of my leg, and I have never spoken to my father since. He made his own decisions and he's forced to live by them, even he knows that, and his children certainly do.'

We hit a bump and the car jumped a little, but she didn't slow down.

'I'm sorry for your loss,' I said, my voice holding firm.

'And after all that,' she continued, tears forming, 'years later I get an interview for a ludicrously well-paid job. And it turns out the job is for one of that rogues' gallery of people dad threw mud at to divert attention from his own mistakes. Do you really think I would let my father hold me back again by mentioning it?'

Suddenly, they came out of nowhere. Flamingos on the

road ahead. She hit the brakes, panting hard, as we swerved to avoid them. I hung onto the handle above the window and my seatbelt as we skidded past the two birds.

'Jesus Christ,' I said, turning to see her, eyes wide. 'Slow down!' Then after a moment, when I realised I had asked her to get us there fast and she was determined to give me exactly what I wanted, I attempted a new register. 'I hope you understand, I had to ask. At a time like this.'

'Oh,' Amelia said, strangely cool, like she was on her way to defeating something that had been hanging over her for a long time. 'Of course.'

'Well. Thank you,' I said as if things were fine between us when I knew they weren't, and how could they be? Yet, I couldn't deny I was impressed by her ability to stay focused while I was holding her over the fire. I thought she was out of control for a second there, but I soon realised how thoroughly in it she was, and had been for some time. Such a brave girl.

But there was nothing she could do when the Porsche came from the parallel road through the trees, hitting us from the side.

*

Sofia

My transceiver buzzed, and I knew there would be consequences if I didn't answer. I'd become so fearful about Robert hearing it, I didn't even take it in the house. I stepped out of the front door into the glaring sunshine, making my way towards the garage.

I finally answered, noticing both cars were gone. But it was just two seconds of white noise before the caller hung up. As I put my handset away, I noticed Ben and JR watching me from the gym, next to the garage. I kept walking along the garage wall, wondering how much they had seen. I wondered if the white noise was a signal that punishment was coming, and if so, what would come next for me. I thought about how the caller would call even when we were in the same room, just to show their power.

And then I wondered whether they were calling to alert me to something. And what was it I heard so briefly? A whisper? Pocket static? A voice within the storm?

I kept walking, until I reached the back of the gym. From there I could hear Ben and JR talking quietly, their voices carrying through an open window.

'Thought no mobiles worked on the island, mate,' Ben said.

'It's not a mobile,' J said. 'Just looks like one. It's a walkie-talkie. It's all secrets. She doesn't even know I've seen her on it.'

The fact Ben was prying didn't please me at all, given where I thought we were with each other, given what I had said to him last night.

'Who's she talking to then?' Ben said. 'Must be someone on the island.'

I heard JR breathe out like he does when he's anxious. I didn't like to hear Ben pushing him, but I also wanted to hear how this played out.

'She says it's for emergencies. Only, I don't know what the emergency is.'

Ben didn't offer anything in response to that. I simply heard them bounce a basketball between them. The sound of it being thrown and hitting hands.

'But, who's she been talking to?' Ben said.

JR stayed silent. I wondered whether I could tell Ben everything, go further than I had last night when I had stepped to the precipice. But no, I knew it wasn't possible. It would only make things even more dangerous for him and the consequences would break me. The caller would punish me and bind me to what we agreed anyway. Nothing good could come of Ben being put in the line of fire. The ball bounced across the tarmac.

'Who do you trust most?' Ben said. 'In the whole house?'

Rubber slapped against the ground.

'Daddy says to keep my mouth shut,' JR said.

'OK,' Ben said. 'I'd never tell you that. Who do you trust more out of me and your dad?'

'You're only ever kind,' JR said. Then I heard him sigh. 'And daddy … scratches. And sometimes he looks at me like he hates me.'

My fingers found my temple, I thought I had been protecting him from this. Ben had won JR over by giving him everything he wanted, never looking at him strangely or trying to correct him. Not trying to teach him anything.

'Know what?' Ben said. 'If you tell me you trust me, we'll go on a little moped ride. But I have to know you trust me.'

'I trust you most,' JR said. 'I do.'

'Then tell me who your mum—'

'But I really don't know.'

I'd been at pains to keep it from JR of all people. I dug my fingers into my palms in relief.

'And I believe you. See? Trust. Now, come on,' Ben said, and they headed outside. I heard them go into the garage.

Outside, I leant against the wall and listened as the moped engine kicked into gear and they drove away.

*

Amelia

My mother's face flashed before me, as the car appeared in my window. But I pulled away and so did the other vehicle. The result was different this time, leaving me some long-felt seconds to reflect on what turns life would've taken if tragedy had been averted the day my mother was driving.

Our two cars ended up next to each other, so close they were kissing, not far from the water. No one was injured, but I was furious with the face looking at me from the driver's seat of the Porsche. Strangely, Kostas seemed just as enraged with us.

'What were you doing?' Kostas said, slamming the car door, sweating, linen shirt unbuttoned.

'You came out of nowhere,' I said, 'you trying to kill us?'

'You were the ones escaping,' Kostas said.

His behaviour had become irrational, I saw it then. He looked like he hadn't slept, all that presence of mind was leaving him. We gazed towards an empty horizon, there wasn't a boat in all of that blue. Just Mr Rathwell's yacht some way away that I'd have no chance of handling.

'What do you think we were planning to do?' I said. 'Swim for it?'

'You disobeyed,' he said, with pleading, worn eyes. 'After all that you and I … How could you leave the—'

'Because we have a verdict coming,' Isabelle said, emerging, a hand to her neck to check for any damage as she walked on, like she was casually fleeing a burning building. 'They're calling now, the lines were down at the house.'

Kostas hadn't finished with us, but we started to close down the distance to the Aegean Rooms, leaving his distressed form in our wake. Isabelle seemed to think she had to get to that phone before it rang out or things would get worse for her.

As we heard the distant sound of the phone ring, Isabelle fumbled with her keys, opening the first hotel room, which hadn't been set up for a guest, and answered it.

'Georgios,' she said. Kostas appeared behind us.

Isabelle was gasping, displaying more fear than I ever had seen in her before. She was worried she alone was about to be arrested for murder. I hadn't seen it until then. No, that's wrong, she wasn't worried, she seemed to know it for certain. I wondered just how much she was willing to do for Robert, how far she would go to stay in his favour. We had established she was around when Isa died.

'I have others with me,' she said, 'to hear this … I assume that's … yes and Amelia, our tutor, and … yes, that's OK? OK.'

She listened, and I noticed Kostas had brought his gun with him, in a holster under his suit jacket. I saw Isabelle notice it too.

'Yes,' she said, trying to push a smile across the phone line. 'I can present myself to you at short notice, if I … What I mean to say is, I'm not a flight risk, I'm not …'

I found myself stepping away from her. Kostas watched my moves carefully.

'I must say,' Isabelle said. 'I feel like I may have been naïve in not having employed a … representative.'

'A representative?' I whispered.

Kostas silenced me with a hand, all his subtlety and sharpness having faded away.

'A lawyer,' Isabelle said, any calm she had leaving her, her hand shaking as she pushed it through her hair and her voice became weak. 'I said a lawyer. Look, the Rathwells can fly a lawyer out at twenty-four hours' notice. I suppose the question is how necessary you feel it would be?'

She was like a wasp under a glass.

'Well,' she said, 'it's not for me to— I'm not used to— I'm sure you have to offer me the option. Don't you?'

She held herself tight where her spine became her neck, eyes closed.

'What do you mean, you have all you need?' Isabelle said.

I sat on a bare mattress. What did Georgios have that made him so confident? Whatever it was, I couldn't feel sorry for her. I was willing to forgive her for having been the one to suggest Bobby and I knew each other beforehand. She was just reporting what she heard. But the way she used my mother to push me in the car, I would never forgive.

'Well,' Isabelle said. 'I won't sign anything without anyone looking over it. I've heard about people signing things abroad and, before they know it, they're in a cell with no recourse and I won't have that happen to—'

I saw her face as something dawned on her. The death knell. What was he saying? I kept my look of concern, while secretly praying for an end to this.

'So, everything's moving forward?' she said, voice cracking as she spoke.

Georgios didn't seem to be doing anything by the book. I looked up, brow furrowed, wondering whether a helicopter was about to emerge, trying not to give away that I was willing it to. Wishing it would land and arrest all of them. Kostas seemed to sense the same and check the sky himself. Then she said …

'The coroner has returned a verdict of accidental death. Death by misadventure.'

Isabelle bowed her head. She held her hand to her mouth and nodded silently as her eyes became wet. Kostas simply nodded like the result was never in doubt. For my part, I was scared. The chances of being fitted up for all this had receded for now, but that had left me trapped here with a killer and no prospect of police intervention. However, I knew what was expected of me; I closed my eyes and drew breath to appear relieved. I knew that if I did so well enough, I might just manage to slip into her confidence, just as I'd asked Ben to find his way into Sofia's.

'Thank you, thank you so much,' she said, taking a huge breath as she hung up. I could almost see the weight lift from her. She glanced at us. 'And thank you both, I do apologise for my manner, I'm sure you can understand the stress we've been under. It's just good to put a line under things so we can move forward.'

I went over, reached out a hand to touch her back, to comfort her, but couldn't quite do it.

Isabelle looked up at us, her face still reddened to a blush. The way Georgios disclosed it did seem strange, his intentions lost somewhere between two languages. But the way she had reacted to him suggested she was guilty of something.

By the time she had cracked her back, pushing her shoulders together, I saw she had recovered quickly, with a resolve about her that suggested she believed we were one step closer to bringing someone – someone other than her – to justice.

'The police would've only made solving this harder,' she muttered.

Kostas had turned his back on us. He threw the door open, the vista of paradise revealing itself beyond. The sun cast a haze over us that was so beautiful I was sure we didn't deserve it.

He gestured for us to leave, and we did so, knowing he would be close behind, having told us nothing about what he had planned for us next.

*

Isabelle

We sped back to the house, Kostas in our rearview mirror and a radio station picking up the whispers of some European disco track in between bursts of static. I was so relieved to be alive and free that I even bobbed my head to it.

I couldn't wait to tell Robert that at least this threat was over. I felt it might even lift his spirits, bring him back to that happier place – that eye of health in between his maladies – and give us clear bright days to live under until the holiday's end.

As soon as we pulled up outside the house, I jumped from the car, Amelia following, feeling to me far more like an ally than she had on the outward journey. She had even told me on the way back that she saw me as 'one of those women that really has her shit together'. It felt good to hear that, to be accepted by one of her generation. I flung open the front door and a quick look in the kitchen and at the den room on the ground floor told me everyone else was outside, a note on the kitchen island simply said, Gone Downstairs To The Beach in Sofia's handwriting.

It didn't seem likely Robert had been left on his own, but it was possible and, if so, this would present the perfect opportunity for us to take in this important news together, alone. As Amelia walked through the house to join the others, I skipped up the stairs.

His door was closed. Unusual. He mostly left it open just a touch, as he said having it closed had come to scare him. I decided he may be doing something private in there.

But I couldn't wait. I knocked and carefully opened the door when he didn't say stop. I saw his legs first as I called his name. My relief returned. We were all alone.

His neck was rolled back at an angle. I ran to him, and gently brought it back into my hands, but he was as cold as a statue. He was dead, of that there was no doubt. And all the screams I could muster from my shallow lungs couldn't bring him back.

My heart fell hard, and I could feel it beat all the way down. I listened to the sounds of a weaker woman than I thought I was. Shock makes us all equal. I grabbed handfuls of my hair in a gesture I hadn't used since I was a teenager. As the shock subsided, my eyes danced around the room, finding nothing but ordinary mundanities. His death was meant to look like natural causes. But when my gaze reached his neck, I knew something wasn't right.

A sound made me turn. My screams had brought another presence, watching Robert and I together through the open door. It was Sofia. To begin with, she locked me in a stare, and said nothing at all. I felt somehow naked, kneeling there. The three of us were together again in this room, only this time one of us wasn't breathing.

We were silent for a good minute, a long time for silence, but here it was nowhere near long enough. It was all that was allowed due to the circumstances.

'Help,' I cried out eventually, releasing all my tension as I did so. But she didn't move.

'Have you called the …' she choked out. Clearly, I'd got to the body before she had, and she didn't believe I'd done it. Murderers aren't usually expected to call the police themselves. Amelia would be my alibi if any foolishness began.

I shook my head *no*, then said, 'Where is …' I waved an arm in a gesture that meant *everyone*.

'At the beach,' she said, her face wan. She was in shock.

Then the banging of footsteps sounded on the stairs. Ben and Kostas arrived in the room.

'No,' Kostas shouted as he kicked out at Robert's bed, then dropped to a crouch to analyse the scene, face in his hands.

'Oh God,' Ben said, looking at Sofia then backing away. 'When—'

'We don't know anything yet,' Sofia said.

'I just came back in to get us all some water and heard you shout,' Ben said.

'Tell Amelia,' Sofia said. 'And make sure JR stays away.'

Ben staggered out of the room, banging down the stairs, the noise echoing around.

Kostas smoothed his hand over the creases of his weather-beaten face, his eyes bloodshot. He knelt before Robert and made to hold his hand in a show of devotion, before pulling back from touching him.

'I … I can't be everywhere at once.'

It was an apology, an expression of anguish and an attempt to stake a claim towards his innocence all at once. He had judged it as murder already.

'If you hadn't left his side—' I said.

'If you hadn't driven off without telling me where you were going—' he said, then turned his eyes on Sofia.

'I could say the same to you,' Sofia shouted before he could say a thing. 'If I knew you were leaving, I could have watched over Robert.'

'But you didn't,' I said, rounding on her, 'so what were you doing instead?'

Kostas looked up at us. We heard the ticking of a carriage clock on Robert's bedside table.

'Someone under this roof knew the exact second Robert's heart stopped beating,' I said, drawing Kostas over to look at two subtle bruises in the shape of thumbprints. 'Because they made it happen.'

'Are these new? He is fragile, bruises easily. How can you tell?' Kostas said.

'I knew every inch of him,' I said, resisting looking at Sofia.

Kostas looked between the two of us. 'I think it's becoming clearer to me who is responsible. And I can take care of it.'

'So,' I said, my hand coming up over my mouth, almost afraid to hear what he would say next. 'Who is it?'

His morose eyes fell to the floor. 'I need proof first. I don't tell tales.'

I knew it would be no use pushing him, he didn't respond to

that. Ever since Bobby, he'd worn a haunted look and a sworn determination not to discount little things, almost to the point of superstition.

'Well,' I said, 'there are things we need to organise now.'

Kostas nodded. He knew what I meant, someone had to go to the Aegean Rooms to call the authorities, and they would have to make it quick. We didn't want to be left alone here with Robert. At least the police would know the route by now.

Before Kostas went, he gave the room the once-over for any other signs of struggle that might point in a particular direction. And beneath Robert's chair found a single pill.

'Is this one of the pills Robert usually takes?' he said to me.

I took a close look. It must've fallen. No real harm there. I scrutinised it before I nodded, with a little disappointment. Kostas stared at me and then left without saying a thing. But just as he was going, I noticed something strange.

'Wait, look. The nails on Robert's right hand are freshly cut.'

Sofia seemed particularly disturbed as Kostas came back and knelt to inspect it.

'He can't do it himself. I didn't do it,' I said. 'Did you?'

Sofia shook her head as Kostas took note of it, then hurried away to make his call.

Sofia's eyes turned cold. Ever since Robert's ramblings on the balcony, she had stopped even trying to look at him with love. I couldn't help but note the lack of absolute sadness on her face as she gazed at him in death.

She simply wandered away to find the others at the beach. I stayed. I wouldn't abandon him so easily. I had the overwhelming urge to kiss him on the cheek, but I couldn't take the chance of leaving a mark. I lay at his feet, looking up at him, this huge monolith, which could neither be hurt nor questioned. Though it terrified me to look it in the face, I couldn't stop myself. After my tears had dried, I wiped my eyes and went downstairs.

I told the maids nothing as I passed them. Best not to let anyone know that death was in the house with them. But I told them to throw away the food that was out on the counter.

Down at the beach, Amelia caught my eyes, white as mist, and I knew then and there she had been told. She was wrapping a towel around JR, having been swimming under a sun so glorious it was like a blessing.

Sofia beckoned her son over, put her hands on his shoulders as I heard her words, 'JR, there's no use babying you because I know you don't want that. Your father is dead.' The child's only sound was 'Oh' before I heard his tears and howls as I made my way towards the house like I was escaping the scene of a fire.

Ben sat, head in hands, on the sand, turning as grey as the clouds arriving overhead. He was comforted by Amelia as I watched on. At such moments, it is not unusual to have an eye on yourself, to feel like you are merely copying the moves of tragedy as seen on television, but this is a dissociation that comes from denial. In this case, however, all of our eyes were on ourselves as the quality of our sadness ran the risk of revealing our true nature.

I went back to my room, pushing my case further under the bed, and looked in the bathroom mirror to see what the tears had done to my face.

I stood there, listening to the rain fall for some time, before I heard the knock at my door. Kostas, his beige suit wet almost to the point of dripping. He must've just come in.

'They will be fast,' he said, with a tortured expression. 'I made sure.'

I gestured him in. It was then I noticed he had lost weight. He had the clapped-out stubbled attractiveness of an aftershave ad, but with grief on his back he looked suddenly old.

'Need scapegoat?' he said, eyes watering. 'This is me. Robert said he plucked me from obscurity, and I often let him down. He was right.'

I could see his outline in the bathroom mirror, where I stayed with the tap running, as he slumped on the bed. Looking at him then, it seemed odd that I was so intimidated by this walking crisis of confidence at the Aegean Rooms.

'Robert said a lot of things on bad days. He spoke very fondly of you on his good ones. Don't torture yourself,' I said. 'If you want to do something, find his killer. You need to keep control of us. Now there's another one dead, and you're no closer to solving the first.'

'Rest assured, there will be no more mistakes,' he said. I could see in his riven eyes that he meant it. Then I got lost in my own image in the mirror, wondering if I looked quite as haggard. I had not forgotten how he seemed to chastise himself for not having noticed the subtle route into the house from the cliff face. Perhaps this job was stretching his abilities, but I didn't say so. 'You know,' he said. 'He told me one evening that people around him were like horseflies, sucking his blood, getting into his eyes. He said they were waiting for him to turn into a carcass, so the real feast could begin.'

'Well,' I said. 'He had a lovely way with words. What is it they say, that owners often start to look like their newspapers. Or is that dogs?'

'Do you believe there was nothing in what he said?'

'I didn't say that.' My eyes flicked back to where he was sitting, as I always thought it best not to let him out of my sight. 'Robert never asked you to watch him twenty-four/seven. You weren't that kind of security and Robert liked his independence.'

After a few years' service, Robert had begun to treat Kostas as a confidant. When Kostas wasn't keeping watch, driving or sailing Robert around, and doing whatever else, they played backgammon and drank his cognac.

'You know, I blew my second paycheck on a suit from Mr Rathwell's tailor, in an effort to be like him.'

I turned and came back into the room to see him drying his eyes, my case and all it contained just under his feet. I hoped he hadn't noticed it was gone when he searched our rooms. I had hidden it in the loft, removing the panel in the ceiling above my bed and standing on tiptoes on it to push it above, in case he started checking on us. Bringing it back down was a mistake.

26

Summering

Amelia

Ben and I sheltered as the early morning crept into the afternoon and the low sun turned red. He held my hand. He seemed anaesthetised, like a patient waiting to be operated on, with a little of that apprehension too.

'Are you going to be OK?' I said.

'We both are. You and me,' he said, turning to lock eyes with me as I felt the heat of his hand in mine. 'I told you before, and I am promising you now. I'll make sure of it.'

But I wasn't sure either of us had that sort of power. We were just two strangers clinging onto each other for dear life. I thought about Bobby's note, but before I could offer my theory, he asked me a question.

'How did someone like you even end up here?' he said, his hand squeezing mine then dropping it in case anyone was near.

'This was a stopgap. I play the violin,' I said, feeling a little silly. Telling him that also made me realise how little we really knew each other. 'Music allowed me to get onto the property ladder, then work dried up and I started to fall. I'd rather starve than ask my father for anything, so I was a month from my house being repossessed when the Rathwells took a chance on me. I think you'd call it selling out, but somehow people seem to think selling out is easy. I always thought I'd walk away from this job at the end of the summer, but now I want to run. But I need J to be OK. I can't let people like this crush him like they crushed me. He deserves better things.'

Ben glanced around then started to speak low. 'He'll come back strong, now his father's gone. He's gaining in confidence all the time. This is what I wanted to tell you. We took a trip out to the bar, JR and I, when I realised what that note meant. I think Bobby wanted the note to be only understood by us in case someone else found it. It wasn't so much *that point when* strangers became friends as *where*.'

'The bar.'

'I realised Bobby wasn't staying in his room, for his own safety. I thought maybe he was staying in the back room, behind the beer fridge. I found his clothes there.'

'You did that? And with JR? Did you tell him anything?'

'No,' Ben said. 'I said I'd left something there, he was playing pool, he didn't see me check the back room. Other than his clothes there was nothing important, nothing useful. I checked the rest of the place, looked in a cooler. Nothing. So, I checked the cash register like he may have left something there. Nothing. Then JR called out, said there was something deep in one of the pockets of the pool table. It was Bobby's phone.'

'Did he know what it was?'

'I told him that it was mine,' Ben said. 'JR said he trusts me, and I swore him to secrecy. But that's not the important part.'

'Have you tried to unlock the phone?' I said.

'That's the thing,' Ben said. 'It was unlocked.'

There was a bang on the front door. Our eyes found each other's. Isabelle had charged me with answering the door straight away. I told Ben to hold his thought and rushed to answer the door. I stood blinking as two medics in light blue shirts entered the house. It seemed ridiculous that they were tasked with taking away the body. The problem of Robert was no longer medical, but practical. But I was moved at how polite and calm they were, how gently they asked where he was, how careful they were with him. Through my tears, I saw them stop suddenly and try to resuscitate. That was when I saw him stir. A twitch in the muscle. That arm flicked out, a sudden punch, all too late. He had returned.

Ben came out and watched it all happen, far less removed, the horror of it causing him to get low and breathe heavily.

But Robert wasn't staying. It was just a reaction left in the nerves that remains possible for some time after brain activity ceases. After a couple of minutes, the medics halted resuscitation, checked their watches and he was pronounced dead, though I started to wonder whether he might rally again, open his eyes and tell them all to go fuck themselves, and then the ambulance would turn around and drop him back here again. But this thought faded as Ben and I followed them out of the door and watched the ambulance leave the gravel drive in the low sun and gentle rain.

I must've seemed mad, that word that follows young women around, because when they were gone, I almost felt like I was going to laugh, until I smothered it with my hand.

The van disappeared, bound for the boat and then the

morgue, which we were keeping busy in peak holiday season. I wanted to ask again about Bobby's phone but then the family started to gather together in the den. The kitchen is large but not comfortable. The den is welcoming, but too small, and requires a group of people who want to be close to each other. All that money and still no good place to sit. After the body was gone, we stuffed ourselves in there, Ben and I sat on the arms of chairs, JR on Sofia's lap, Kostas and Isabelle sat far closer than was comfortable. And we said nothing for a long time, knowing only that we had to be together. Safety, they say, exists in numbers. Here that meant, while we were all together, it would be difficult for one of us to attack another without witnesses.

Later, when the rest dispersed, Ben and I stayed in the den and overheard Kostas and Sofia talking in the kitchen.

'Georgios called,' Kostas said, 'I thought the lines might have stayed dead, given us some time to think, but no such luck, the contractor off the island Robert used to have shouting matches with fixed the problem in record time. Georgios said he was working another case when he heard the news, and he decided he wouldn't have time to get to us before the storm came in. He felt he had to call to give his condolences. He took details of how he was found, said he would take a look at the body himself once the van made it back. It all made sense, but at the same time it didn't exactly feel by the book, even if island policing is a little unorthodox. Then he said to expect more calls.'

We listened extra carefully after he said that. What was clear was that Georgios would want to know where everyone was at the time of death.

'He asked after Isabelle,' Kostas continued. 'Said she seemed quite heightened when they spoke. Said, after this, he couldn't imagine how she must be feeling.'

'I can't either,' Sofia said. 'Did he ask about me?'

'Yes,' Kostas said.

He sounded drained as he relayed it all. But then his voice took on a darker tone. 'You know, I had this feeling you *wanted* an investigation. That you wanted to pull out of what was agreed between us?'

'No,' she said, 'not true.' She sounded a little afraid.

'Do you think you know the police here better than I?' Kostas said. 'The last thing Robert would want is his own death to become gossip. Those tabloid rags with their biases and campaigns will make it all salacious. Will you let me handle this?'

'Yes,' she said after a long hiatus.

'Good,' Kostas said. 'He asked about Amelia and Ben too.'

Ben glanced to me in the half-light as we stayed quiet in the next room.

'I told him the young man and the young woman seem to be taking it in their stride,' Kostas said.

'Was there any indication whether he would be visiting?' Sofia asked.

'He didn't say. It's so strange how one tragedy seems to bring two, he told me. But then he said it was not the first time he had seen this. In life. And in his line of work. I said that was often the way.'

As the night went on, the phone line holding strong, we would be asked to describe the specifics of our day, right up until what the medics had discerned was the time of death.

'Can I ask something?' she said, just as we thought the conversation was over.

'Oh, anything,' Kostas said.

'Why would someone cut Robert's nails?' Sofia said. Her words followed by a long pause.

'That's a detail I'm still working on. Currently,' he said, before a long pause, 'I have no idea at all.'

27

The sky turned

Sofia

By evening, the beach and the pool were being hammered with rain, the sand turning to mud that rolled brown into the churning waves. The chlorine of the pool mingled with rainwater and flooded onto the flagstones, the puddles flowing up to the patio doors. The storm had finally found us.

I was drying my eyes as I came back into the den, having spoken to Sir Anthony. Robert's body had been taken away only a matter of hours ago but things had happened fast. I was embarrassed when I saw them all assembled silently there. I'm sure everyone heard my raised voice over the line. It wounded me that Isabelle of all people was sitting there judging me when I returned.

JR was in bed at least, but when I sat next to the others, we were close enough to hear each other's breath.

'What did he say?' Isabelle said. And I could barely look at her. I fixed my jaw and thought about what Kostas had told me he'd found in her room. But that would have to wait.

'I told him the doctor had just called, the one who had seen Robert many times, and he was happy, given the extent of his known illnesses, that an inquest into his death was not needed.'

There were various shades of reaction in the room, all quietly rendered at first.

'The medics didn't find any marks on him, at all?' Isabelle choked out, so pointed, and solely in my direction. She seemed very happy to keep Bobby's murder in-house and under wraps, but Robert's was making her waver, despite what we had decided. But she should've been less bold, in company. The way she acted like she was the only one who cared for him made me want to reach out and slap her.

'If they were searching for surefire signs of asphyxiation, or even *strangulation*,' Kostas said, analysing us all as he spoke, 'they'd be looking for a fracture of the hyoid bone at the bottom of the tongue, or at least blood in the eyes. But the latter comes from the strain of the victim, and the former from the strain of killing, and Robert didn't have enough left in him to make that kind of struggle necessary. When an old man with an underlying condition passes away, it takes clear evidence to prove it wasn't those conditions that killed him.'

'Unless someone is really prepared to push for a full autopsy. And that's exactly what Sir Anthony said he was determined to do,' I said, another shade of discomfort entering the room.

'And what did you tell him?' Kostas said, narrowing his eyes on me, as if he hadn't told me exactly what to say if Anthony said that. Letting Anthony push for the autopsy would inevitably reopen the investigation into Bobby's death, leaving us all under scrutiny, even Kostas.

'I told him he was a sick man who was finally at peace,' I said. 'I told him he should listen to the doctor and let him go.'

Isabelle called me a liar with a look and then quietly spoke with subtle power. 'You know as well as I do that one of us did this.'

'I don't know that for sure, do you?' I said. 'I told him I was his wife and that he should respect that. He agreed it was my decision before the line died again. It's never been very reliable in a storm.' Our conversation had been set to a soundtrack of rain so thick it sounded like one long mist of white noise. 'When Bobby died, we all committed to containing this. That's what we decided,' I said with feeling.

'But things are different now,' Amelia said. 'Aren't they?'

'Yes,' Kostas said, plainly. 'They are.'

I felt Isabelle's hand on me, but it was the coldest comfort. A physical lie, designed to keep me on side. But that ship had long sailed.

'Still,' Isabelle said, with a triumphant tone, 'it sounds like Anthony might push for an examination on the body's return.'

Though she was still touching me, her words were a threat. As if an examination of Robert would worry me more than anyone else. She had locked me in the car, disagreed and undermined me in Robert's room, and now was pointing blame at me. And then there was what I'd found out about those pills. But I held it all in.

'When do you think they'll release the bodies?' I said, looking across to Kostas.

'Two or three days,' Kostas said. 'We'll have to arrange the funeral of course.'

We would have to brace ourselves to be descended on at

a grand ceremony back in London. As for family, they were nearly all dead themselves and the ones who weren't were not talking to him.

'Three days?' Ben said. 'We can't stay that long. We need to go.'

'No one's moving anywhere,' Kostas said.

'Someone can stay behind though, can't they?' Ben said, eyes wandering to Isabelle, who had kept the doe-eyed look she had when I saw her next to the body.

'Even if someone were willing to,' Kostas said, 'as of right now, we can't get a boat in this weather. Or a helicopter. So, sit tight, relax, breathe.'

The ability to stay breathing was clearly what Ben was worrying about, but he didn't say it. The rain started to clatter against the windows. Hail. Thick spheres of ice.

'I could stay,' Isabelle said. 'That is, it may not be my preference, but I am willing to stay.'

What a bleeding heart. Every word of hers stabbed. I couldn't let her remain so seemingly selfless any longer, I pulled away from her grip and leant back to put some distance between us.

'You'd like that, wouldn't you? To escort his body home. To control it all up until his last moment, just like you did with everything else in his life.'

She gave me a pleading look like I'd slapped her out of the blue. But the pressure had been building underneath for some time.

'I see what you've been doing. How you've been pulling Robert's strings, controlling him.'

I had planned to do this in a calmer way, but here I was, I couldn't stop. 'When I spoke to Sir Anthony, as he's executor of the will, I asked him to confirm the contents of it.'

Isabelle was so still. Her only movement was to blink twice. Not a hint of shame.

'Yes,' I said, 'that's right. I always thought Robert had some surprise up his sleeve, but it was just as he said, the estate was to be divided between all living relatives. Except Bobby.'

'So, that's why he wrote those letters, because he knew he—' Isabelle said.

'Oh, and Isabelle. You're in it too,' I said.

The others tried to hide their shock, but the awkwardness was too much to bear. That was why it was useful to have them there, to see her breathless and uncomfortable.

'Now, wait a minute,' Isabelle said, 'he did mention the possibility, but you know Robert, I never thought—'

'I assume you know what Munchhausen by proxy is?' I said.

'No,' Isabelle said, deflecting with a tight laugh. 'You'll have to educate me.'

'I will,' I said. 'Sometimes people like to keep others sick. Mothers with their children, husbands with their wives, even carers and their patients. Most of the time it's because they get off on being needed, but sometimes people have other reasons. Gaining control of a money pot for example, one where you can pay yourself thousands of pounds—'

'Ludicrous,' she said, standing, and unable to stop herself from shouting. 'Robert told you why he gave me that money.'

'But Robert had been doing everything you told him for a long time. Because you'd kept him dependent, doped up on just the right blend of pills. Until, in the end, whether something was his idea or your idea became difficult to remember. All those little steps backwards he made, because of his strokes, who knows if you were really just keeping him that way, with your little pills.'

Kostas produced a packet of OxyContin from his pocket. He'd told me earlier that when he'd seen that pill on the floor, he'd wondered why he hadn't found any pills amongst Isabelle's things when he first searched her room. So, he'd gone to her, distracted her with a story of self-doubt as she admired herself indulgently in the mirror, and found a stash that amounted to hundreds of these pills in a case below her bed. I saw her piecing it together as her anger found focus on him.

'You little bastard,' she said, staring at him, seated, while she stood stranded in between us all.

Kostas simply shrugged.

'I need them, that's why I have them. If you must know,' she said, and it cost her to say it.

'Go on,' I said. 'It'll all come out anyway. I've always known there was something fundamentally fucked up about you, I'd just like to, finally, know exactly what it is.'

'It started with a horse riding accident a few years ago. I began taking these, just the normal dose. They made the days easier, I found, and not just bodily, mentally. By the time I was supposed to come off them, I had begun to rely on them, they put everything back in place, and I had to take enough to really feel the world contract, and that means you have to keep up the dose, or go bigger, like I did. But I could never tell Robert.'

'Because Robert wouldn't respect an addict,' I said, biting into the words, as I stood. 'Wouldn't continue to give you thousands of pounds of gifts, wouldn't—'

'Wouldn't love me any more,' she cried. One swift pull and there it was between us, like a bad tooth. The others were dumbfounded, wanting to crawl off somewhere else no doubt. 'I'll tell you another reason I couldn't stop taking those pills. It was the pressure of being in a … relationship with a powerful man, when the last thing he wanted to do was make it public. Because my face didn't fit. He had the modern trophy wife who looked so good in magazines but in practice was just that little too wilful for him. So, I had to have him only in private, slaving away behind the scenes for nothing but promises, for a long time, ever since—'

'For about two years,' I said. It felt good that there were other people to hear this. It should've been humiliating, but somehow it was purifying.

'And you know,' Isabelle said, eyes suddenly wide, nodding, her hand over her mouth as it dawned on her. 'Because, recently, you've been having me followed.'

'No,' I said, shaking my head as I leant towards her. 'No, recently you've noticed. They've been there for a long time. I still loved him, I just knew he got something from you too, some joy of life, so I let it happen even though it hurt me. That's what love is, it's about lying to yourself until the very last second. But I always wanted to know what that something you did for him was. So, tell me—'

'Tell us,' Kostas cut me off, 'why you were nervous when you took Georgios' call at the Aegean Rooms,' he said. 'If you'd done nothing wrong, why be so afraid? Wasn't she nervous, Amelia?'

Amelia stared at Isabelle. It must have felt like a pile-on, but it was the time for it. 'Yes, she was,' she said.

'Because,' Isabelle said, that old reticence returning just like when she'd been questioned about the money. 'Because Robert has committed many financial indiscretions both here and at home, tax irregularities he insisted on, money for bribes to put into proxy accounts—'

'But,' Amelia said, 'what does that matter when compared to murder? When I was in there with you, it really felt like—'

'Because, darling, let this be a lesson to you: never put your name on anything. Stupidly, I put mine on everything. The story breaking back at home that Robert was so anxious to ignore is about him paying little or no tax. Georgios knew I was named in the story, and it's just the tip of the fucking South Pole. I helped Robert cover it up, I co-signed the forms, out of love and duty. And I'm only one call from the authorities away from going down for it. And if they ever allied that kind of joint enterprise, to … to something worse he'd done …'

The tears came, it was like watching a statue weep. Or a great wall, and it was coming down. I felt for her. She was Robert's greatest defender, even when he'd started to slide from the man I loved to something else.

'I don't know if he did anything to Bobby, but I admit I was afraid he had. I'm sure some would believe I co-signed on that too.'

Outside, the driving rain sounded like a falling wave.

'I don't think you have to cover for Mr Rathwell ever again,' Ben said. 'I think we all can see that and—'

He was cut off by a loud grating buzz. It echoed around the building. We looked at each other, our faces pale. Someone was pressing the button on the gates.

I went to the window and saw a car there, beams cutting through the dark and the rain. Someone wanted to come in. Another uninvited guest.

'The police? Medics?' Ben said.

'Can't be. Someone else,' I said.

'How did someone else get on the island?' Amelia said.

'Whoever's out there, we need to let them in,' I said.

'We can't,' Amelia said, 'who is it?'

'We have things to discuss. You all may be drawing your conclusions, yes, I see that,' Isabelle said. 'But bear in mind, while it's easier to blame all this on a dead man, he didn't kill himself. Someone here did. Robert was defenceless when it happened. No trial, no jury, just one of you.'

'One of us,' Ben said. 'And how do we know what story is breaking back at home? What about Robert's first wife? About her suicide that maybe wasn't a suicide,' he said, looking back at Amelia. 'My mother told me before I left that she'd heard Isa's family want to have her exhumed, they believe the science has moved on and they may be able to prove what they couldn't back then. Only, Robert won't tell them where she's buried, never has. What if that's the story breaking at home?'

I saw Isabelle's blood run glacial. 'You fool. You little fool, you've no idea what you've got yourself into. You're in over your head.'

The blare of a car horn out there. We would have to act fast or risk looking guilty.

'That's not the story,' Kostas said, reaching back for his gun as he assessed the view from the window. 'Sofia may not have wanted to know but, in my position, I had to. It's about a tax scheme. You're just another person stirred up by conspiracy on the internet. I wish everyone would leave poor Isa in peace.'

Ben put his hands to his head. I turned away and pressed mine into the cold glass of the window, drawing my face nearer to see who was there. I saw an older woman, her head out of the window yelling through the hard rain. And I knew who it was.

'It's Jeanette,' I said, and Isabelle gasped.

'Who's Jeanette?' Amelia murmured.

'We can't leave her out there,' I said, eyes glazed. She pressed the buzzer again and again. She waved and I waved back.

'Who is Jeanette?' Ben shouted.

'Robert's sister,' Isabelle said.

'Wait,' Kostas said before anyone could answer the door. 'Shall we tell her right away?'

'Of course,' Isabelle said.

'We can't,' I said. 'What, tell her that her brother and nephew were killed as soon as she walks in the door. It'll look more than suspicious.'

'But it's true,' Amelia said, locking eyes with me.

'Let's leave out Bobby, let's wait,' Isabelle said. 'She can't have known he'd even be here. But the news of Robert needs more immediate attention. The longer we wait, the stranger it will seem.'

'True,' Kostas said as Ben stared at the car, beeping its horn again. 'We should tell her about Robert, but only when the time is right. Keep it nice and natural.'

The boys were dispatched to help the older lady as Isabelle turned to Amelia and I.

'She knows where to find the boatmen that'll drop you here for a price on the way to the larger islands,' Isabelle said. 'That's how she got here. She's family, just like Bobby.'

The mention of the word family was enough to civilise us, as if we had just remembered to act like one.

'We'll find out who killed Bobby and Robert,' I said. 'But first we just need to get through this. Together.'

PART 3:

But let's keep it a secret, shall we?

28

Let me in

Amelia

'Oh, come in out of that wet nonsense, darling,' Isabelle said.

We were a strange welcoming committee, some of us committing hard, others less enthusiastic. The formidable form of a soaked auntie Jeanette seemed to bring half the weather inside with her.

'It's disgusting out there,' Jeanette bellowed, 'absolutely disgusting. They didn't want to bring me across on the boat, five minutes more and they wouldn't have been able to, rough crossing. Come here, Sofe.'

Jeanette gave Sofia a squeeze. There was a squeeze for Isabelle too but when she saw Kostas the welcomes stopped. Ben and I, the help, at least got warm smiles.

'Sorry, I'm being loud, aren't I? The little one and the big one asleep, are they?' Jeanette said, pointing upstairs.

'Oh, yes,' Sofia said.

'Indoor voices then,' Jeanette whispered, a finger to her mouth.

What Isabelle clearly wanted to greet her with was: 'Why

are you here?' But that wasn't appropriate and appropriate was what we were striving for. But no matter how hard we masked our feelings it seemed obvious that something was wrong. Even if, with the exception of Ben, who had developed a vague melancholy stare, we all were remarkably composed.

'I know, I know,' Jeanette said, taking her waxed jacket off and throwing it on the wooden coat stand. 'I know I'm days late, couldn't get the right flight, which slightly misses the point of a birthday, but misery guts doesn't like birthdays anyway. And I didn't want to call ahead, it would ruin the surprise.'

She must've been sixty-five, a good deal younger than Robert, and strong, burly, strong enough to easily wield two large tweed-patterned cases and a travel bag. She dropped them with a tired slap on the floor and breathed out with relief.

Ben scuttled down around her feet, grabbing her cases for her. He was right to get out of the way, his tension would have been plain to see, so it was better for him to play the faithful manservant. I joined him, lugging her heavy bags upstairs to the spare room on the first floor. The room was made up, and it was late, so at least she would be kept off the floor where Robert was supposed to be sleeping.

'Don't be long,' Sofia called up to us from the bottom of the stairs. 'We'll have that late dinner.'

We'd already had dinner, but it was clear she wanted to keep us together.

'Are you all right?' I said to Ben, once we were alone on the landing together. It's a question I've always hated when aimed at me because it leaves you so self-conscious. Everyone knows what it really means: your current mood is a problem. But it was the only question to ask.

'Yes,' he whispered back in a bark. 'Why wouldn't I be?'

I noticed the hand I reached for was quivering. 'You're sweating,' I said.

'It's a hot country. Hot climate,' he said, dead behind the eyes as he leant into the wall.

I looked out the window at the stacks of rain coming down outside.

'Look,' I said, taking him into my room, 'look in the mirror.'

He did. What he saw staring back didn't look good.

'Maybe I've got heatstroke,' he said, 'I feel sick.'

He placed a hand over one eye as he looked in the mirror. 'Can everyone see it?' he said.

'No, no. I don't think so,' I lied, and he sensed it.

'Kostas told me he noticed that the nails of Robert's right hand were cut,' he said, rushing to close the door. 'Whoever did this is out of their mind. I thought I was safe because I didn't know anything. I thought I could keep us both safe. But they won't stop, and one of us could be next.'

'Who won't stop?' I said.

'Sofia told me some stories about Robert. About how he really was strong enough to kill Bobby, that he was sick inside. I think she wanted me to protect her, thought she was in danger. Then Robert turns up dead.'

'When did she tell you all this?' I said.

He ignored the question, stormed out of my room. I followed him into his, trying to stop myself from feeling an ache inside from wondering what intimate hours they had spent together. He tried to slam his door, but I caught it. As

I stepped inside, I saw his bathroom door close and heard him muttering behind it:

'I knew they were trying to frame me. They must have put that blood on my shoes. Picked me because I was an easy target.'

'OK ...' I said. I wasn't sure if he was onto something or was coming undone.

I heard him drinking from the tap. My mood plummeted too. It felt like he had been holding this back for a while.

'I shouldn't have taken that money, the twelve grand,' he said. 'It'll seem like a bribe. You were right, they've bound me to them. It's a weight, pulling me down to the bottom.'

'Just stay calm,' I repeated.

'I waded into a fight in a bar in Soho to see what it felt like to punch someone and be punched. I did it again, protecting a girl from a sleazy guy in a bar. Got a police caution for assault. I think they chose me because of that, because I had a history of fighting back, because it would make me a likely suspect.'

On the other side of the bathroom door, I didn't know what to think. The extent of his anxiety made me feel more composed by comparison.

'Now, I don't even think Robert could've done it. All the things we heard are hearsay, he was an outspoken old guy, nothing more,' Ben went on. 'Everything else was just reputation.'

'Maybe she turned on Robert the same way we just saw her turn on Isabelle. Do you think Sofia pursued him?' I said, putting it together. 'After they met? You think she killed Isa? Then Bobby?'

'No. No, I don't think so,' Ben said, sucking in breaths. 'She seemed just as scared as us. You wanted me to ask her some questions and that's what I found out.'

There was a silence beyond the door. There was nothing we could do there and then until we knew more. I had to calm him down so I could get him to act normally downstairs. It's an unnerving feeling, that responsibility. You have to put your own fears away because, as much as I felt overwhelmed, we needed composure.

'What was on the phone you found back at the bar?'

'Numbers and figures,' he said, 'and I don't think you want to know the rest. Bobby was killed because of it.'

'No, no secrets,' I said. 'Not from each other. Listen, I'll keep us safe.'

He gave a dark laugh at that, as if safety was long gone. 'It's screenshots of Robert's accounts. Bobby's emails show he sent those images to the papers a few days before he got to the island. He leaked the story. It got him killed. And now I have it, so what do you think happens next? I saw all this coming so long ago, but I walked right into it.'

'Please, I'm with you,' I said. 'We'll call their bluff. Share it with them all so we have nothing to hide.' I heard him breathe heavier at the thought of that. 'Just put on a good face now.'

'The only question is whether they choose to make me the killer or the next body,' he said. 'I don't think a good face can save me. But thanks.'

'Just try and breathe through it,' I said. 'Stay calm now.' And without speaking, the two of us sat there breathing, in and out, in and out, on either side of the door. I don't know how much time passed, but at some point there was a knock on his bedroom door.

'Yes?' Ben said, struggling to keep his emotions inside.

I flinched as Kostas' voice came from behind Ben's bedroom door, sounding far steadier: 'It's dinner. Come. Eat something. We are all expected.'

As his footsteps went away, we remained silent.

'I could tell Jeanette that Robert and Bobby were murdered,' Ben said. 'But then they'd kill me and you and her too.'

'Try and put your fears away,' I said. 'We don't know anything for sure. Just try and be yourself.'

'And who's that?' he said. 'I'm not sure any more.'

I hesitated at the strange question, deciding he needed bolstering. 'You're …' I said slowly … 'a good influence. Friendly, if a little shy at first. Very proper, but with a mischievous side,' I said, feeling my voice crack at the truth of that. 'A world of contradictions. But with a sense of humour, justice, duty. So, can you come downstairs, and do your duty, for everyone involved?'

And after a long hiatus, I heard the lock of the bathroom door slide open and his voice came again: 'OK. I think I can play it.'

29

Dinner

Sofia

'Thanks so much for making a fuss of me,' Jeanette said, dropping a heavy hand on my shoulder and squeezing. Kostas, Amelia and I were sitting, while she wandered, holding court with a glass of plonk in her hand. I looked up at her and smiled and, at that moment, Ben entered the kitchen, murmuring a quiet hello. Kostas patted Ben on the back and he visibly twitched.

The maids had headed through the gates to their rooms, but the fridge was always stocked with fresh dolmades, feta and other local produce. Ben busied himself putting it all together.

'Looks wonderful,' Jeanette said, shaking her pill box and popping a couple. Everyone was on something, it turned out. 'I won't be having the tomatoes or anything too acidic. My ulcers.'

She had had that problem for some years, I remembered. The coffee she had on arrival and the plonk she was knocking back as we sat there probably wouldn't help. But then, these choices were what got her into that state in the first place. She often admitted she should take better care of herself.

'I'm sorry I didn't say a proper hello,' Jeanette said, sitting, as Ben leant over her to lay the food on the table, the cutlery coming down harder than he intended. Finally, he turned his head to face her for the first time that evening.

'I've been treating you like the lobby boy,' Jeanette said to Ben, 'but from what Sofia says, you've quickly become part of the furniture.'

'Really?' he said. 'No. Feels like I've barely been with the family five minutes.'

He looked in my direction. Jeanette stared at him like an onlooker observing a drowning man.

'Fast friends with JR, Sofia was saying,' Jeanette said. 'Fast friends with everyone. Even Robert, now *that's* something. *That's* the kind of person who only comes along a handful of times per century.'

Kostas laughed as he sipped his Zinfandel. We could've said it then, it might've felt natural, but none of us wanted to be the one to do it.

The nerves were catching, like some infection. The rain outside started to sound to me like choral voices in a distant room.

'No, I wouldn't say,' Ben mumbled, having gone back to that posher voice he used at the interview. 'I mean, if Robert was fond of me,' our hearts were in our mouths – he had just referred to Robert in the past tense, 'if he likes me, I'm flattered of course.'

'Here's to good friends,' Jeanette bellowed, toasting us all. She had enforced a bright and bustling energy on the house and the further she dragged the mood that way, the more the revelation about Robert's death would seem like we were withholding.

Boisterously, she banged her fist on the kitchen table a few times. We must've all been staring, because she threw up her hands with a smirk. 'You caught me, I'm trying to wake the old man. Can you blame me? I want to see my brother, after all this time.'

'Oh Jeanette,' I said, looking at Kostas, 'I'm sorry to have to tell you this, but Robert ...'

'Needs his sleep, I know. I just keep picturing that lift starting to come down and then there he'll be ... no, no, I know, *very naughty*,' she said, looking at me when she said those last two words.

For a few minutes I managed to keep the conversation going, surprised at how automatic it all was. Ben rallied and joined in after a while, the laughs nearly in the right places. Meanwhile, I felt extraordinarily thin, like I'd been scraped back to the flesh.

'Robert, Robert, Robert,' Jeanette kept saying. I had the sudden urge to blurt out who had a hold over me there and then, but I knew what the consequences would be. If I took her aside surreptitiously, my keeper might be apprehended, but all the truths I would have to give away to do it couldn't be put back in the box. They would damn me even as they did my keeper. And it was too late for that now.

'I always thought it was such a shame he couldn't find the right person to start a family with when he was a younger man,' Jeanette was saying when I tuned back in. 'But he had particular tastes. And finally they were all met in our dear Sofia.'

She smiled at me across the table. 'You wooed him, didn't you, Sofe? A campaign of love letters, so he told me. So modern for the younger woman to do the chasing.'

I saw Ben flinch, then catch my eye. Maybe she had come here to say something specific. Next, I felt sure she'd mention the fact he was still married to Isa at the time.

'Would you like some bread and honey?' Ben said to her. 'It's all local.'

'No, thank you,' she said, 'good for allergies, I hear. And in all my years coming here I've never tried it.'

'It's very nice,' he said, searching for something to say.

'Oh, I'm full as it is,' she said, standing suddenly. 'Bedtime, I think, but don't worry, I'll have more energy by tomorrow.' And when we simply smiled back, she wandered over to the lift. I needed her away from there for her own safety. I saw Amelia fold her arms tight. 'But before I go, I should just say a little hello to my big brother.'

'You can't,' Kostas said, and Jeanette gave him a dark look. She had seemed determined to barely acknowledge him before that.

'Oh, I know how protective you are of him,' she said. 'You see, I thought the surprise was for Robert. But it seems I was a surprise for all of you.'

'What do you mean?' Isabelle said.

'I was invited. Natty little envelope with lovely brief message. *Just an ordinary dinner for eight at a grand house*, it read. *We'd be so pleased to have you. But let's keep it a secret, shall we?* Then the address and date of Robert's birthday.'

We froze, glasses in hand.

'But,' Isabelle said, reformatting the question. 'Who sent you the—'

'I know who sent it,' Jeanette said. 'It was you Sofia, wasn't it? Always nice to have surprises to spice up a weekend away.'

I felt their eyes on me.

'Of course,' I said. 'Robert does get so very bored. Unless there are surprises.'

The others glanced at me to register their shock.

'But this one shouldn't be too much of a shock,' Jeanette said, not moving away from that lift. 'Robert and I had been back in contact over the phone of late. I've been lobbying to get us all back here for some time. So, I was glad you didn't all come back without me. Now, I know you think I'm naughty, but I'm going to wake my big brother—'

As she pressed the button for the lift, the voice came.

'I'm sorry, Jeanette,' Amelia said.

Jeanette paused.

'Robert passed away last night.' Amelia said, stepping forward.

Jeanette's hand was frozen on the button as the lift appeared in front of her.

Amelia focused her eyes on me and it wasn't hard by then for my tears to come. 'We've been beside ourselves, as you can imagine. We didn't know how to begin to tell you.'

Jeanette's face turned. The others held their breath. For a moment it was only me facing the force of her emotions. I stood. Her hands tensed as she came towards me, but then she opted against a hug and stood there, face covered by a temple of fingers. And for a good while there was only sobbing. I went closer but opted not to touch her, softly explaining that Robert had gone gently, the others bowing their heads out of respect to the tragic details.

'Why leave it so long?' she said, a weight hitting my gut

249

at the realisation we should have told her sooner. But then, shaking her head in admonishment, she clarified her meaning, 'why did I leave it so long to get back in touch?'

'You can't blame yourself,' I said, in a gasp that held some relief. 'No one could say you, of all people, has anything to answer for.'

She nodded as she placed a hand on my face and then something altered in her eyes; a new thought we weren't privy to was held in front of us for a few seconds.

'Do you know what?' she said. 'I've had a long journey, I think I'd better head straight to my bed, though I know I won't sleep. Who wants to—'

'I will show you to your room,' Kostas said.

'Not you,' she said. 'I'll take the girl. But I suggest you all come up soon. You look awful, now I know why. Let's get some rest.'

I saw Amelia shake herself loose, as she took Jeanette upstairs, the rest of us exchanging sharpened glances before we slowly began to follow her. All of us apart from Ben, who hung back, waiting for Isabelle, I noticed.

When the other doors closed, I listened at the top of the stairs. I could just see the tops of their heads and the space between the two of them.

'I know everyone wants me to be quiet, but I can't do that,' he said, realising his voice was too loud when she hushed him. She grabbed his hand and squeezed it, and not in a kindly way. But Ben couldn't be dissuaded. 'Was Isa's death made to look like suicide too? Who was around back then? All of you, except Sofia?'

'Oh, she was there in spirit,' she said, seeming to relish it.

Jeanette knew about my letters to Robert back then, so of course Isabelle did too. 'They were in correspondence,' she said, evenly.

He took a breath.

'Then. Did she know Isa was trying to take everything?' he said. And all this had started with him trying to discount me. If I was charitable, he sounded like a man who wanted to know what he was getting into. But the insinuation in what he said next was far from charitable. 'If Isa managed it, then the man Sofia was pursuing would be worth a fair amount less.'

I held my breath.

'Perhaps,' she said.

It burnt to hear him talk like that after all we'd done and shared. If he doubted me, he should've come to me first. He drew breath. 'Then that might be reason to—'

'Look, whatever you're thinking, Isa did it herself and it was terribly sad. Not just because Robert loved her so dearly, but because it seemed to start the domino of events which is ending here. Whatever you've been told, this isn't the kind of story you think it is. It's a tragedy. And it's Robert's. That's the curse of Robert Rathwell and don't let anyone tell you otherwise. Isa's death punished him, Bobby's destroyed him, then someone murdered what was left of him. And we'll deal with them as soon as Jeanette's gone. Isa came to collect her things the day she died, I let her in. At some point she was left alone in the garden and that's when she did it. Whatever my feelings towards Sofia, she wasn't anywhere near the house that day.'

I'd been quite convinced she wouldn't speak up on my behalf. My estimation of her changed quite sharply then. It seemed she really was trying to find out what was happening here, just as I was. As for Ben, he had taken an idea his fears had handed him and started running with it. He was a scared child charging in all the wrong directions. I cursed myself for thinking he could protect me.

As they broke apart, I quickly went to bed, closed my door and locked it behind me to keep him out.

The nocturnes

Isabelle

That night I considered knocking on Sofia's door. After Robert's death, I felt I had to try to soothe the divisions that had emerged between us.

I also needed to voice my concerns about Kostas, which were swelling with every moment. He had a sad resolve about him, the way he defended Robert's honour. You could say it was all to make up for his faults in not staying with Robert every moment he could, but it seemed to me more in line with how Kostas had always doted on Sofia. I remember that day in the Bahamas when he took a photo of her entering the sea, the picture on the wall. Everyone seemed to think it was wonderful. An artistic side we didn't know he had. But the truth was I'd seen him take photos of her before, just at a distance, making out he was snapping a bird, the sky or the trees, careful that no one would think he was taking a photo of her. But I knew what it was.

I opened my bedroom door in silence. So quiet was I in fact that the figure across the landing, standing in front of her door, didn't even appear to hear me, despite being just a matter of steps away.

I edged closer and still he didn't move. 'What are you doing?' I said.

Ben stood stock-still in front of Sofia's closed door. It's possible he followed a noise.

'What *are* you *doing*?' I repeated. 'Are you asleep?'

I stepped closer, still he didn't move. I stood at his side and passed a hand in front of his eyes. Suddenly he stirred and turned to me sharply.

'Sorry,' he said. 'I was just thinking … that … d'you know, I think I must be half asleep.'

I wondered why he could possibly be here. Did he want to apologise to Sofia for the suspicions he'd told me of downstairs?

'Go back to bed, everything's fine,' I said.

But that didn't seem to calm him at all.

'What about you?' Ben said. 'What are you doing up at this time of night?'

He had regained some of his boldness.

'I heard someone outside her door and wanted to see what was going on,' I said. 'So, you see, you needn't worry. I hear everything. Even you.'

We both turned to look at the door, safe in the knowledge that neither of us would be venturing beyond it tonight.

'I need to show you something,' Ben said. I didn't go at first, then I was wandering downstairs after him and suddenly we were at the door of his room and he was beckoning me in.

Inside, he reached under his bed, removing a floorboard before he emerged with something black in his hand. When he flicked on his bedside lamp, we stood there looking at the broken cable ties. The same kind that must've bound Bobby's wrists.

I looked up at him, waiting for some kind of confession.

'I found these in JR's room today,' he said. 'On a shelf behind his poster. I don't know where he got them from, but I wanted to get to it before Kostas did.'

The fact they'd been hidden wasn't good. If Ben's story was true, why had he been sitting on it so long?

'I've been thinking,' he said. 'Maybe JR caught Bobby, the bad boy his dad told him about, in the middle of the night. Did something with his knife. Then, maybe he was very angry with his daddy. I haven't told anyone until now, because I didn't want it to be true.'

I wanted to laugh it off, but then I considered what people had said about JR in his young life, the things we had thought so extreme and irrational. I thought about the scratch on JR's hand and how he was given to rages. Robert wouldn't have been such a difficult light to snuff out.

'You were back before we were,' I said to him. 'You, JR and Sofia were in the house when Amelia, Kostas and I were out. Don't think I hadn't noticed. Did you leave him alone upstairs, even for a second?'

Ben struggled with it, he shook his head for a long time, but I couldn't tell whether he was thinking or deciding what to tell me. His lips remained closed, but then he began to nod, with a reluctant look on his face.

'When I asked who took the knife,' I said. 'He said he thought it might've been you.'

Ben shook his head in disbelief. I couldn't tell if he felt JR had been calculating, or he was just a disturbed child, telling tales and watching where the pieces fall.

'I hope you know that's not true,' he said. 'And what about the cat?'

My hand went to my head, I was hot with shame. I had to put the story straight about that animal. But this wasn't the time or place to talk about that.

Under the lamplight, Ben was whispering again. 'When I first saw the cable ties, I thought maybe they were put there, just like the blood was put on my shoes.'

I didn't want to touch the second part, but the first made sense. 'JR couldn't have done it. The idea is a joke, it's the imagination running wild, it's hysteria. Give the ties to me,' I said, and Ben wavered, but then passed them over. I took them, using the cloth he held them in, and started to go.

'We will find out who's doing this?' Ben said, with a rising inflection that made him sound like JR. I wasn't sure what to say as I looked at him there. So, he changed his question to something more concrete. 'Will you keep that safe?'

I simply nodded and he whispered, 'Goodnight' as I left him, heading back up to my room. I remembered my father talking about international relations, and how the main thing that staves off all-out war is balance of power.

I wandered past Sofia's room. It wasn't true that I heard everything in the house, I did have to sleep sometimes. But as I've got older I've needed less sleep than most. When I got back to my bed, I lay awake in thought.

Ben may have been trying to get into Sofia's room when I found him, of course, because he had been fucking her in the night hours. I crept into the corridor to confirm my suspicions about that last night. I felt, had I not disturbed him, he would've come to the inevitable conclusion that if he was still welcome there, he would have known it.

31

The unravelling

Amelia

When I woke that morning, the others were already up. I heard voices from JR's room as I stepped quietly into the hallway and heard Jeanette being reunited with her nephew. Stopping by JR's open door, I listened to them talk.

'If you like, we can share things,' she said to him. 'I don't like secrets anyway. Now, when you have money, you start to worry about who is trying to take it. It's supposed to make you strong, but it can make you weak. It can make you disappointed in wonderful things. It can make you care about having all the power and success when it'd be better to have no expectations at all. So much so that you might worry about people like me. Even if all I want is a visit every so often and a card at Christmas. That's why I haven't seen you in so long. But it wasn't his fault, it was the money.'

There was a long pause. 'I loved dad so much,' JR said eventually, and I heard him tear up and Jeanette hold him.

I'd never heard him say anything like that before. Even as things were falling apart around him, I saw JR becoming something else, something better, I hoped. It was like his senses were opening up and he was defeating the childhood melancholy that held him back.

Wondering where the others were, I descended the stairs, hushed voices drawing me towards the den. It was like the walls of the house were whispering.

'It wasn't JR. The cat,' Isabelle said, my ear to the door as I blinked slowly in shock. 'It's gone on too long already, and I'm to blame.' I heard her voice crumble on the last word. 'After I saw him burying it, I feared what his teachers were saying about him was right, and I suppose I ended up exaggerating what I saw. I told Robert it was brutal to do something like that. I thought it was odd when he disagreed. Then piece by piece, over a matter of days, he admitted to it and made it clear he would've seen me changing my story as disloyalty. Robert went hunting often, that generation view animals differently, he said it was a pest that needed putting out of its misery.'

I heard Sofia gasp and swallow this reality before a dying sigh. They had all started a summit early that morning without me, but I refused to be left out. I threw the door open and slipped inside.

'Oh, I'm starting to understand many things Robert was capable of,' Sofia rasped, starting when she saw me. Kostas, Isabelle and even Ben offered me only a sidewards glance.

Isabelle barely noticed me, however. Looking like she was coming apart from herself a little, she shouted, 'No, now that's another matter entirely. You had your suspicions, based on hearsay. The most terrible thing he did was to that poor little animal. I understand why you think things got even darker. Everyone did. But he was no worse than any other men of his age. Can't you see that? Kostas, you tell her.'

All eyes went to him.

'Some of you wanted to condemn a boy on little evidence, let's not make the same mistake,' Kostas said, lowering the volume. 'Mr Rathwell was not the sum of the worst things he did. Someone took advantage of him.'

Sofia went to speak, but then just stared at him.

Ben glanced at me and took a breath before he spoke up: 'Look, I'd love to stay respectful, but I can't stay quiet.' He pulled out a phone and threw it to Kostas, who caught it and started to study what was on it. 'I went back to the bar, found Bobby's phone. He was leaking Robert's accounts to the press. There's the motive. Robert wasn't just embarrassed by Bobby, he knew he wasn't morally flexible enough to take over his legacy. And he was right, Bobby was actively trying to bring him down and he knew it.'

'I see,' Kostas muttered, scrolling down, before staring back at Ben with a steel gaze. 'I'm keeping this.'

'Do,' Ben went on, growing in spirit. 'Kostas, I think someone put OxyContin in Bobby's food, so his blood would be full of it when he was found. I think someone searched everyone's rooms that night we were at dinner, that was the only time we were all out of them. I think someone confiscated JR's knife. You've already shown yourself very willing to search our rooms behind our backs. And after you took it, the knife ended up in the killer's hands. You and Mr Rathwell arrived at dinner last. So, I hate to test your loyalty, but who was it? You or Mr Rathwell?'

Isabelle cried, losing control: 'This is grotesque, casting aspersions against a man who isn't here to defend himself. Who's barely cold in the ground, it's vile.'

'It makes sense,' Ben said, bringing things back to a whisper, 'and I think you're starting to realise it. Rathwell was a strategist, that was how he made his fortune. He wanted to shut his son up, so he came up with a plan. Maybe he even asked you to steal Isabelle's pills for him, Kostas?'

'You're a natural storyteller,' Kostas smirked. 'But JR is a smart boy and he suspected it was you who took his knife with the rosewood handle. Everyone knows of the evidence on your trainers.'

I saw Ben's jaw clench. 'Someone has been planting evidence on each of us, to turn us against each other. You don't want to believe someone has made a fool of you, or that Rathwell did this. But I think he was working with one of us.'

'The person who left these in JR's room,' Isabelle said, her voice weak, as she placed cable ties on the table between us.

Sofia shook her head as she saw them. 'Who would do that to JR?' she said, her eyes searching out Kostas.

'I don't like to point fingers without reason,' Kostas said, shaking his head as he glanced at Ben.

Ben knew he couldn't be a bystander any more. I wish I could've helped, but I just watched in stunned silence.

'While you're figuring it out, remember this,' he said, 'there's plenty of reasons someone would want to fit me up. And what would be in it for me? I, out of all of us, have nothing to gain.' He looked at Kostas. 'But I think that when you realised Robert had made you an accessory to murder you took your revenge.'

Kostas laughed, sitting deep in his leather armchair, voice so comparatively cool: 'Stories, stories, stories. I see, the investigator becomes the investigated, that's a good one. I was with Isabelle and Amelia when Robert was killed. But Ben, the possibility of Robert's innocence seems to be making you lose control. Do you often lose control? Sofia tells me she's concerned at how you've behaved since Robert's passing. That is what she told me and, after all, she knows you best out of any of us. My conscience is clear, friend. How is yours?'

Kostas' words seemed to speak to my suspicions about Sofia and Ben. My stomach held waves. I held out hope it wasn't true.

'Do you tell your friend Amelia here everything you get up to?' Kostas said. 'Because I don't think you do.'

Ben looked at me, shards of breath falling out of him. I had been so naïve. I thought it was all him and me, there was strength in that, but suddenly it was all a lie and I felt so weak again. I couldn't trust him with my life or my feelings. I felt a sickening ache inside me.

Ben sat down, reduced to silence. Kostas ran a finger along his jawline with a smile. Sofia stared at me, giving away nothing.

I turned on my heel and strode from the room in silence, slamming the door behind me. Anger overwhelmed me as my head pounded at Ben's betrayal. He had used me. I had asked him to get close to Sofia, but they had a deeper alliance already. My breath was tight, my skin tender.

I wanted to phone the police, get it all out in the open, but the line appeared to be down again, and I knew now I had no allies here. I was vulnerable and could easily be silenced for good. My thoughts went to JR. It was him I cared about, not Ben, and I needed to know he was OK. I charged up the stairs, but he wasn't in his bedroom, or Jeanette's.

I went back down and through the kitchen. The maids

passed – holding the last of the trestle tables because we were to have brunch on the suspended viewing deck over the cliff face – but they hadn't seen any sign of him. I charged down the steps to the beach, taking them three at a time. But I couldn't see him there either. The throb in my head consumed my body, all of me beating fast. I fought back the tears.

I closed my eyes, muttering the words that had been said in that little room so I could remember every one of them. It was then as I stood on the beach staring out to sea that I decided to document everything. To spend my rare free waking hours writing down what happened here, recording it all in minute detail, so it could act as my statement. They would all have to suffer the consequences. Even Ben could go straight to hell. Containing the scandal was the family's main priority. Making sure no guilty person went free was mine. I would save myself with the truth.

But that was for the future. Then and there, I opened my eyes and realised I was going nowhere. My feet had sunk deep into the wet sand. Then there was a sudden roar and a clutch of sand flew up behind me. It felt like someone had reached into my ribcage and squeezed.

Looking down, I saw JR and Jeanette in a pit they had made. They had been lying there, buried under towels and sand, waiting for someone to come along they could scare.

I breathed in desperate lungs of air. I couldn't scold him. And certainly not her. I just about managed a smile. I was incrementally learning that I could deal with a great many things.

'We wanted to get under the sand,' JR said, 'to where the dry parts are.'

Expressionless, I sat down on the deeper sand they had exposed, soft as baby skin, and the three of us looked out to sea.

'Heard you having a summit,' Jeanette said, 'I thought we better leave you to it.'

I gave her a gentle smile as the salt wind licked my complexion.

I glanced at JR, deep in mourning, I could tell, I knew it well. He was becoming a mature boy. I was so proud of him. I had thought I was alone after what I'd been told about Ben and Sofia. But I wasn't, I had J. And we just needed to hang on.

32

The pleasure of our company

Isabelle

We ate on the suspended deck, so Jeanette could see the panorama of the waves below, but the wind was up so the tablecloth was jettisoned early. We held on tight to our cutlery. Robert was weighing heavy on Jeanette, as he was on all of us, but she began the meal not with a reminiscence, but with a complaint.

Jeanette pointed her fork at Kostas as she chewed and said, 'Be a love, I need far stronger coffee than this, could you fetch some?'

Sofia had dismissed the maids, now more determined than ever to keep people who didn't need to be there out of the house.

Kostas just smiled and stood, reduced to the lowliest member of staff in one sentence. But JR jumped up, keen to play the waiter, saying, 'I'll go,' as he wandered towards the house, leaving Kostas to beam at Jeanette as she spoke.

'I've been thinking about the word synecdoche,' Jeanette said. 'Have you heard of it before?'

'No,' Sofia said, a little cautious of where this tangent might lead. 'I don't think I have.'

'It means when part of something represents the whole,' she said. 'As in England played the West Indies at cricket. Well, of course, ha, it wasn't England itself, but a team of its best players. Do you see?'

'I see,' I said.

'And Rathwell,' she went on, 'well, say that name and everyone in the country thinks of Robert. But Rathwell is a name for the long line of people that he represented. A lineage of fathers, mothers and children, falling through the ages, and it's only because of the choices of so many Rathwells that Robert ended here in this house, finally. Where we're all sat. That's what heredity is.'

Grief makes philosophers of us all. I'm sure she had a good point, but I was intent on getting Jeanette away from here as soon as possible.

The others made muted noises of agreement and JR placed Jeanette's coffee down, sitting discreetly.

'Robert has shaped all our lives,' Jeanette said, 'whether we're Rathwells or not.'

'So true,' Sofia said, looking nervous.

The morning wind brushed us with its touch and a glass fell, Ben catching it and holding onto the stem. Further away, on the edge of the orchard, a green can toppled over, spilling its contents onto the grass. Amelia got up to right it, as weed-killer could put a great patch in the turf. When she returned, Jeanette's eyes were on Ben, while Amelia could barely look at him.

'Do you know, Ben,' she said, 'I think I recognise you from somewhere. Where would that be?'

Under the spotlight, Ben wilted, shaking his head like he was afraid or embarrassed.

'He's an actor, you see,' Sofia said. 'You must've seen him on television.'

This caused Ben to break out into a shy smile as he nodded, eyes on the table.

'That must be it,' she said. 'What have you been in?'

I spoke up to help too. 'Oh, don't ask him to list his credits. Actors hate that.'

'No, go on,' she said, 'just for me.'

He raised his hands, reddening. 'Well, what have you seen?' he said.

'No, no,' she said. 'There must be something particular. What have you *been in*?'

It had gone past uncomfortable. '*River City*?' he said.

'What's that?' she said.

'It's on Scottish TV,' he said.

'No, no,' she said, 'that's not it. It's … something else?' she said, looking at him ever closer.

'Do you go to the theatre?'

She just shook her head. 'I'll get it. Don't worry, I'll get it. I've seen everything.'

There was a pause, but he cut in before it went on too long. '*Casualty?*'

She screwed up her face. 'That's it,' she said. 'With the defibrillator. Saved a life?'

'Wow,' Ben said, looking brighter. 'Amazing.'

'There you are, see,' she said, buoyed by her victory. 'Here we are, surrounded by musicians, actors. Robert wanted the biggest slice of life he could take. And this setting, and these people gathered here today, are the surest sign that he realised it.'

Kostas placed a hand on Sofia's shoulder, but soon retracted it. The wind threatened to take the baseball cap he was wearing that morning off the cliff, so he pulled it down tight.

Jeanette took a big sip of her coffee to keep her going, then locked eyes with Kostas. An uncomfortable silence followed and, sensing something coming to a head, I said, 'Amelia, perhaps you could take J to the orchard, I imagine he's bored of all this adult talk.'

'Yes,' Jeanette said. 'And we have more adult talk to do.'

Amelia paused, then stood up and led him away, JR looking back with a strangely wise expression.

'I want to see the room where it happened,' Jeanette said. 'It may seem morbid, but it's important to me. I have one brother. I want to know every detail.'

She went to stand but listed a little and sat. I wondered whether she had started to slur, but it could've been my imagination.

'I'll take you there,' Kostas said, standing and putting a hand under her arm, which she immediately slapped off.

'No, n ... not you,' she said, taking a sip of her coffee when her mouth seemed to go dry. She had started so eloquently, but now she was struggling to get her words out. I wondered if she was drinking again. She had struggled with that in the past. 'And n ... no ... not you either,' she said to Sofia.

Sofia looked shocked and I spoke quickly before the situation got out of hand. 'Jeanette, this might not be the best time.'

'Oh, I've always known what's going on,' Jeanette said. Her eyes looked glassy and unfocused, but she struggled through whatever was impairing her. 'I heard you all arguing over your place in the household, I had to take JR away. Don't you care about him at all?'

'Of course,' Sofia said. 'He's everything to me.'

'Ha, well,' Jeanette muttered quiet words to herself as she reached for her water. 'You can continue whatever it is you're fighting over. Young Ben can take me to the room.'

Jeanette looked to Ben who tried to stay calm as he went over to her, but Sofia couldn't contain herself. 'Don't ever say I wouldn't do anything for my boy,' she shouted. 'This is all for him. Everything I've done—'

'Everything?' Jeanette said with a crooked look of triumph on her as she stood. 'What about the things you do with your security man? Behind closed doors? Is that all for JR, is it? For … Robert?'

She swayed like a tall boat on a rough ocean, just as the wind threw a glass onto the oak boards below us and it shattered around her.

Sofia looked to Kostas, who hid his gaze, his hands flat on the tablecloth to stop the crockery from lifting clean off. He wasn't saying a thing. Ben was quite ashen then.

'That's not—' Sofia said. 'That wasn't—' but she found it difficult to deny it. I had no idea. And I prided myself on keeping an eye on even the smallest details.

'I was in the garden one day,' Jeanette said. She seemed to have regained control, I wondered whether it was simply rage that had been affecting her. 'I looked up to the house and there the two of you were, in your room, Sofia. I think you didn't realise how good the sightline is if you're at a certain point in the garden, or perhaps you were just overtaken by passion. You were pushed up against the wall next to your window and that greased pig was whispering in your ear. He pulled the blinds down with one hand, but it was too late, and I told Robert over a Scotch that night. Of course, he didn't want to hear it, that's why he asked me to leave. That's why I haven't been asked back for so long. Because I was disobedient, I told a true story that didn't fit with the one about the trophy wife who really did love him, so I had to be removed.'

'That's not what you saw,' Sofia said. 'Tell her, Kostas?'

But Kostas merely muttered, 'Jeanette, you should be careful of your blood pressure.'

'Oh, do shut up, you horrible little man, you're … the weasel under the cocktail cabinet, nothing but a …' she pitched forward, steadying herself with a hand on the table. 'Robert said I was trying to discredit his wife to get myself back up the food chain, make myself his most trusted woman again, said I was telling *tall tales*. He was sleeping with his eyes open again. Except for the fact that he did believe me … knew it was true … I could see it …'

That's when Jeanette's legs gave out from underneath her. Her body going limp as she dropped, cracking her head hard against the table before she hit the deck.

*

Sofia

I screamed as Jeanette hit the ground. Sprawled on the wooden boards, she reached for her throat. The bruise on her temple protruded so quickly where she hit the table, indigo and scarlet forming fast around it. But there was no blood.

Isabelle went to her. We knew two things: she was

unconscious, but she was also struggling to breathe. Isabelle had done her first aid training and so checked her airways. They weren't blocked but her pulse was fading. She tried to pump her heart but when she went to give her mouth-to-mouth Kostas stopped her, saying it was too dangerous, which seemed obscure at first.

But I also knew that to truly keep the heart going using CPR is a messy thing, you have to be prepared to break a rib. I wondered whether he was wary not to leave a mark on the body. Isabelle stepped back, unsure what to do, then she pushed Kostas away and kept on pumping at Jeanette's chest.

'Get her inside,' Kostas said.

The weather was closing in and we didn't want her to get cold. We moved her as quickly as we could, past the pool, onto the patio. Ben had the legs, Kostas the body. But by the time we got her back inside the black-steel patio doors and into the house, minutes had passed since her fall and we knew it was hopeless. It was done.

We stood back. A foam had escaped from her mouth. Her body was devoid of oxygen and the blood had ceased to pump.

'She was poisoned. And by something particularly potent,' Kostas said, looking up at us all.

'We don't know that for sure,' I said. 'Poisoning can look like many other things. The body struggles, it fights to hang on, it gives in. It could've been her heart. The woman had a bad stomach and insisted on filling herself with toxins. Poisoning can come in many forms.'

'I'm sure,' Isabelle said. 'Odd she was in the process of defaming you when she did it.'

I stayed quiet. Yes, Jeanette had been defaming me, but I had never given myself to Kostas despite his overtures. However, he did know something about me and Adam Sands.

'Sofia would be the most fortunate poisoner in history, to time this in such a way,' Kostas said. 'Jeanette starts to attack her out of nowhere and one minute later she collapses.'

'What about you?' Isabelle said to Kostas. 'You were being defamed too and she clearly hates you.'

My eyes wandered outside to the orchard where I'd seen something left out behind a tree that morning.

'Weed-killer,' Ben said. 'Someone left the weed-killer out. Isn't that—'

'That might ...' Isabelle said. 'That has arsenic in it, doesn't it? Very old-fashioned, but it would work.'

'But I stayed sat right here,' Kostas said. 'It was JR who brought her the coffee.'

I felt my face fall, as I pawed at my collarbone, faintness coming over me at the mention of JR. Ben scratched his arm as he glanced back at the green can. I looked at her and scoffed, she couldn't seriously believe a boy, however extraordinary, whatever predilections running through his family line, would do this.

'But I don't even believe it could be concealed in coffee,' Kostas said, pacing with a different kind of verve in him. 'At least it's bitter, I will give you this, but even the strongest coffee in the world wouldn't conceal enough weed-killer to kill someone that quickly.'

'What if it didn't have to be that much?' Isabelle said, speaking rapid-fire. 'You saw the pills Jeanette took. She takes them to line her stomach and they're supposed to stop her being sick. If this was done by someone who knew her condition, they would know that without the reflex to be sick she would've died of toxic shock sooner rather than later. You could've prepared the coffee earlier somehow.'

'That still leaves why she didn't notice the taste, spit it out,' I said. 'But you are right about one thing, if someone knew she took such pills for her stomach, that would be useful, and how easy would it be to switch them. Isabelle, you seem to have a very willing doctor. I wonder if you could get hold of anything else that might be dangerous if ingested frequently over a short amount of time?'

'If you really thought I did this,' Isabelle said, 'you're even more foolish than I thought.'

Before anyone could reply, I looked back out, beyond the pool and the suspended deck, to the orchard and saw JR and Amelia coming back our way. J had clearly decided he was being kept busy and wanted to know what the adults were doing.

'We have to move the body,' I said.

Ben and Kostas approached Jeanette again. 'This way,' Kostas said with no time to waste. They brought Jeanette's body behind the kitchen island and left her there, Kostas disappearing upstairs towards her room as JR approached the door with Amelia in tow.

We managed to stay calm enough for his questions. We explained that Jeanette had upped and left, that she had been called away urgently and jumped on the boat home. Meanwhile, Ben walked Amelia onto the patio and I could see him explaining what had happened.

J looked between us, sniggering like it was some kind of game. He was finding her sudden leaving difficult to comprehend, and for good reason. Suddenly, he disappeared in the direction of her room and Amelia, seeing him go, went after him.

We heard the lift, and we looked up with bated breath to see Kostas coming down. He had done what he needed to do up there and avoided coming across JR and Amelia coming up the stairs. He also had a new kind of determination about him.

'Well,' he said, 'at least we know who was sending those letters now.'

And at that point, I didn't have a single idea who he meant.

*

Amelia

I followed JR up the stairs, breathing hard.

'She can't have gone so soon, she was just there,' he said. But when we opened the door to Jeanette's room it was empty. All her things were gone. Not to be easily fooled, JR opened every wardrobe, but there was nothing there. He went out into the hall and benignly looked up and down. No sign of her. I saw his eyes darting around, his mind working overtime to solve the puzzle he thought the adults must be setting him. I wanted to teach him how not to be dominated and lied to. Yet, there I was, telling those lies to him myself, and telling myself it was for his own good.

'She really must've left in a hurry,' I said. 'Grief does strange things to people. You know that. It's in most of the books we've read together, J. She probably just needed to get out of here.'

The silence on the ground floor drew JR back down the

stairs. 'I want to check mum's OK,' he said. There was a sense of responsibility in him that had never been there before.

He charged into the kitchen and everyone tensed, leant over the island, waiting for his fit of anger. But instead he hugged his mother tight. They closed their eyes. I bit the inside of my lip.

'Whatever she said,' JR said. 'I'm on your side. I love her too, but not like you.'

There was that word again, his emotional life was blossoming, and it was so strange to see. His sense of perception was sharp too. He had seen the tension in his mother's smile.

'You OK, Amelia?' JR said, noticing something in me too.

'Just feeling a bit nauseous,' I said.

'You look pale too,' he said to Ben.

'I think I'm coming down with something,' Ben said.

Then JR pointed up at the low clouds, glowering at us, instantly distracted. 'Wow,' he said, pressing his face against the Crittall doors. Everything looked tidier, I noticed, as if the others had been busy while we were upstairs, and all was normal again.

'Electrical storm coming,' JR said. Every new event in his young life had begun to offer him an opportunity for wonder. It almost made me cry. 'A lightning strike travels at two hundred and seventy thousand miles an hour,' he continued. 'It would take fifty-five minutes for it to reach the moon.'

I put my hand on his shoulder.

'If you count the distance between the lightning and the thunder you can tell how far away it is,' he said. 'Because of the difference between the speed of light and the speed of sound. It's five seconds for every mile.'

I caught the eyes of the others behind his back, as we watched his enthusiasm and the heavy weather growing. They must've seen how hollowed out I was. We stood there, watching lightning over the sea together, so far away, but getting nearer all the time.

33

The family plot

Isabelle

After Amelia and JR left for the beach, Kostas said we couldn't leave Jeanette in Robert's room as she would start to leak. It was probably those words that made me comply in the beginning. I hated to think of her up there.

I lobbied for her to be placed somewhere, wrapped in plastic, until the police could come, but soon talk turned to scandal again and how, as Jeanette lived alone, had few friends and was given to being away for long periods on a whim, it would be a long time before she was missed. Ben looked uncomfortable, catching my eye. Kostas said that if the police found out she was dead, there would be no keeping any of this quiet. They would shine a light on all of us. Two deaths could be explained away. There would be no coming back from three. And all I really wanted at that point was to get off the island alive. There was also my share of the will to consider. After all, if the police did start digging into our affairs, there would be no controlling what came out. We mentioned scandal again and again like it was a mantra or prayer.

I was about to say that none of it mattered, that we should phone for help, but the words wouldn't come. When everyone else stayed silent, I didn't want to leave myself exposed. I thought some of them would put up more of a fight, but all I saw was a room full of shut mouths. They were scared to speak, of course, worried that they would be the next one to die. Whatever the reasons, as lightning flickered across the sea, we agreed to bury her. Though the storm was heavy, the burial had to be that night, that's what Kostas said. The ground would be softest then, and we'd need all the help we could get with the dig.

Amelia was the only one who refused. When she heard the scrape of Jeanette's body being dragged her way, she looked at us with reddened eyes and said she could have no part of it. And suddenly I, with all my secret doubts, didn't feel the purest amongst us. But the right thing to do never left my racing mind from that moment on.

Sofia told Amelia she understood, stroking her arm, saying she would keep her company inside while it happened. Amelia didn't look enthused by that, but it was clear it was the lesser of all those evils open to her. Sofia had already told the maids to keep shut up inside their lodgings for their own protection that night, from the storm, she said. Ben was an obvious choice to join Kostas, because of his strength, and because he didn't seem like he had it in him to disagree. Then eyes started to flicker my way, as cleaning up everyone's mess was what I did best. Sometimes I wondered if I was doing this just to spite myself, or to prove to my very deceased and very critical father that nothing could break me.

So, there we were, all of us remorseful and compliant. It

was as if no one wanted this covered up at all and no one was responsible. Because that was how it had to seem.

As soon as JR was in bed, we knew we were to wait another hour, until eleven when night would fully cover us, even though we were miles from the nearest island. I sat looking at the clock with ten minutes to go, watching from the bathroom window as Kostas wandered into the orchard to pick the spot.

That's when I took my chance, opening the door quietly and ghosting along the hallway. Everyone else was nowhere to be seen, they had all seemed to take at face value the suggestion that the phone lines were down. But, I hadn't tried them myself, and perhaps the contractor had managed to get them up and running again at his end.

I had decided to go along with things until we were back home and safe, then I could tell all I knew. But our chances of safety were becoming slim to none.

I crept downstairs, the telephone glaring at me. I couldn't let someone get away with this.

I had seen Amelia and Sofia go into their rooms and felt Ben must've been in his too. Kostas was outside, and JR was asleep. The phone was right there. I picked up the receiver, turning my back on the rest of the house to keep my voice down as I lifted it to my ear. My eyes followed the cord from the phone to the socket, running along its every movement. I saw the place where the line had been cut, the mess of wire. My gaze stopped on the two ends, lying apart on the floor. I was frozen, my hand still clutching the phone, as my mind ticked along, listening to the deathly silent phone. I don't know why, I squeezed it harder for a second. Holding on for dear life, perhaps. Then I felt a hand on my shoulder.

I jumped, dropped the phone, it landed hard on the marble floor.

'The line's been cut,' the voice said, behind me. I turned, slowly. It was Ben, his head virtually next to mine. His eyes glowed as he lifted his hand to his lips.

'Don't,' I said.

'Shush,' he said. Suddenly he gripped me hard, looking about him.

'I found the telephone line like this just a second ago,' Ben said. 'I don't know who did it. But I've been thinking, we can't go along with this.'

His desperation was palpable.

'What was that?' I whispered, but he didn't seem to hear it. He stared right into me. 'That,' I said, so quiet it was just breath and a tap of the tongue.

We stood in the dark hallway and listened. I thought I could hear the pat-pat of something approaching. As I looked along the corridor, a shape appeared at the end. Ben gripped my hand. Then I held my breath when we saw the glint of metal emerge from the dark.

Kostas stepped forward, pointing his gun our way. He rubbed the butt of it against his damp forehead to scratch an itch before he spoke. 'You people just won't do as you are told,' he said.

I gave Ben a look.

'Slow, slow,' Kostas said, pointing the gun between both of us.

'You did this,' I said, 'and we're not covering it up for you.'

Kostas smiled, with those eyes that had been lying for some time. This had been a long time coming between us.

'What proof do you have?' he asked.

'I saw you with that weed-killer this morning,' I said. 'And back in London, it's one of your unofficial jobs.'

'That's very circumstantial,' Kostas snorted.

'You planned to kill Bobby with that knife and make it look like suicide,' Ben said. 'But it didn't go as smoothly as you intended. Then I saw the blood on that paving stone.'

Kostas seemed tired. It looked like he'd done a lot of work to get to this point. He didn't even bother batting that away.

'And you're pointing a gun at us,' I said.

We heard the rain come down out there like white noise.

'I just knew you'd need some persuading to do the right thing,' Kostas said. 'We stick to the plan, we protect Robert's good name. This is how it has to be.'

I felt sure Ben would keep talking, but he seemed to lose confidence. How Kostas thought he was doing the right thing we did not know.

'Come on,' Kostas said, 'you can run but I have the car and boat keys, and if the weather doesn't kill you, the swim would. Plus, there's only one gun. I would've preferred it if you did this willingly, but the other way is fine.'

We were marched out into the weather, Ben and I glancing to each other as we realised this was how it had to be, any thought of disobedience quashed. The next thing I knew we were counting the gaps between the thunder and the lightning. I didn't think we would really do it, but a gun pointed at you tends to change things. Anywhere within a ten-mile distance was dangerous, we had decided, as lightning has no trouble moving that far. But given the frequency of forks in the sky, we didn't have the luxury of ten miles. We gave ourselves five miles, that meant we needed to maintain a twenty-five-second gap.

I looked up to the house and saw smoke billowing from the chimney. Sofia and Amelia had met as planned in the kitchen. I wonder if he had forced their hand with a weapon too. Or whether they didn't know the turn things had taken. When my look lingered Kostas told me to get back to work.

Ben and I plunged our spades into the mulching ground and flung the dirt back towards the largest of the pear trees.

'Thought we were supposed to stay away from trees in this weather,' I shouted to Kostas.

'We need the cover from the rain,' Kostas said.

It didn't feel wise to be holding a metal spade either, but I'd made my point.

'Just so we are clear,' I said, 'you think she sent the letters? Is that what you think?'

His eyes wandered to both of us, but he said nothing.

My skin tingled as I looked down at her. We ploughed our flashing spades into the ground under a dark canopy of looming cloud,

'You think Jeanette brought us here?' I said. 'Robert told me about those calls between Robert and her, that they weren't always so friendly. You think she sent her message to Bobby to add extra pressure, pretended she got one too, but secretly planned to extort the money while here? She said she had been in Robert's ear about coming back here this summer.' I watched Ben digging into the ground, his hooded top clinging skintight wet, his hair wild.

'I don't think anything like that,' Kostas said. 'I thought it was possible when she arrived at our door, but a blackmailer would be far more careful with what company she kept, where she slept, what she drank and ate. I knew by the time her body hit the ground she knew nothing of this. If all she had was a belief Sofia and I were having an affair, then she had nothing. Jeanette may have seen us talking close, but it wasn't love talk, more of a disagreement.'

I didn't dare ask what he'd said to her in that room, and he wasn't about to offer it.

I caught Jeanette's eye as she lay there soaked through, flat out on a shower curtain. Her look was as playful and knowing as it had been when she'd arrived and I'd been trying to get her inside to save her from the rain.

Lightning pierced the black canvas like the sky was about to cleave clean in two.

'Then,' I said. 'Why did you kill her?'

Then came the crunch of thunder like a ship hitting rocks. And Ben started to count as he worked away, sweat on rain on sweat.

Kostas didn't answer to that charge. Instead, he said, 'The blackmailer was Bobby alone. And he wasn't coming here because he was a bleeding heart. He was furious he wasn't in the will and wanted his father's money and was happy to drive his father into the grave while he did it, even though Robert funded his whole lifestyle. Bobby was a bad, bad boy.'

Ben stopped digging.

'*How do you sleep?*' I said, though I kept on talking fast before he thought it was a genuine question directed at him. 'It was aimed at Robert, about his ex-wife's death. Simple as that.'

Kostas shrugged. 'Not quite that simple. He kept the meaning elusive to trouble you all. Lit a fire in a house of secrets to smoke you all out. Sofia may well have something to hide, but it's not about me.'

I glanced up at Kostas, not wanting to say a word on that matter. He simply put the gun in his holster, rolled his shirt sleeves up past his biceps and started to dig too.

'I have to admit,' I said instead. 'I thought they meant me and my little pill problem. '*How do you sleep?* Given all those pills you take. A pretty practical question really. And they're right, the pill relaxes you, but take too many and they're hard to sleep on.'

'Thirty-five seconds,' Ben shouted. We nodded to each other, seeing the hole we'd made, a decent shape but nowhere near deep enough yet. Another great light show began above us, and Ben started digging and counting once again.

'So, everything you've done is for Robert's protection?' I shouted.

'Just as you say,' Kostas said, showing me the whites of his eyes through the rain. 'This is my job. And always has been.'

I had to ask the obvious question. 'Then why is Robert dead?'

He breathed through his nose as he gritted his teeth. 'I'm not going to lie to you. Take my admittance as an article of faith. Bobby needed dealing with.' I saw the steel in him as he said it. 'But I didn't kill anyone else. Bobby had an accomplice. I believe they are responsible and they are amongst us.'

I stopped digging, my muscles shaking they were aching so much, my breath high in my chest. Nothing sounded better than getting out of here. But Ben looked even worse for wear.

'As much as I want to find out who did that to Robert, I don't want to go to prison for protecting him from Bobby,' Kostas said, panting in the rain. 'All I want is to get out of here alive.'

Ben and I paused to look at him after he said that.

'You mean, you're going to … let us out of here?' Ben said, grabbing desperate breaths.

Another rupture above us, like heavy artillery.

'When everything is set right. The day after tomorrow,' Kostas said, 'it clears fast on these islands. As soon as it does, we will sail.'

'Thirty seconds,' Ben said.

We looked at the ditch filling with water, the job not nearly done. I looked down at her again. I felt standing water in my eyes. She was a good person, full of life and hope. I still believed that. No matter what she did or didn't do. I would see she was remembered when we got home. I just didn't know how yet or what I would do to see justice prevail.

More fireworks in the sky.

'It's getting closer,' Ben said, I could see there were tears in his eyes too. 'We need to—'

'We need to rest in shifts,' Kostas said, his voice shredded. 'One of us rests while the others finish the hole, then we swap to lift the body down. We'll be done in a few hours, long before morning light comes.'

'You'll let us do that?' Ben said.

'I don't see that there's any other way. You try to escape,' Kostas said, revealing the gun again, like he was showing a horse his whip. 'It's a small island. I'll find you.'

'You go inside first,' I said. My back ached, I popped another pill. I was a glutton for punishment, but I also knew Ben was done for the time being, given how hard he'd worked.

He wanted to disagree but didn't have it in him and, after a wet pat on the back by Kostas, we watched him head back to the house. I imagined Ben would tell Sofia and Amelia about what Kostas had revealed. But I had a feeling Kostas no longer cared. He had the gun and we had nowhere to go.

I turned to Kostas, leaning on my spade as Ben went into the warm. Kostas' biceps and shoulders flexed as he dug, rain revealing his imposing muscular core.

'What did Robert have on you then?' I said, and his blank look had no challenge in it at all. 'Sometimes I think I was flattering myself that he didn't know about my pills. Leverage made it easier for him to trust people. What did he have on you?'

'Nothing,' Kostas smiled, through the effort and weather. 'The leverage was that I came from nothing, and he put me in his beautiful world. I was grateful. He was my friend.'

It's true, it wasn't hard to see how much he admired Robert. Kostas had a lot in him, his endurance was impressive, and he was fast, his broad back straining as he straightened, like some powerful workhorse. If I tried to grab that gun, it would be a foolish move. But still, I was done with playing nice.

'You don't really believe this will just go away, do you?'

'Of course not,' Kostas said. 'I just need the others to think it's a possibility. I was thinking on my feet. You get used to it, in my profession. But you and I know Robert's killer isn't going to get away with this. Let me tell you what's going to happen. Let me tell you how we make sure justice gets done.'

It was rich coming from him. I began to dig again as the thunder sounded like a snare drum, but this time we didn't even bother counting. Instead, he just talked and talked.

34

Perfect sunrise

Amelia

I woke early, when the rest of the house was asleep, to watch the changing colours of morning from my bedroom window and write feverishly in my journal. The darkest blue at the sky's peak to deep pink nearer the horizon. The storm had broken, and everything left behind was cracked and beautiful. It felt undeserved. So perfect that every other sky was just a sad, printed imitation.

I had been party to a terrible thing, though I hadn't seen her expire or be disposed of. I tried the phone line as soon as they went into the storm. When I saw the cut cords lying across the floor, I knew it was too late. I could only feel better when I wrote everything down, telling myself I would use it as soon as I could.

I slipped my thin notebook into my pocket, deciding to keep it close at all times. Then I went into the hall to see Mr Rathwell's door open, with JR and a very tired Ben staring out on the balcony.

I went and sat down. JR said nothing, just put an arm

around me. I saw he already had his feet on Ben, who looked harrowed at what had been forced on him the night before. In many ways, I felt I could only take my stand because he complied. Part of me didn't want to see him, but he was a difficult person to hate. When he reached for my hand behind JR's back, I squeezed it then let it go. The thought of him and Sofia clung to me when our hands touched. But when he looked up at me, sullied and lost, I did manage a smile. He needed me as much as I needed him. We talked about what we would do when we left the island, which must have seemed so casual for JR, but held so much comfort and hope for Ben and me. Then, when talk turned to family and friends, JR put a hand on Ben's arm.

'What's your family like?' JR said.

'Oh,' Ben said. 'Not so different to this.'

'That's hard to believe,' said JR.

I gave a soft laugh when Ben couldn't, finding some catharsis in the levity J brought. I held JR close and marvelled at his ability to rise above all of this.

'My mother's not very well as it happens,' Ben said with a change of tone, his face reddened with emotion ... 'J, I'm just so tired.'

But JR just tapped him on the back and excused himself: 'I'll get us all some coffee.'

I stared at him, this young man, as he left. I realised I didn't give Ben enough credit for his part in it. Or for the ways he had kept me from harm.

'Hey,' JR said, 'I saw someone lit the fire last night. No fair, I wanted to do that.'

Ben just shrugged. 'Sorry, buddy, someone got cold, I guess.'

As JR left us, I decided not to fill Ben in on the details of the fire as they ran the risk of compromising him even more. I recalled Sofia spent most of the night bleaching the patio of all traces of Jeanette and, when I didn't help, it gradually became fine to remove myself upstairs. I'd torn out the pages of my bible and placed the notebook inside it. By the time I'd come down, the pink marble fireplace in the kitchen was blazing away, the logs covered in firelighters, as Sofia gave Jeanette's personal effects to the flames.

'Anything that won't burn can be buried,' she'd said to me as I came into the room. There was a fever about her, as if the energy of her spring cleaning could protect her from the reality of it. Her words searched me out, asking me to sign off on what was happening by being informed, but I remained blank.

She told me we would say Jeanette never made it to us, muddy the timescale, so the deaths didn't run together.

'This isn't what I want either,' she said as if to scold me for thinking otherwise. 'But it's what we have to do.'

The longer I sat beside Ben on the balcony, the more I began to relax, as if my body forgave him before the rest of me. Soon, my head was on his chest; it felt so good to feel the warmth of someone else, the only person I could trust. Even if he had tested that idea almost to breaking point, I needed him to believe in him, and needed him to believe in me too. I felt his hair on my neck, his soft sweatshirt under my touch, the smell of mud and the ghost of old rain, petrichor they call it, a subtle scent that humans have an instinct to hunt for. I felt like we had hunted each other out, Ben and I. The words in my notebook that looked disguised as a leather-bound bible would separate us from them.

'Let's stay together, until the end, whatever happens,' I said. He'd said the same to me once.

I felt him lean in to kiss me on the forehead. I chose not to push him away this time. But I felt the mark it left.

'There's a plan,' Ben said. 'For getting us out of here.'

There was something sinister about plans made in this house when you weren't around, but I was relieved to hear him say those words. It must've been made late last night, after I'd gone to bed. It made me wonder if he'd been to bed at all.

'Kostas virtually confessed it all, had us at gunpoint,' Ben said. My blood ran cold. I thought of Kostas' face, so reassuring in every moment, when it was just him and me. I thought of Bobby, Robert, Jeanette. 'Didn't deny killing Bobby. But he wouldn't admit to Robert, says he was devoted to him. Isabelle says he was obsessed. Says she didn't know why she didn't see it. It was right there in front of her. He loved Robert so much he wanted to be him, so he's taking his life, Sofia and all.'

I looked into his listless eyes and couldn't believe the way he was talking.

'Then let's go to the police, let's do something, let's—'

'He has a gun, he knows the island, he's the only one who can man the boat. He's clever, he's planned this out, cut the phone lines, taken all the keys, and he's killed before,' Ben said, his voice low. 'We can't go anywhere he doesn't want us to go.'

'So,' I said. 'How do we get out?'

'He wanted to get us all together tonight, so he could *explain everything*. I think he's lost his mind. Sofia said, whatever he wanted to say, she wanted JR as far away from it, and its consequences, as possible. She persuaded him to discuss it on the boat over to the mainland. JR will be far above us, taking a helicopter ride across to Lesvos with the maids. Conditions should be fair enough for us to go tomorrow,' Ben said. 'Until then, we're going to keep things as steady as we can.'

'We play along?' I said.

'Play along,' Ben repeated, when he found the courage to squeeze my hand and look at me. 'Yes. Something like that.'

I looked at him. I'd wondered what the secret to his ease was when we first met. Even if it was a trick, some method of deluding yourself that everything was fine, it was one worth learning. I hoped a little of it had finally rubbed off on me.

'This is just a normal holiday,' he said. 'At least for twenty-four hours.'

*

And so that day we walked to the red sand beach as a family. We were more united than we had ever been, in appearance. Ben and I walked amongst them, as if we were stitched into this dark tapestry as much as the rest of them. As if we weren't hostages.

We soon reached the cliff along the dirt path, flanked by rustic stone walls, not far from the ruins where we were to descend to the red sand beach.

The redness was more vivid than I could have imagined. The salt scent was rich, the air perfectly cool on my skin.

JR ran off, his feet kicking up splashes of red as his mother called for him to be careful, and I watched on behind with the others, trying not to think about how happy these people would be if Ben and I were dead. The sun beat down on us through thick air. I was just a witness, a walking camera.

JR charged back in my direction, clawing at my bag for the snorkel and masks. Then, as I saw Ben, Sofia and Isabelle drift further down the beach, I noticed Kostas was hanging back for me. Somewhere inside, I held a breath. Predictably, he wanted to talk.

'Don't go too far,' I said to JR as I handed over the clear plastic items.

'Are you coming in the water?' J said.

'Just try and stop me.'

We watched him cross the sand and plunge into the sea. Once his head had disappeared and the snorkel poked out of the water, Kostas began.

'You will be well looked after, you know,' he said.

'I think I already have been,' I said, playing dumb. 'What are we talking about, danger money?'

'Something like that,' he said, three words Ben had said not so long ago. 'The payments will appear in your account from a company name. It will lead back to Isabelle, in her role as a patron of the arts. She's just supporting a young musician. With a disability. Think of it as a mentorship.'

'I see,' I said.

My heart fell. Was this why Ben was willing to play along? Money. He had already taken that twelve grand. He and his mother weren't well off, he'd made that clear. Had Kostas managed to make putting up any fight against him so hard and the money so attractive that he was happy just to let it be?

'And what if I don't want the money?' I said, noticing his anger immediately.

'That would make me very unhappy,' he said, giving me

a look like his hand was around my throat. 'Everyone else has decided to do the right thing.'

We both looked out as JR emerged, then waved as he readjusted his mask.

'I wouldn't want to make anyone unhappy,' I said.

'I wouldn't,' he said, 'if I were you.'

Inside, I was shaking. But from somewhere I found a little bravery. 'Can I ask a question? Just one.'

'Depends on the question.'

'Are you carving up the estate between you all?'

I watched the others at the end of the beach. Sofia and Ben had their feet in the water. Isabelle eyed them, further away, sitting on the red sand.

'Sofia is learning to come to terms with what Isabelle meant to Robert. We brokered a three-way split. Sofia won't challenge the will.' Then sniggering as if feeling my next question. 'The third part being JR's. I don't get a cut of this money. Just my small fee.'

He was talking like he was just another put-upon hired hand in a job that wasn't worth the hassle. The tone was strange. But otherwise, it all started to fit into place. Sofia, despite telling me she didn't want it this way, was going to escape with her ex-husband's money. And Isabelle had named her number too. I began to wonder if they had all been in on this from the beginning.

'We discussed it last night after you went to bed,' Kostas said.

'And you're assuming I'll take the money,' I said. 'But what if I don't? You don't need to buy my silence, I'm giving it you for free.'

He spoke through a sigh at first: 'The difficulty with free things is that they don't have any value. Everything worth having is worth something and money has the advantage of carrying an insinuation with it, which is useful for us. Money also has the advantage of being money, which is useful for you. It'll be three million by the time it's done. Think it over.'

Halfway through his words, he really had started to sound like Mr Rathwell. Three million pounds. Seven dark figures lurking into my account that could solve all my problems.

'I don't have to think it over,' I said as I searched around in the bag and gestured to JR that I was coming in.

Kostas folded his arms as he looked at the horizon: 'Don't be a stupid girl—'

'I'll take it,' I said.

I couldn't be the only one to refuse. It would be my death sentence. But I would capture every word in my notebook, write it all down as soon as I could. I was doing all I could to prevent any more bloodshed, especially my own.

I walked along the warm sand, biting my lip, away from him and towards the spot JR had drifted to. But just as I was about to wade into the water, I saw Ben had beaten me to it. I wondered if he really had been silenced, because if he had, I wouldn't be able to spare him. I planned to tell the whole truth, even if it meant throwing Ben to the lions. After all, hadn't he already made a choice of his own? Men have the ability to turn a blind eye in a way I have never allowed myself. Their hapless nature is read as charming, their charm is read as charming. While someone who looks like me has to prove themselves at every turn, and if we finally achieve something through guile and hard work – being all things to all men and women – then we're treated with greater suspicion than before.

As my eyes watched the snorkels on the skin of the water, I realised Kostas had followed me, like a stray dog. He wasn't finished.

'I managed to fix the phone lines this morning, made some calls. We leave tomorrow,' he said, low. 'I know for sure who killed Robert and Jeanette.' He looked me in the eye and I couldn't tell if he was mad or if he was telling the truth. Just because we're paying you to keep quiet, doesn't mean justice won't be done. It will be nice and tidy, you'll see. Then once we get to Lesvos, the rest of you will go your separate ways.'

'What about you?' I said.

'Oh,' he said. 'I'm going to charter another boat and take off on my own for a while. I made enquiries about it a long time ago.'

It figured. 'And on the boat,' I said, searching for some clue as to what Kostas had planned. 'I know Ben isn't much help, but if you want me to do anything, I was a decent sailor when I was younger.'

'Don't worry,' he said, removing his sun glasses to double-check where Ben and JR were. 'You won't have to *do* anything.'

His mouth creased into what might normally be a smile, but expressions had begun to take on other meanings.

He left me to my thoughts and went back to join the others. With a numb feeling spreading through my body, I removed my foot, slung it on the sand, grabbed my snorkel and headed towards the water. I felt the nerves of my empty foot tingling as it dragged along. I submerged myself in the cool water. The mask tightened around my nose and the silence of the deep took over.

Down there, the sea was like a marble ballroom, almost too clear to be real. I swam towards Ben and JR, who were helpless-looking. I saw them attacked from the side by the weight of water, the tide jostling them against their will. It looked so smooth from the shore. As their legs kicked, bubbles shot out behind them. Their movements sent ripples down to the sea bed, kicking up sand. Triangles of quaking sunlight cut through the silent water.

Ben kicked out hard suddenly, then turned to see me, his face as pale as it had been yesterday, hair like thin straws of seaweed. He looked at me, his bare body vulnerable next to the sharp rocks. He stayed so still, in that nowhere place. It felt like we were finally under the covers together, but while anything could be said in an intimate moment like that, here we could say nothing at all. I couldn't admit what I still felt for him, despite what he had done. And he couldn't say sorry, and tell me what he felt for me too. With the translucent pipe in his mouth, as his wide eyes stared at me from behind the mask, I couldn't tell what he was thinking at all.

35

The reckoning

Isabelle

The next day we loaded everything onto the boat, cases, hold-alls of all shapes and sizes, everything, leaving only JR and the maids behind after everyone had been told about their special arrangements.

The sea was calmer than we had expected, Kostas was more than able to handle it. I had convinced him that if we did this on a boat, that special someone had nowhere to go. Being a man of the sea, he liked that, it felt like home territory.

Behind closed doors, voices whispered, and everything had set itself in place.

JR was learning to cook with the maids when we left, which we told him would be very important when he went away to boarding school. It was difficult for him to swallow as he'd never seen a single person cook around him in his youth who wasn't employed by his father. It's possible he knew something was out of the ordinary, but this new version of him was suddenly keen to try new things.

On the deck, the sea beneath us was calm as we headed out

into the blue. Other boats occasionally appeared in our sight-line, which forced us further out in the direction of Lesvos. Kostas skilfully handled the yacht with some help from Ben, who was faring far better than Kostas thought he might.

'Let's find a clear route,' Sofia said, 'so it feels like there's no one else under the sun but us, for miles around.'

This line had been discussed, and she delivered it with utter conviction.

We dropped anchor, there was one single boat in view of us, cutting through the ocean fast, and quite some way away. We waited for it to disappear.

*

Two nights ago, when Amelia had gone to bed and the storm raged, I passed Kostas the spade, soaked from head to toe, and went inside to sit by the great fire Sofia had made.

I sat, trying to stay calm. Kostas knew he was holding all the cards. And seeing me as a woman of tact, with a deep commitment to his master, he trusted I would act accordingly. He had learnt to measure a person from Robert, judging me to be a planner who saw logistics in all things. Yes, he had me pegged.

'I didn't want to bury her, I want you to know that,' I murmured to Sofia. 'Kostas admitted it, killing Bobby, he's confessed. He cut the phone wires and he brought a gun ...'

'He's had me at gunpoint for longer than that.'

She gazed back into the flames. As we spoke I saw the light catch in the standing water in her eyes.

'Kostas has me in the palm of his hand,' Sofia said. 'He

has a habit of calling me from his pocket, even when we're in the same room. I have to go somewhere to speak instantly or there's trouble.'

The idea of a long-standing joint enterprise between Kostas and Sofia was unravelling, shifting in the air, like the great blanket of sea stretched out beyond the house. Some of it had occurred to me a long while ago, other pieces slotted into place once their relationship was suggested by Jeanette, even though Kostas denied it.

'So, when did your affair turn into leverage for Kostas?' I said.

She stared at me in something like disbelief.

'There was never an affair with Kostas,' she said. 'He has something else …'

She faltered.

'You don't have to tell me what it is,' I said. 'But tell me this, did Kostas write those letters or Jeanette or—'

'No, Bobby did. But I wrote the invitation to get him here,' Sofia said. Finally, it all started to unfold before me. 'Robert was paranoid and getting stranger and stranger, but he still couldn't bring himself to take any action against Bobby. However, he did often tell Kostas what a disappointment he was to him and Kostas felt sure Robert was about to cast him away into obscurity. So, determined to prove his worth, Kostas forced me to write to Bobby and help manoeuvre him here, so he could make Robert believe he had turned up unannounced.

'Kostas said he was going to sort out the problem, and, oh God, I knew how unhinged he was, but I hoped he only wanted to rough him up. After watching Ben and Amelia with Bobby at the bar, Kostas came back to stir Robert up into giving him the final go-ahead. Then, on the way to the Aegean Rooms where he planned to creep into Bobby's room and slit his wrists, he noticed the lights were still on at the bar. And when Kostas saw Bobby drive off in the direction of the Grand House, he followed, winding himself up, telling himself it had to be that night. Bobby too had decided that speaking to his father couldn't wait. At the gates, Kostas watched Bobby dismount and, to his horror, take a route he hadn't noticed was possible.

'As cocky as Kostas was when he told me all this during our call the next night, he admitted his mistakes. Behind his façade, Kostas was never a good security man. Bobby crept along the cliff face and into the garden for old time's sake, with the energy of a man determined to kick up a fuss. Kostas hurried through the house and into the orchard, only to see Bobby had passed by him in the dark. He was nearly at the house when Kostas put his hand over his mouth. Those indentations came from the struggle to get the plasticuffs on, the blood was a scratch from Bobby fighting back. Doing it with JR's knife was a little flourish to horrify me further into my silence. Placing him against a tree was a little echo of Isa's death Kostas hadn't intended, but he enjoyed history repeating itself, he said. Once Bobby was dead, I imagined Kostas thought Robert would be thankful. That it might allow him to take Bobby's place in the will.'

I looked at her, unable to believe what she had been party to, and she saw it all in me. 'So, you didn't know he wanted to kill Robert? And Jeanette?'

She shook her head. 'God, no, they were never part of the plan. In fact, it was me who invited Jeanette, just like

I employed Ben. I thought the more witnesses there were, the harder it would be for Kostas to do anything violent. And, it was hard, Ben saw his first mistake – the marks on Bobby's wrists – and Kostas was forced to go along with the idea of murder. Then he had to think on his feet, trying to make each of us suspicious of one another, put the blame on Ben's shoulders, and he made me play my part. Once he'd gone that far he must've seen a chance to go further, with Robert himself. Robert wasn't as pleased as Kostas thought he would be when he came to his senses and learnt that Bobby had been killed. Then when Jeanette came, who'd always despised Kostas, I think he had to kill her in case she saw through it all. She would've contested the will anyway once he was that far in, so she had to go, I suppose. And I brought her here—'

'So, what's his endgame?' I said. 'How does he get to that money?'

Sofia swallowed, this woman without an exit strategy. 'After he gets out of this, he has told me that after some time we must marry, at least legally. And he'll get what he always wanted, to be Robert. He's crazy, but he has a hold over me that has consequences for J's future.' She hesitated, staring in the direction of the orchard. She wiped a tear from her cheek.

I turned it all over in my mind, started to talk it through. 'He's done what he needs to do, he has the gun, and he now knows all about the financial fraud I've committed, just as he does your secret. We're bound up in this in more ways than one.'

I let out a long breath. 'But the police, how was he so confident he could control them? And why slit Bobby's wrists to make it look like his mother's suicide?'

'Sadly, suicide often runs in the family. He thought it

300

suggested a boy who never got over his mother's death, he liked the symmetry of how it all appeared. And as for the police,' she said, 'Georgios was in Kostas' pay this whole time.'

I felt hollowed out. I considered the fact that Georgios didn't even question me at first. Rather than threatening me, he may have thought I was in on it.

'Any other questions?' I had said.

'Should I have?' he had said, not to challenge me, but because he believed I was calling the shots. That was why Kostas was so sure it would be fine.

'But this isn't over. Even if Jeanette and Bobby's deaths might go unpunished,' Sofia said, 'Sir Anthony will push for a full autopsy on Robert back in London. We'll all be implicated. It's too big …'

'What are you saying?' I said, my breath shallow. 'What are you asking me to do?'

She looked at me for a long time. Until her remorse started to harden into something else. 'You must've thought about the logistics of this. Someone *has* to take the fall. There's no other way.'

*

The other boat was just a dot on the horizon and soon would be gone, so I gestured to Kostas to begin, then withdrew to the back of the boat and took out my phone as had been discussed. We'd just reached the point out there where there should've been some signal.

I was to call the police, ask for Georgios and tell him Ben had confessed to the killings in a moment of weakness. We'd hammered out our stories last night accordingly, rich with detail that could only lead back to Ben. He could tell his own story of course, Kostas had assured us, but with us all as witnesses, he wouldn't stand a chance.

As I reached the back of the boat, I knew what was to come next. Kostas had told us he had immobilised people many times, and with Ben's back turned he said he would place an arm around his neck and get him to the deck in one swift move, then bind his wrists. We'd then turn the boat around and deliver him to the waiting police on the shore next to the station, and say we were ready to make our statements.

I looked up from my phone, my eyes caught by a tiny dot on the horizon, and that's when I heard the shouts, the sound of a blunt instrument on a skull. I wondered how much he struggled. I considered again what a series of acts I'd been complicit in and I waited for the moans to subside, but that wasn't happening as quickly as I expected.

I tucked the phone back in my pocket, having not made the call at all. And came back around to the front of the ship to see Kostas bloodied and leaning against the starboard side of the ship, as Ben approached, wielding an oar like a deadly weapon.

Kostas' plan had suffered some adjustments.

*

Sofia

I shook when I saw Kostas' blood run onto the deck. It's strange what necessity makes you become. We had passed our vices to each other, in the name of both protecting a young boy, or getting what we deserved, or just staying alive, until together we were here.

*

Two nights ago, before a roaring fire, I had explained it all to Isabelle. I knew what Robert meant on the balcony when he muttered, *They talk and talk*. It wasn't a group of people, but one in particular. I knew he meant Kostas because he talked endlessly at me too. Once I was here, I found one of those old transceivers placed amongst my things, he must've put it there when we first arrived. Even when I saw the blood on the patio, I had held out hope that whatever had happened wasn't fatal. He had told me to make Ben clean it up, and my room to disobey was small, so I had followed orders. It didn't look like enough blood after all, and I always held out hope Kostas was a pure fantasist.

'And what about Ben?' Isabelle said, by firelight. 'You vetted people yourself because you wanted someone who had a record of defending himself, maybe even losing control a little. But why did you invite him into your bed? Was that part of it?'

I thought no one else knew. I was speechless, and suddenly she was speaking again.

'I imagine you got his fingerprints somehow, Kostas placed blood on his shoes. And the cutting of Robert's nails? Something about planting more DNA on Ben?'

'Something like that,' I said. 'You'd have to ask him. I didn't do any of it. He talks and talks, but he still doesn't tell me everything.'

'He even left those cable ties in JR's room—'

303

'That was a threat he might do something to JR,' I said. I had managed not to mention Kostas to Ben, even as I spilt the truth about Robert to him, and after the cable ties turned up I was relieved I didn't. 'Kostas knew I wasn't being wholly obedient by then. And no, I didn't pick Ben to set him up. But I did want someone who would fight for me, protect me. And I did keep him close, closer than I even intended to, because I was scared.'

'For your life? J's? Or of your secret coming out?'

Her soothing had turned to accusation. If she was implying that if I cared less for my own plight, I would've saved a lot of bloodshed, she was right. The guilt clotted inside me. My hands were pins and needles.

'I can't do this,' I said, wandering to the black steel doors. A rich life can make it hard to be good. I felt like I'd rather run out into the storm and throw myself into the sea than admit to her my weakest parts. 'Doesn't everyone want to save themselves?'

She approached from behind. 'Darling, I don't understand.'

And how could she? I'd held back for so long, even co-opting people who didn't know what they were getting into. If I wanted a real ally, I had to confide in a way that pressure had barred from me. The truth was the only thing that could stir her compassion, it was too late for anything else. What Kostas had on me was about to come loose.

'Robert had Kostas follow me in the days before JR was even conceived. When Kostas found something, he decided to keep it for himself. Does the name Adam Sands mean anything to you?'

'No,' she said.

I exhaled. 'As I'm sure you know, I signed an agreement that made sure I wouldn't marry Robert and disappear months later, a letter arriving in the post telling him I wanted half of everything. He wanted an heir and, as I wanted a child too, this eccentricity didn't seem too harmful to me. I had a test to prove my fertility and all was fine, my position was safe. It was a little demeaning, but I was hardly in a bargaining position given where Robert found me. But the child didn't come, and my future became more unsafe as the days went on. Robert revealed he would never agree to be subjected to tests, believing himself utterly fertile, but the truth was quite different.

'Meanwhile, he became disappointed in me, I wasn't the obedient type of trophy wife he had hoped for. Still, I did love him, but his dissatisfaction meant we were moments away from divorce. That's why I started IVF. I searched through databases of men, looking for eyes that were green with a curve of brown, or other markers of heredity. Then I found Adam Sands' eyes. He had even been in the army as Robert had as a young man, and they were so similar in other ways too. Except Robert went into business and Adam became a doctor – he was far cleverer than Robert, it turned out. Robert saw J's intelligence as confirmation of what he suspected about himself.

'After I'd put Adam and Robert's photos next to each other, I made arrangements, and nine months later JR and I were safe. But Kostas said JR and I would be left with nothing if he exposed the lie. Robert would close off as many work possibilities to me as he could, and I would be back in a bedsit, but this time with JR. Kostas has waited, whispering that name, scattering photos of me around the house, gifts that were really warnings. He explained how the prenup would be watertight even postmortem, how, even though Robert is dead now, I could have everything taken away and be thrown back into poverty. I knew enough law to know he was right. Sir Anthony would see me in court if he thought I'd duped his oldest friend. I thought Kostas just liked leverage the way Robert did, but now I realise he wanted to be stitched into the Rathwell fortune or he would push me out of it. The day simply came when he didn't want to take any more orders. He could wait no longer.'

I pressed my face into the glass, staring out at the orchard and the small shadows and movements within it. Isabelle came to join me, our shoulders touching. Somewhere down there, two bodies were digging hungrily, under a pitch-black sky and great sheets of rain.

'I could never have hurt Ben. And though I feared what Robert became, despite what I knew of you two, I loved him too,' I said.

She seemed to know it. I had given her everything. I hoped everything was enough.

'So, how do we get out of this. You and I?' she said.

I shook my head. 'I'm not sure we can.' I knew how powerful and sharp Kostas was, even if he was a little crazy. I'd walked the line of not disobeying and keeping myself useful while attempting to put things in his way, but he had won every time. 'But we can try,' I said, lifting my gaze. 'We tell Kostas we're going along with it. Then we make another plan.'

*

As Kostas was preparing the knot, Ben hit him with the oar and grabbed the rope he was holding.

Ben said he'd started getting into fights after watching American anti-hero films of the 1970s. He never threw the first punch, he told me.

'The urge to fight,' Ben said on our long night together, 'is simple. Like the sensation that hits a dog when he realises he has to lie down, eat or sleep. A dog isn't self-conscious about being a dog.' And I saw it in him. Ben, even sleepless and strained as he was, took to defending us all so naturally.

Seeing Kostas there bleeding, legs ready to give way, his head split open to the skull, made me want to stop it all, despite the things he'd done to me. And what he wanted to do next: force us all to back him up in some harshly lit courtroom. That's why, in my mind, this wasn't murder, this was true self-defence. By the time Isabelle came back from making that call she never intended to make, it was nearly done.

But Kostas wasn't finished. He leapt up and kicked the wooden wheel of the helm, changing the angle of the rudder beneath us and in turn bringing the boom attached to the sail swinging our way. It missed us, we fell to the starboard side of the boat as it listed, but it hit Ben. And we were too far away.

Kostas recovered, bearing down on him. He scrambled away in the direction of our luggage, under the seating. Ben didn't get there in time to stop Kostas kicking his back, sending him sprawling into the pile of bags. Kostas stamped down on his spine again and again, then breathed out hard in joy as he powered his foot under him and up into his sternum. Ben struggled to breathe, his ear bleeding, as Kostas pushed the hair back behind his own ear and bent down to finish this by lifting him over the side. Ready to let him sink deep beneath the ocean. We could only watch on.

That's when Kostas felt a pain of his own. Amelia had swung herself around from the ground and, with full force, kicked him in the shin with her prosthesis. I could see it all, she just couldn't let that happen to Ben, couldn't let another man dictate her life. Screaming in pain, Kostas bent to drag her along the deck, and Sofia and I were too far away to stop it. Ben pulled at a long black zip on one of the bags. Kostas noticed and let her go, but he wouldn't get to Ben in time. Ben reached inside, turned, and hit Kostas with the croquet mallet, the force of it sending Kostas to the deck for good.

I saw Amelia watching from the ground as she crawled away. She looked like she wanted to stop Ben from going further, but I intervened.

'This is how it has to be,' I murmured. Gradually she realised what we were planning to do.

Ben turned, grabbing the Prusik knot Kostas had prepared from the gleaming wooden deck. He slipped it around Kostas' hands and tightened it.

How could Kostas ever think that we would want a trial, that I would wish to take the stand and defend my story against an attack from some other lawyer, that I'd want the whole thing stretched out longer, with the four of us in league against Ben but always in fear that one of us would turn, for years and years? It would never end.

'I think Robert preferred desperate people,' Ben said, breathing heavily. 'Single-parent children with troubled family lives, with bad or distant fathers. That was what was so attractive about you, Isabelle, me, Amelia. Even you, Sofia. Robert knew all of us were in search of a father.'

'Robert asked me to kill her,' Kostas spat, his bloody lips

murmuring. 'Isa. He asked for my clothes and gloves to dispose of them, but then he kept them, covered in DNA. Said he didn't trust me out in the world, with our secret.' His mouth gave us one last warm smile as he began to lose consciousness. It was like he didn't think it was over yet. 'But still, I lived to serve him, he paid me well. I didn't kill him, one of you did.'

'I don't believe a word of it,' Isabelle choked out.

He had no chance of convincing me he didn't kill Robert; as for Robert's part in Isa's death, I hoped it wasn't true. After Robert died, I'd started to believe my husband wasn't all bad, and I wanted it to stay that way.

Ben heaved Kostas up to the side of the boat with great effort. Kostas hadn't considered that I would fight back, that I hadn't really organised a helicopter for JR, because we were planning to come back. He'd left himself so vulnerable that he'd even looked into going on a trip and told me he had informed Georgios not to be surprised if he disappeared for a while.

It hurt me that he'd put me in this position. The pressure was so strong in my ears I barely heard the voice behind me.

'Don't …' Amelia said, leaning against the starboard side. 'Can't we just let him …'

But it was time. She merely wanted to tell herself that she was against it. I wished I had the luxury of thinking the same. People, I think, are far too worried about how they justify things to themselves.

Kostas looked like a helpless child when Ben pushed him overboard, hands tied behind his back with the Prusick knot he'd made himself. We all watched him flail around in the deep mass. I watched Amelia go to sit alone, place her earbuds in and even begin to read a bible. Then, even stranger, she started scribbling in it, as if her life depended on it.

Amelia

I knew that trauma could make events difficult to recall so I started with the feeling that, even after everything, I was still desperate to pull him back onto the boat and put a stop to all of this. Then I let the rest flow as much as it could. Powered by fear. Aided by adrenaline. My nose bleeding like the guilt was seeping out of me.

Then I sensed someone above me.

Isabelle gripped my wrists as the boat powered back to the shore with Ben at the helm. I felt myself shake under her grasp. The blood from my nose sat on the back of my fingers, but Isabelle barely seemed to notice.

Everyone was in deeper than I was. It made sense they would want to get rid of me.

I cursed myself for not picking up an implement from the kitchen in the night, but I was too afraid they were watching. I could've dug something sharp into her thigh, I could've twisted it, as I had been taught to do once at self-defence. But without that knife, with her standing over me with positional leverage, I would have to wait.

I closed the bible and looked up, my headphones still in my ears playing meditation music.

Ben, who was currently steering us home, had told me he'd spent every moment of alone time over the past couple of days reading about how to single-hand a boat like this, pod-drives, thrusters and all. Now I knew why, but while I knew he was a better sailor than he had let on, he had certainly never done this on his own before and would have his hands full. He couldn't have known Isabelle was bearing down on me, looking to take care of the last loose end.

'Don't blame yourself, you couldn't have known,' Isabelle said, so quiet, sitting next to me. It was all so calm. Having seen such brutality, the fact that it was over and may even have been the right thing to do was difficult to accept.

My throat felt too dry to speak.

'I'm sorry we kept you in the dark,' she said. 'But we didn't know how you'd react. And this was our only chance.'

Something made me think this was white people closing ranks, as they often did. And not telling the likes of me a thing. But another part of me was fighting to believe that it really was over. It certainly seemed that way. What had appeared savage, was the only way we could save ourselves.

'I hope you see this was justice done,' she went on. And I was starting to. Though I should've known she had an insurance policy either way. 'And look, the fact you were here makes you an accessory to everything that's happened in the eyes of the law, particularly as you helped Ben.' It wasn't a smile that I saw behind her eyes, but it was a form of triumph. 'This isn't a threat, it's just a reminder of how things are. Remember that … and we can be friends.'

I took the earbuds from my ears: *Just let the traffic in your mind slow to halt*, said the app. And I said …

'Then let's be friends.'

We got to our feet as she held the small of her back with one hand and passed me another white handkerchief for my nosebleed with the other. She stroked my hair and walked away.

I wiped the blood from my nose with my fingers, the flow ending as quickly as it came. When I looked up, Sofia was staring at me. She held my eyes defiantly until she could no longer. She went to the edge of the boat and looked out at the distance where Kostas, weighed down, was making his way towards a trench of the ocean. It was good to see the death didn't come easily to her.

She beckoned me with a turn of her hand, and I found myself drawing close to stand at her shoulder. Then, with a jolt, she turned. Her eyes were red shallow pools.

'I really am so sorry,' she said, her voice cracking, her accent running the words together. It was like speaking to the true her that lived underneath for the first time. But I was no longer the forgiving kind.

I left her there, staring out as she gripped the side of the boat, her golden hair running down her back, as I went to Ben at the ship's wheel.

He was muttering to himself, trying to find that old ease of his, so he wouldn't seem conspicuous when we landed back at shore. I sat deep in the banquette and watched, trying to do the same. All the while, reminding myself that soon I would go to the police and clear my conscience, to stop my head from throbbing.

I watched Ben shudder as he fought to come to terms with what had happened. Isabelle meticulously went through what looked to be a mental checklist of how to clean the scene, disinfectant in hand. Next, I heard the scrape of her scouring away at the side of the boat, slowly turning it to perfect white again.

Ben had already washed himself clean. Almost perfectly. There was just one long spark of blood that ran from his forehead down past his ear.

Then I saw a boat coming towards us, blossoming in size and speed.

I considered that spot of blood that everyone else had missed. It stared at me like a tick on a piece of homework. For the first time in a while, my head stopped pounding.

'Ben?' I called. But it was like he couldn't hear me. Like he was, in many ways, no longer there. 'Ben?' I tried again as the boat got closer. It was close enough that I could see how well-manned it was. I saw the Greek symbols emblazoned on it, and below that, for a second, I thought it read: *POLICE*.

'Ben?'

36

A richer life

Isabelle

Ben should've weaved further away from them, even through general etiquette, but he had neither the skill nor temperament as the boat came upon us. As they got closer, Amelia leant over and wiped a large red mark from Ben's forehead with the hanky I gave her.

They must've seen it. They just waved.

Written on their boat, below some Greek writing, was *PARADISE*, and those sunburnt men on the stag do waved and shouted something in Italian as we passed them by. We headed for shore, all of us in an eerie stillness, expecting another fly in the cream at any second, but that fly never came.

Three more days and we would make our escape.

*

Our bodies were heavy and tired at the house in those three days, from the adrenaline that had been coursing through us for so long. We finally rested our heads on loungers, blessed by the returning sun, saying little, just feeling the breath in our chests. This was the holiday we all really needed.

I saw Amelia and Sofia become comfortable in each other's presence in the last days at the house, as if some recognition had occurred between them. Amelia's relationship with Ben, however, was more complicated. At first, one would come into a room, only for the other to leave. It was like they were circling each other, waiting for the other to make a false move, or else the right one. Sometimes they had brief and wary conversations. Then one afternoon, I saw them withdraw to the cinema, and I followed, just in case. Waiting in the cool of the projection room, I watched them sit in the red velvet seating. I sat myself in an uncomfortable plastic chair, out of view, and listened.

'Sometimes it seems like,' he said, with care, 'you're wary of me.'

'I'm not,' she said, instantly. 'It's just difficult. After what we've been through.'

'I'm still the same person I always was,' he said.

I stood a little, my head next to the projector, to see them. She nodded. He put his hand close to hers, but she pulled away.

'I promised you we'd be safe. No matter what … I had to …' he said.

I heard her breath, but was it indignation or emotion?

'It's suddenly about us? Or is it about JR? Or Sofia? Or yourself? I'm not sure who you're fighting for. No,' she said, when he had reached out for her touch. 'I asked you if there was anything between you and Sofia and you lied. I thought we had an understanding.'

I think, given all that had happened, she wanted to put the

affection she had for him away for good. If she saw him back home, she would only be haunted. I know I would.

'Just know, I got closer to her because I thought it would help us. You said we couldn't be bystanders, that we had to find out what we were implicated in. And ... then it all just ...' he stayed open-mouthed, but no more words were coming out. He couldn't explain the unexplainable. He muttered something, cursing himself or maybe this place. Then after a long pause he simply said, '... I'm sorry.'

He stood and I left before he wandered away, remaining unseen. It sounded like a break-up, from whatever they might have had.

In a last act, Sofia asked me to make a delivery to the refugee camp consisting of the rest of the perishables and anything – lamps, electrical goods, everything not nailed down – that could be of use. I suppose I should have had more faith in her goodness. I had taken on some terrible habits over the years. Though it would've felt trite to tell her so.

Under a colourful handmade sign that read 'WELCOME', white tents climbing up the dusty hill as far as we could see, the people of the camp seemed more hopeful, thankful, bright, than I could've expected. Sofia had stayed on Korpios with J, so Amelia, Ben and I handed out our wares. Amelia locked eyes on Ben talking to some of the refugees. He seemed to focus in on one man in particular need, separating him from the group, and after a while, Ben palmed him something as he looked around. When we returned to the car, Amelia asked what it was. I looked at Ben to make it clear he was OK to tell her. I had given him the permission of course, otherwise he never could have done it. It was Kostas' passport. Amelia seemed somehow conflicted about it, taking it all in with her eyes, but she appeared to come around. I thought it was a very good idea. It might be useful for Kostas to seem like he was still moving around.

Bobby and Robert's bodies would have to be moved. I would be collecting them on my last day at the house and escorting them back to England in the jet. Georgios told me this was a break with tradition as usually a man would escort a man home, just as a woman would collect the body of a woman. I told him Kostas had disappeared on his travels but not to worry as I'd been doing a man's job for quite some time. He seemed fine with it but didn't wholly understand. I suppose he'd never met a lifestyle assistant before.

In those last days, JR saw a change in all of us and I saw his pains ease, if only incrementally. We swam together on the beach downstairs, cheering him on. Gone was that grey airless feeling that we'd held inside us. As with each hour that passed, we realised it was more likely that there would never be that knock at the door, or that ring on the Bakelite telephone in the hall, that everything had finally reordered itself and was settled.

I had insisted on taking them to the airport, mostly because I wanted to make sure they went, casting them into the sky as I had watched Kostas plunge into the sea and would watch Robert dissolve into the ground. I stayed looking on in the gleam of the departures hall until they all went through. Sofia and JR would have a longer wait for their flight than Amelia and Ben, but we had an instinct to stay close to each other until the last minute.

When I came home, I shut the large front door, and I was

finally alone with my thoughts and my devils in the Grand House.

I teared up as I thought of Robert. I regard the money I will receive as payment for being the custodian of his good name. And, if Robert was seen to be implicated in murder then he would've been removed from being the CEO of his own companies, it would have had financial ramifications to those left behind and, most importantly, the charities he gave millions to. His history would've become a series of lurid facts, with every other achievement of his life just notes in the margins.

I can understand the belief in gossip; he traded in it, selling stories which weren't strictly true, and he died because of one. It was true that Isa's family had requested to have the body exhumed and Robert refused. They may pursue it through the courts, but Isa Marnell had a history of severe depression, and Robert paid for her treatment.

I went through Kostas' personal effects and found his gun. Checking the chamber, I found it had never even been loaded. He had done nearly all of his darkest work with words.

I had been offered the island as part of my settlement; a suggestion Sofia had made. I ran my eyes along the beautifully empty beach, bag packed up at the house in the hallway. Then I saw something wash up on the tide. A black shape against the perfect white sand. I approached it carefully, then slowly bent down to pick it up. It was Bobby's gift, that plastic gun was back to whisper old things to me.

Charging up to the house, I threw a few twigs onto the ashes of the fireplace and got the thing going again, eyes wet, thinking of that poor boy. My job was over and I was finally letting it all in. Twenty minutes later, I watched the plastic gun melt in the fire. The fumes it gave off made me withdraw. The smell would linger, clinging to the walls with a toxicity that would last long after I was gone.

JR, in an intuitive moment on leaving, said, 'I have a feeling we'll never come back.'

Intuition is a quality his father possessed too, passed on more by nurture than nature as it turns out. I for one can't wait to see what kind of man life carves him into. Because he's right, I can't ever come back here. And having paid the tireless maids and every other outstanding bill, I allowed myself one last look at the view as I planted grass seeds over the uneven ground under which Jeanette lay. I decided I would bankroll a search for her when news of her disappearance surfaced, which by then would be a long while since that boatman dropped her off on the island. I had the advantage of knowing it would have either been old Dimitris or Chrisos, who in a lifetime of ferrying people from island to island I had come to realise never even remembered me, and certainly wouldn't keep such a thing as passenger records. I would let the trail go cold after a year or so, then set up a memorial fund for orphans in her name. She loved children so much, though neither of our fates gifted them to us. This was as much of a tribute as I could offer.

My eyes red and hot with thoughts of her and heat from the fire, eventually I dragged myself outside and dangled my feet in the pool one last time, shaking off the quiver, feeling a touch like a schoolgirl. I leant back on my hands and turned my face, without cream, to the raw three o'clock sun. It felt like the first rest I'd had in ten years.

That's when the phone rang.

I rushed up, staggering to my feet and drying them on the

last towel as it rang on. Just my luck that I was left here to deal with this myself. I tried to predict how that bastard Georgios would catch me out in his search of Kostas. The others may have been stopped at departures to share the blame, that would be something, or they might be extradited depending on how much the police had on us, so at least I wouldn't have to endure the ignominy of this, the trial, the spotlight, on my own. But for now, I concluded, I would have to bear the entire thing on my back, as always. I breathed one short blast of air and answered the phone.

'Isabelle?' Sofia said on the other end of the line. I breathed a sigh of relief. 'Something's come up.'

'Is it important?' I said.

'I would say so.'

'Police?' I said. 'I knew it.'

'No, no,' she said, 'nothing like that.'

I sighed. 'Then, whatever is it—'

'Look, I've … there's no other way than to come out and say it. It's Ben, he … Well, I have something to tell you.'

37

Goodbye

Sofia

Ben placed his hand on JR's head as he hugged him close, ruffling his hair and drawing in his scent. There's a scent mothers get from their children, that nature puts there to make sure we safeguard our young. I liked to think that's what I'd done.

'Will you come and see me at school?' JR said.

'Oh,' Ben said, looking at me. 'I'll be busy doing my play. They don't give you many days off at the Royal Shakespeare Company, I'm in three different shows there, so …'

JR's face had already fallen, not so much because of what Ben was saying, but how he was saying it. JR may not have known what a break-up felt like, but he'd seen one in movies and he had become so emotionally astute.

'What I'm saying is,' Ben said, 'I won't see you for a while, but you will see me again and in not so long. That I can tell you for sure.'

'OK,' he said, doing that miffed look kids do when they get emotional and can't express it. But JR wasn't that boy any more and did find the words. 'Thank you for being with me at this important time. It's meant a lot to me.'

Ben was taken aback, and I could see he was trying not to tear up.

I looked over at Amelia in the queue for coffee, flicking through a little bible then placing it back in her bag. I didn't know she was religious.

'Why do people never believe me?' JR said, in a moment of introspection. 'When I say things, like with the cat, I never lie, but everyone seems to think I do. What should I do?'

'I don't think there's anything you can do, mate,' Ben said. 'I suppose when the adults are lying, it's difficult to believe the one person who's telling the truth.'

JR took the words in.

'You're a good guy, Ben,' JR said. 'The absolute best.'

Ben looked away at first. 'J, you've always been a better guy than me. Whatever happens, let's stick together. Deal?'

JR looked up at me as if he didn't want to say yes before reading the small print. But soon he said, 'Deal' too, just as their flight started boarding.

'And remember you're cool,' Ben said. 'And everyone is going to think that at your new school too. But don't be arrogant about it.'

'I won't,' JR said, tearing up. I sensed Ben wanted to say more but before he could JR was drawn away by Amelia, so she could go and buy him a science magazine and give him one last squeeze that I knew would break her heart a little. And suddenly Ben and I were alone.

After a hesitation, I leant in to give him a kiss on the cheek and then drew back to look at him.

'We were never friends,' I said.

It was supposed to speak of intimacy that surpassed anything mundane, but he seemed to take it as a denial of any closeness we ever had. But goodbyes have to be cruel, and so I left the sentiment as it was.

'I thought about knocking on your door in the last few days,' he said.

'You never needed to,' I said.

'You asked me to stay close, to look after you. But I doubted you,' Ben said.

'You too,' I said. 'But I think we can be forgiven for that.'

The queue was moving. JR and I had another hour until our flight, but Ben knew he had to get going.

'And thank you,' I said.

He frowned. It all felt criminally insufficient. Stating all that had passed between us was the bone stuck in my throat. I saw he had developed a twitch that involved hard blinking, quite different to the poise he so often had.

'You don't need to thank—'

'You're a good man,' I said. 'That story you told me about helping the girl get to the refugee camp, that's who you are—'

'It's not. I mean, you don't need to say any of this—'

'And everything *I* did, I did for J,' I said. 'But you weren't part of that, I … whatever we did, it meant something—'

'You used me,' he said and although it came from nowhere for me, he seemed to have wanted to say it for some time. 'What do you think, from a law point of view? You were my employer, whether I wanted it or not, there was a power imbalance. I felt pressured and confused.'

He wasn't smiling, but I felt sure it couldn't be an accusation. 'We used each other,' I said.

'Fuck you,' he said with a smile. It wasn't just the words that made me think of Robert, it was his eyes, something his mouth did. 'You don't know anything about me.'

Then he was smiling, but I couldn't bring myself to smile back. Something awful had been birthed between us. But we had realised at once that talking it away wouldn't make it any better, it would only make us sicker. Crowds of people rushed around us, but we stayed completely still.

'Good luck with your play,' I said, I knew I had to go. 'Goodbye.'

'So cold,' he muttered. 'You sound like Robert. Mum always said he was cold.'

I looked him in the eye. 'What did you say? Your mother ...'

'Did I not say?' he faltered. 'She knew him.'

'But why didn't you—'

'There is no play by the way, no Royal Shakespeare Company. I only said that to seem like I had other things going on. I needed to price myself highly, it's an audition technique really. Never lose the sense of your own importance, especially when others try to dismiss you. Not that any of that stuff's ever done me any good, until now.'

'Oh,' I said as I began to tighten inside. In one way he seemed to take great pride in having tricked me, but behind that I also saw a deep shame. It wasn't such a big lie. What I really wanted to talk about was his mother, but I was also afraid to.

'I suppose there was no TV job we gave you that twelve grand for either?' I said.

He grimaced. 'Sorry. No TV job, my mother begged me not to go because of what she knew of Robert. But I couldn't tell you that, could I? I told Amelia. But then I couldn't tell her everything. Mum didn't want me to come, was distraught when I told her what I'd done, because she knew why I was coming here.'

I paused, sensing something awful about to happen. 'Why were you coming … Sorry, how did your mother know Robert? When—'

'Don't talk about my mother. You pity her, do you?'

'No. But I would love to know how she and Robert—'

We both started to fall apart at the same time.

'She's at stage three of her cancer, but I left her. Like everyone always did.'

The red sundown light streamed in through the tall glass airport windows. I didn't want to go where this was going, didn't want it at all.

'She's got no money, nothing. And nor have I, no direction, no …' he said.

'Whatever your mother …' the place was spinning … 'whatever she thinks …'

'When she decided to be a serious actress, mum changed from her stage name back to her real one. You probably found her acting credit Celia Bowman, but no picture,' Ben said. 'Robert would've known her as Kitty Maurier. At least under Kitty she had a couple of catwalk jobs. After one of those, she met Robert. I think he may have remembered her if he'd heard the right name and seen a good photo. But then you were searching for Celia Bowman. And there's nothing at all under that name. I've checked. Her career simply wasn't remembered. Makes me sad.'

Amelia was waving, I had to dash to save JR from being caught in the crowd as they streamed past him, jostling him, the single stationary part in all that panic.

'Goodbye,' I said.

But he held onto my coat and, when I tried to pull away, he whispered into my ear.

'I needed to find a way to speak to my father,' he said. 'He's a hard man to pin down. Mum had an affair with him, very short-lived, many years ago. She said there was an understanding between them, he knew I was his. But if he didn't want me, then she didn't want anything from him. You know, he didn't even bother offering hush money, things were different back then. All he gave her was a black opal on a chain.'

I closed my eyes, remembered Robert mentioning it on his balcony.

'I thought he could've been pleased, to have me, to know me, but I wasn't something he wanted,' Ben continued. 'She told me about all this when she first got her diagnosis. She didn't want him in my life, but I sought him out. And when I finally saw him, in the flesh, when I spent those moments alone with him, I knew he was my father, and I think he felt it too. I think that's why he said he'd killed two sons, I triggered a memory. I was almost heartened he thought of me, that he saw abandoning me as killing me. Anyway, any recognition faded, but he knew. Just like when I met Bobby, I knew the same.'

I stayed there not moving, my body had become stiff.

'And then I had to stay in that house, knowing Bobby had

done nothing but tell the truth, but dad did plenty. Kostas killed my brother, I wasn't going to let him get away with it. I'm a real shark now. It's strange, I didn't enjoy doing it, but it did feel right.'

'You're wrong,' I said, picturing the similar way their mouths puckered when they smoked together, as I watched through a crack in the doorway. How Robert said it felt like he 'knew him always'. How they said blunt things to wrong-foot each other, with the same dead-eyed look of glee. Quite shark-like, it was true. JR didn't have that at all. How funny that the one son he threw away was the only one capable of taking over his business. 'I'm sure there are many women who think ...' I looked into his eyes, brown with a curve of green above the pupil. I thought Adam Sands' eyes were like Robert's, but they weren't as close as this. 'You can't be—'

'We're not wrong,' he said. 'I've thought about this more than you have. I listened to my mother tell me so many stories about him. It all added up. I set internet alerts for everything that mentioned Rathwell. I couldn't believe you slipped the name into your ad, I guess you hoped for a better standard of candidate. Must've been strange when hardly anyone got back to you. I paid to get past the paywall, to apply, and once I had, I got in touch with the site and pretended to be someone who worked at the house, asked to change the email address that applications came through to. You're not great with technology, as you said when we first met. Or safety. But me? I left nothing up to chance.'

'It's not true,' I said, watching the face before me change. 'I'm sorry, it can't be.'

'It is,' he said. 'I'll test myself against JR.' It stung even to think of the consequences of him doing that.

'I won't let you bring him into this,' I said.

Ben looked over at JR. 'Then we won't. Just in case I'm wrong. There are other ways. I kept a cigarette butt from the one I gave him.'

The fact he had been scheming to this end all the while flashed before me. I saw JR coming back to us and Amelia waving to Ben as the gate was closing.

Then I held his face in a way that from a distance must've seemed fond and, in a way, it did have a little motherly love about it.

'You'll never be part of this family,' I said.

And he held me back. 'Oh, Sofia, I already am. And I'll get everything that's coming to me.'

As a thick swathe of people passed between us and JR, he pulled me close and kissed me on the mouth and we lingered, his head to mine as he whispered one last sweet nothing …

'You won't see me for a while. But you'll be hearing from me.'

38

How do you sleep?

Amelia

By the time I hit the airport that day I had decided I would go to the police when I got home, with my little bible and the journal held inside. No matter who the truth rebounded on, I felt the law should decide what to do with it all. I thought that was the right thing to do.

But I never did. Maybe I couldn't do it to Ben, given I'd pleaded with him not to be a bystander. We said we'd stay together until the end whatever happened, after all. And if I'd told the truth he would surely have been punished most.

All of this, of course, was conditioned by the fact I still had feelings for him, sharp and tender, the kind that wounded me if I thought about them for too long.

But I never let go of that bible. So there was always time.

The next few years brought the most sustained period of work of my life and undoubtedly saved it. I performed some of my favourite pieces, with the most wonderful musicians and conductors, touring to what felt like every major European city and every concert hall I had ever dreamed of playing.

Philip Glass, Shostakovich, Purcell, Prokofiev, Vaughan Williams, Holst, Debussy. The ability to get lost, to be a body performing a function within narrow but fulfilling guidelines. I played for the joy of obeying the rules, I played like my past never existed and the future would never come, I played to avoid my reflection.

Once a performance was over, I would leave the theatre and stroll through Paris, Budapest, Ljubljana, Leipzig, Berlin, Vienna, Bern, St Petersburg, then meet up with the other musicians for a drink at some local bar if my spirits were up to it.

I began to feel more myself, whoever that was, my thirties revealing the fact that my twenties had been a period of suspended animation, when you are presented with all the moves of adulthood and told that if you learn them and play them then you will become whole. You're allowed to live in a house, pay rent, you're forced to stand in post office lines, but it's not until your thirties you realise that your true self was waiting there all along, and you finally slip into your own skin. It's possible I'll feel the same when I reach my forties, I don't know.

My sole wish – not to be left alone with my ghosts – had been granted. A will to work in my chosen profession, which had waned due to the difficulty in finding consistent opportunities to do so, soon began to return. I rarely thought of the little octet that once held me captive on Korpios, and when I did, I wondered how I'd been so intoxicated by proximity to that lifestyle. Those old tensions strung tighter than bow strings. And that's before I even thought about the deaths, which I tried not to.

Contemplation is overrated. It's our angriest critic.

I ignored the amounts that fell into my bank account at regular intervals, making sure I never spent any of it. Nothing lavish or luxurious, though it was tempting. I cordoned it off, away from the cleaner money that sat there, which I didn't want lingering with the dirty. Until finally I decided to use it. I decided on a system of regular anonymous donations, to be dispersed amongst various charities over a number of years, until one day all of it would be gone.

I began to see a woman, who was ten years older than me, a very pretty Hungarian first violin named Max. We met playing Dvorak's *New World Symphony*. Pop classical, my father called it, but I never saw it as that. Some things are popular, I told Dad, because everyone can recognise they're good. That shut him up.

One night at the Brooklyn Academy of Music, we played to a particularly appreciative crowd and I told Max and the others I would see them after my nightly walk.

I remember I took an awkward route, as I'd strolled in all the normal directions on previous nights. This time I wandered down the BQE, the Brooklyn–Queens Expressway, with all its screeching tyres and sudden horns, and a thought about Bobby sneaked past my defences: the gusto with which he entered the fray, like a percussionist who loved the crash cymbal and always came in too early.

Sometimes Jeanette's face comes to me, with all her vibrancy, because she was the one person who died who didn't do a single thing wrong. Then Kostas' face comes to me too and, when it does, I breathe deep and try to think of something happier. Of dolphins and orcas, but they reside in the sea too.

I wish I could use my meditation app but even that has been cruelly stitched into the memory.

It was only a year after our trip that Isabelle consented to Isa's family having the body exhumed. I followed the twenty-four-hour news channel each night, watching each bit of the fallout again and again. The first shock was where she had been buried, in the garden of the London house. It didn't mean anything in itself, but it didn't look good for Robert. Only Robert and Isabelle knew where she was buried – the whole time she was there, in that house.

Isabelle was magnanimous on the news channels when the DNA results came back. The science had really come on since the first examination, a man who had been employed by the Rathwells had killed her, named Kostas Rota, no one else's DNA was anywhere near her. Though Mr Rota had since disappeared, presumed to be in hiding, the Rathwell Company would be co-operating in a worldwide search for him. Mr Rathwell was cleared of wrongdoing. If he had known she really was killed, he surely would have allowed her to be examined sooner, to clear his own name of any lingering rumour, they argued. Isabelle and Sir Anthony played the scandal so well, so contrite, denouncing the scandal around the company that had begun with tax issues and sleaze and promising to turn things around. Whereas the current news cycle was all argument and little apology, they went the other way and managed to save the company. They announced the business was transitioning away from its previous interests in mining and had acquired Mr Rathwell's widow Sofia Rathwell's company so they could diversify into renewable energy. That name Isabelle talked about, Rathwell, falling through the ages, had come to mean something else again.

I'd blotted out all their faces for such a long time, since that news. This time when Kostas came calling, as I walked, I considered him then let him go. The red taillights of cars headed past, smoke rose and gathered in a New York haze. And I started to try to make peace with what had happened.

Finally, I strolled into Williamsburg, a hipster neighbourhood that had cooled over time as the bearded men had had children and the pipe smoke became less ironic. It still felt too cool for our crowd of musos, but I headed in search of Maher's Bar where they were gathered all the same. That's when I heard my name.

I turned and he was just standing there.

Six years on, Ben was thirty and the years looked well on him. He wore less formal but more expensive clothes, no longer the old-fashioned movie star, an affectation from his twenties, he had settled into what appeared to me a character both more and less himself. This is a thought I've had before, a side effect of encountering someone lost to you for some years: *So that's who you always were*, the thought goes. But also: *You've been led astray from who you really are, what has time done to you?*

'Oh God. That's you, isn't it?' he said. 'I mean, that is *you*?'

I opened my palms with little energy, having been used to keeping my gestures small in the intervening years. I was embarrassed to get a welcome so loud on the street, with all the grandeur it implied of me.

'It's me,' I said.

He crouched and put his hands over his mouth. Not

a gesture in his repertoire when I knew him, but things had changed, inevitably. He whispered, '*Oh my God*' repeatedly into his hands as he stood and approached me with force.

I flinched as he came for me, but it was no good, soon his arms were around me. And it felt more normal than I imagined. This body that I had feared at night, comforted me. And yet, it felt better than that, somehow extraordinary, somehow special.

We stayed in a quiet hug for longer than I ever had, as I have a propensity to find silence and closeness together either too uncomfortable or too sexual. And one inevitably because of the other.

'I'm trying to think of something,' he said, 'less bland to say than "How've you been?"'

'I'm trying to think of something less guarded to say than "Fine",' I said.

'I'm meeting people in,' he babbled as he checked his watch, 'forty minutes. That's time for one drink, right here, right?'

He pointed to the nearest bar and my body clammed up.

'I don't know,' I said, 'I've got to meet Max and my friends.'

'I'm sure *Max*, I already love him by the way, great guy, and the *friends*, wouldn't mind me stealing you for forty minutes. I owe you that much. In fact, I owe you—'

'You don't owe me anything,' I said, but it sounded less passive-aggressive than I thought it would. And I did take that drink.

The place was all rough wood cladding and low lighting, an expensive bar masquerading as cheap, winking at you about how expensive it really was. He insisted on Old-Fashioneds and the music was a kind of cocktail jazz that had recently become hip.

'I read about it, in the papers,' I said. 'Did you get as much as they say you did?'

He nodded in an upward motion, not saying yes yet, just taking in the inevitability that I had heard about it. Him becoming one of the family, an heir no one knew existed. Ben's presence with the family on the Greek holiday on which his father died was a detail not found in any article.

'I'd say I've got enough not to have to worry,' he said. His voice had become a touch transatlantic, and in such a short time: 'But then, jeez, there isn't enough money in the world to stop the worrying. For anyone, I mean. Not just ... you and me.'

'And are you still acting?' I said, ignoring that last comment with a slow blink.

He laughed as if he didn't know exactly what I meant by that, but soon regained his composure: 'Isn't everyone acting? I'm not being paid for it, not that I ever really was. Ha, no, I work in apps now. I've got a start-up. Think Uber, but with a mentoring element, relationship fostering, trying to use Eastern thought to solve that work–life balance problem. You get it?'

'Not really.'

'It's difficult to describe. That's what's good about it. That's why it's going to be a success.'

He even moved differently, there was a languor in his limbs, a lazy ease that reminded me of his father and maybe Bobby too. Not that I would ever mention it. They were the dead elephants in the room.

'You still play your ... music?'

I nodded, it was the first time I had felt the need to be

humble in a long time, as if my achievements and my realisation of them both happened at once and made me blush.

'I played tonight in fact. At BAM.'

'Holy shit,' he said, then repeated it a couple of times before letting it sink in and holding my shoulder. 'That's, I was going to say incredible, but it's actually totally credible, from someone as amazing and clearly talented as yourself. I'm so pleased when people get exactly what they deserve.'

And there was a glow about him then. That orange warmth had returned, I saw a survivor in him rather than any other harsher labels.

'My mum passed away,' he said, his hand still on me, the weight feeling comfortable. 'We did all we could. The best care, everything she deserved, we stayed at the best hotels, ate at the best restaurants, whenever she was strong enough. Luxury, a little late in the game, but luxury all the same. And whenever we did something extravagant, she said the same thing. That all she really wanted was to spend time with me.'

I noticed a single tear that the rest of his face was trying hard to ignore.

'I'm so sorry to hear that,' I said. 'Can I ask, how did *she* feel? When it all came out?'

'You want to know if she felt angry? Or vindicated?' he said, leaning in and talking low. 'Neither, not really. She wished I hadn't done it. But then, she knew why I needed to. When she first got sick, she said she'd seen Jeanette in Harrods once. I must've been sixteen by then. She knew exactly who Jeanette was, had even been to a party at her house. She told her what Robert had done, but Jeanette, dear Jeanette, of course, wouldn't hear it.'

Hearing him say her name stung and he saw it.

'But somehow mum didn't push it. She just walked away. Told me she decided, then and there, never to concern herself with that family again. Because it wasn't the money, none of it, for her or for me. It was the principle.'

His mother may not have felt vindicated, but I did. This was a story of heredity, where everyone fell back into their rightful places, without as much blood and violence as in some royal family histories. But he didn't need to burden himself or me with whether it was *right* or not. What did *right* even mean? I reminded myself to hold onto this thought and repeat it when I needed it most. We talked for another hour and then he released me back into the wild.

'I wouldn't want to keep you from Max,' he said.

I looked out at the Hudson River and the Brooklyn Bridge in the distance, all the lights of Manhattan that stood behind Ben. I'll always remember it.

'It was genuinely nice to see you,' I said. His smile said he understood the implied caveat that referenced my expectations, and he took it on the chin, said the same words back, and went on his way.

Now we are married, I think back on the meeting and wonder how planned it was. It would've been easy enough to search my name and recognise the opportunity to wait until I was playing in his town. The city isn't so quiet at night, there are plenty of bodies and lights to lose yourself in if you want to track someone then approach quietly. But he'd never own up to it, so I don't ask.

What I knew was not contrived was the way I fell for him. He met me a couple more times in Brooklyn and when the tour ended Max and I parted, her saying she thought there was someone else and me denying it. She said something about heartbreak being the hardest pain to get over, that you can actually die from it, and I cried over the phone because I hadn't felt anything so strongly for years.

Ben had been devoted to me that whole time, it was clear to me then. He flew me back to Brooklyn and I never left. He said such fond and sentimental things to me that afterwards neither of us were the same. I still tour, but I'm always headed back here, and when we have a child, in about twenty-nine weeks, I know I'll be living here in Park Slope, with its fields full of nannies walking their children, for the foreseeable future. Which works for me, because Ben is here with all his ambitions and his surprises after my concerts. And I love him, to the flesh of him, to the soul, this amorphous man who changes often but will always fascinate me whatever form he takes and seems to hold the other part of me.

He sometimes asks me whether I still think he's a terrible person. I tell him, no, you're my family.

And then I think of how the Rathwells chose people to work in the house who seemed lost, and how lucky we were to have found each other there, when all other possible families had slowly deserted us, throughout our lives. I think about what different versions of ourselves we were then. Sometimes it feels like our past happened to other people.

I decided to put my fears away the night before our wedding. I took my bible from beneath my bed and went for a walk along the Hudson River, holding it tight. Pausing beside the water's edge, I rested my arms on a wooden rail and began to read.

*

I'd always thought that if I saw someone drowning the instinct to save them would kick in automatically. And that's true, it does. But you can suppress it.

*

Then I threw it into the murky water, forcing myself to stay and watch it sink.

As the bible disappeared into the dark, I wondered about what Ben had inherited from his father. Mr Rathwell may not have been a killer, but he was ruthless, and was it that otherwise negative trait that allowed Ben to save us? I wonder what bad things I've taken from my father and made better. Or if heredity is just a flicker inside us, intermittently distracting us from who we really are.

And this real him, and this real me. Have we risen above the terrible things that happened because we're fundamentally good?

*

One night, some months later, I was searching for a sapphire ring Ben once gave me that I'd misplaced. He was so good with gifts. They weren't just extravagant, they reminded me how well he really knew me. Having looked everywhere else, I'd decided it must've somehow ended up on the top shelf of the bathroom cabinet, but I could barely reach up there. Teetering, I strained, pushing my fingers to the very back. I felt something. Fingers splayed, I managed to pull it down, but it wasn't what I was expecting. It was a clear plastic box.

When I saw what was inside, I felt unsteady on my feet. I turned, sensing someone behind me, but there was no one there. When I turned back, the box rattled.

Though I couldn't understand what it was filled with at first, the chill it had given me was immediate. I looked closer. Inside were small, curled, almost transparent, shards. I lifted them up to eye level, nearer the light, to examine them closely. Then I realised exactly what they were. They were fingernails.

I swallowed hard, steadying myself as I wandered back to bed, breathing deep to stay as calm as I could. Ben smiled at me when I entered the room. He was awake, reading a play.

I placed the box on his bedside table. He looked at it. Any other person might've wondered what they were. They looked like artefacts from another age. Something dug up and preserved. But I saw in his eyes that he knew. Of course he did.

Then he told me everything.

He said he wanted to tell me so many times. When everyone was out, back at the Greek house, while our car was colliding with Kostas', Ben had gone to confront Robert. I remembered he had mentioned that he felt like Robert wanted to talk to him alone. The thought of Ben going to him made my chest ache.

He thought his father had come to realise who he was, that this was why he'd taken a liking to him and in private he would admit it. But when Ben breathed deep and told him who he was, Mr Rathwell looked blank. So, Ben went on, telling him everything his mother had told him. But, nothing. The only flicker of recognition came when he mentioned a gift Robert had given his mother. A black opal.

Gradually, Robert's face turned. His father was about to acknowledge him at last, it seemed. But instead, he began to laugh. Then, when he finally caught his breath, he simply dismissed it out of hand.

As Ben stared at him, so many things Sofia told him swimming through his head, he felt it was impossible that Robert hadn't killed Bobby, his brother. That was what stirred him to do what he did. That and the cruel look, the laughter, the fact he said his mother was a liar. Suddenly Ben's hands were on his throat.

They say strangling takes a long time, but it was over before he knew it, Ben said. He had thought of his mother, dying of cancer after a life of struggle, as the last breath left Robert's lungs. Then Ben found himself cutting the fingernails, for proof, to prove the old man wrong. It was as if someone else was making the decisions, he said.

We lay there most of the night in silence. The next day we got up and went on as normal.

The next night, I woke and asked him to explain Jeanette's death again. Toxic shock from weed-killer Kostas put in the honey she ate, Ben said. And I said I thought it was in the coffee she drank. And he paused. I remembered Kostas maintained he had only killed Bobby right up until the end. And once again, my mind began to race. The most terrible feeling, as I lay alone with my husband at night, is that I realised I didn't even need to ask.

But Ben spoke anyway. When Jeanette arrived, he remembered her face from the department store. He hadn't mentioned that when his mother met Jeanette back then, that he was there too. Sixteen years old and a few feet away. Jeanette had given him a long look that day before she shook her head. And when he saw her at the house, he felt sure she would remember. She even said he was familiar. And if she remembered, if everyone found out who he was, what with the bloody trainers, they would surely think he was the cause of everything. This outside force that had come to do them all harm.

He was surprised how well Jeanette's face had burnt itself into him. That's the last thing he had to say about Jeanette. That's what he told me in the dead of night. And after he did, I was in no doubt what he had done.

He can't have been in his right mind when he chose to poison her, I thought, as I lay there. It was all that pressure, that danger, all those thoughts rushing at him. The real him could never have done what he did. Then I wondered if I'd ever known the real him at all.

After he said it all that night, I was so afraid to ask if this was why he had sought me out in Brooklyn. I held it all deep within, hoping I could escape what I knew. Then, after a long while, Ben slept and my pulse died down. He was my husband. I didn't even have my bible any more. And I wasn't sure a woman could testify against her husband. We were a family now. Bound together, for better or worse.

I didn't think that meant I was enabling anything. And if I was, I started to tell myself I was enabling a victory of sorts. Of one generation over another. I was seeing justice done. Helping to right a wrong. The underdog coming back to claim what was rightfully his, I told myself.

One morning, I woke to find Ben moved as he sat at the kitchen island surrounded by newspapers and post. I couldn't quite figure out whether it was good or bad news. He was shaking, of that there was no doubt. As I got closer, I saw he was crying even, hands over his mouth in that gesture of *oh my God*.

'There's a letter,' he said, when he looked up at me.

I put my hands on him, curled my arms around him from behind, and couldn't tell whether that tautness in his muscles was needing me, or trying to push me away.

'Who from?' I said.

He lifted the offending piece of paper, to read the words once more, just out of my line of sight. Words I had a feeling he was reading for the fourth, fifth, sixth time.

'It's from JR,' he said. 'It says he wants to tell me all the little things he knows. The letter begins: *How do you sleep?*'

Acknowledgements

Thanks as ever to Catherine, for her love and support, and for surviving a worldwide pandemic with me.

To Juliet, whose understanding and perceptiveness about books is almost otherworldly. The fact she does it all with such a light touch is barely credible.

To Finn, a terrific partner in crime for making this book what it is. As smart as he is exacting as he is handsome.

To Rhian, for a particularly warm, thoughtful and coaxing copy edit.

To Lisa Milton and all at HQ for the continuing support as we novelists were stuck in our homes, mining for gold, and occasionally walking the streets. Missives from the frontline of publishing and general care was very much appreciated.

To Duncan Robertson, Tom McHugh and Jo Kloska for various thoughts and and/or early draft readings. Honest book blokes all.

To the man who found my laptop with this book on it after

Thomas Cook went out of business mid-air and my bags were nearly lost. It was his first day, and the beginning of a heroic career in luggage retrieval.

And to Clementine, that disturber of my sleep and writing hours, that small discoverer. For all the mistakes as a father I will inevitably make, forgive me. In turn, I hope you never learn of the endless nights you put me through, because you'd surely never forgive yourself.

Rx

ONE PLACE. MANY STORIES

Bold, innovative and
empowering publishing.

FOLLOW US ON:

@HQStories